**"There is more,"** Cam interrupted through gritted teeth. **"The dancing is just part of it. For this plan to work, we must do more."**

"More?" she echoed. "What more could we possibly do?"

"It's simple, isn't it? When I dance with you, other men want to dance with you as well. Therefore if you want gentlemen to come courting, I must court you as well."

For a brief moment, Maddie wondered if *Principles of Geology Volume III* had indeed dropped on her head and she was in a dream conjured up in a comatose state.

"It would be pretend, of course," he added quickly.

"Pretend." Still, heat gathered around the suddenly constricting neck of her collar. What did she think he meant anyway? That he would court her for real?

"So, what do you say, Miss DeVries? Do we have an agreement?"

## Author Note

Modern steelmaking as we know it didn't start until the development of the Bessemer process in the 1850s. There's not much in the history books about the role of women in the iron furnaces and steel forges, but we do know that women became vital to the steelmaking industry during World War II. With the men at war, women took up jobs in factories, including some of the most dangerous ones in the steel industry.

While Rosie the Riveter, much like Maddie in my story, is a fictional character from Pittsburgh, there were some real-life women who contributed not only to the war effort but to the women's rights movement in general.

The Women of Steel from Sheffield kept the city's steelworks industry running during both World Wars so Britain's forces abroad would be well armed. They did this while still looking after their children at home. Today, a sculpture commemorating their contributions stands in the city.

Across the pond, American women also took up jobs they were later forced to give up once the men came back from war. However, many remained or later on inspired the next generation to enter these industries once exclusive to men.

Alice Peurala, a Chicago steelworker, sued her employer, US Steel's South Works, in 1967 when she was being denied a promotion after years of service simply because she was a woman. So, she sued them and won. Her lawsuit also compelled steel companies to fight against racial and gender discrimination by signing the 1974 Consent Decree. Peurala formed the Local 65 Women's Caucus and continued to fight against inequality until her death in 1986.

Thank you, ladies, for the inspiration. We will continue to fight the good fight.

# PAULIA BELGADO

---

## Game of Courtship with the Earl

HARLEQUIN
HISTORICAL

# HARLEQUIN®
## HISTORICAL™

PLEASE RECYCLE
THIS PRODUCT IS RECYCLABLE

Recycling programs
for this product may
not exist in your area.

ISBN-13: 978-1-335-72382-6

Game of Courtship with the Earl

Copyright © 2023 by Paulia Belgado

For questions and comments about the quality of this book,
please contact us at CustomerService@Harlequin.com.

Harlequin Enterprises ULC
22 Adelaide St. West, 41st Floor
Toronto, Ontario M5H 4E3, Canada
www.Harlequin.com

**Printed in U.S.A.**

Born and raised in the Philippines, **Paulia Belgado** has worn many hats over the years, from office assistant, flyer distributor, singer and nanny to farm worker. Now she's proud to add romance author to that list. After decades of dreaming of seeing her name on the shelves next to her favorite romance authors, she finally found the courage (and time—thanks, 2020!) to write her first book. Paulia lives in Malaysia with her husband, Jason, Jessie the poodle and an embarrassing amount of pens and stationery art supplies. Follow her on Twitter @pauliabelgado or on Facebook.com/pauliabelgado.

**Books by Paulia Belgado**

**Harlequin Historical**

*May the Best Duke Win*
*Game of Courtship with the Earl*

Look out for more books from Paulia Belgado coming soon.

Visit the Author Profile page at Harlequin.com for more titles.

To Jason, the best husband and dog dad ever.
Never stop nerding with me.

Mahal kita.

# Chapter One

*London, 1842*

Extracting valuable materials from useless objects was a concept familiar to Miss Madeline DeVries of Pittsburgh, who had, since the age of five, learned the science of metallurgy from her father.

When heated to a high enough temperature, a hunk of ordinary ore lost its impurities and turned into something extraordinary.

*If only I were like ore*, Maddie thought. *And I could be rid of my flaws*. Then she, too, could be extraordinary, like iron, born from the smelting process, changing the world as she knew it.

At this moment, however, Maddie would settle for just being *ordinary*, if only so the other guests at the Worthington ball would stop staring and whispering as she walked by.

'Gads, they grow them big in the colonies, don't they?'

Maddie would have laughed, except she'd heard that insult before.

'What do they feed them, do you think?'

Now that was a new one.

Her shoulders slumped. Really, she should have been used to it by now. After all, seven years had passed since that unfortunate summer when she'd grown a foot taller. From then on, she'd towered over all the women—and most men—her age and beyond.

Her father, Cornelius, pragmatic and calm as always, had merely patted her hand and assured her everything would be all right, then gone back to discussing the day's production numbers.

Her mother, Eliza, on the other hand, had declared it a complete and utter tragedy.

'Who will marry you now?' she had cried. 'Where will we find someone who won't have a neck ache each time they look up at your face? Your prospects in this town are meagre enough as it is.'

It was a silly statement, because Pittsburgh boasted a large population of eligible men, but what Mama really meant was the lack of men that were of their newly acquired social standing. With the seemingly unquenchable thirst for building and commerce and progress all over the United States, the DeVries Furnace and Iron Company's business had flourished. Their family grew rich, elevating them from their humble origins.

From then on, there was no stopping the tenacious Eliza DeVries from achieving her dream of taking her place at the top of the social ladder. Not the closely guarded societal borders protected by the old rich families—not even the borders of *America*. And that's why they'd travelled all the way to London—so that the DeVries family could gain a foothold on those elite drawing rooms by joining the families of England's nobility through the marriage of their two children.

*Or at least, one of us.*

Maddie's spirits sank even lower as she glanced at

her sister. As usual, a gaggle of beaux surrounded the prettier and daintier DeVries daughter, eager to catch her attention.

Caroline was not rock, nor ore, nor iron. No, to anyone with full capacity of their senses, the younger DeVries was like gold: glittering, shiny, and beautiful. In her light blue taffeta gown, her blond curls arranged artfully on her head, and her skin glowing under the candlelight, she shone like the precious pure metal, valuable by itself with no need for any external process to remove impurities.

Glancing down at her own attire made Maddie groan with woe. In an attempt to create a more delicate appearance, Eliza dressed her eldest daughter in the frilliest frocks in light pastel colours, which did nothing to mask Maddie's considerable height. Indeed, it only drew attention to her size, and she ended up looking like an over-decorated wedding cake.

Tonight's outfit was a particularly frothy concoction of pink tulle, white French lace, and lilac bows down the front of the skirt and sleeves. It was a dreadful combination, and Maddie could only wish she were a wallflower, unnoticed and unremarked upon. Instead, she had to endure the stares, the pointing, and the not-so-very-subtle jabs at her person.

The stirrings of a waltz distracted Maddie for a moment. Envy rose in her as she watched the delicate ladies take their place with their dashing, handsome partners. How she longed to twirl about the ballroom again in some gentleman's arms. The last and only ball she had danced at had been months ago. Sometimes, she wondered if it had been all real or just a dream.

When the dancing began, Maddie decided she had served enough time in the main ballroom enduring everyone's gibes. Surely she could find some relief from the gawking guests. She spied the doorway on the other side of the room where several ladies disappeared through.

*That must be the retiring room.*

She weaved through the throng of people but halted when she heard the familiar voice of her mother. Glancing around, she found Eliza DeVries in the company of a group of well-heeled matrons.

'…yes, indeed. My Caroline has been taught by the best tutors since she was a young child.' Her mama's nasal tone was unmistakable, and Maddie had to stop herself from rolling her eyes as her mother extolled the virtues of her younger daughter.

'Finest in the Americas, maybe,' came the snooty retort from the woman on her mother's left.

'I'm sure you have many excellent teachers back home, Mrs DeVries,' the crisp, polite tone of the Miranda, Dowager Duchess of Mabury, interrupted. 'And I find both DeVries girls to be lovely, in both disposition and their individual talents and characteristics.'

Maddie couldn't help but smile as she met the Dowager's knowing grin over the back of Mama's head as her mother held court with the other women.

The DeVries family couldn't have asked for a better sponsor for their season in London than the Dowager. Indeed, attempting to navigate it by themselves had been a disaster. When they'd arrived in London at the beginning of the year, they didn't receive many invitations. So, they had hired a guide to assist them, the Honourable Miss Harriet Merton, who in turn had managed to obtain the assistance of the Dowager Duchess in launching the young American misses. The Dowager had invited them to stay with her in Highfield Park in Surrey. There had been three of them in the beginning—Maddie, Caroline, and Kate Mason, daughter of New York industrialist Arthur Mason. However, Kate had married the Dowager's own son, Sebastian Wakefield, Duke of Mabury. After the wedding, Papa had decided that he wanted to see the rest of England—and perhaps take a rest from the tediousness of husband hunting as well—so he took the family on a tour of the countryside.

Maddie had thought they would be invited back to Highfield Park, where the Dowager would continue to host balls and parties for them. However, the Dowager had wanted to give the newly-weds some privacy. So, she'd taken up residence in London and asked the DeVrieses to stay with her, which also allowed the two girls more opportunities to be out in society. They'd arrived a month ago, and they had attended some ball or soirée nearly every night since.

'Yes, indeed, Your Grace,' Mama tittered.

One of the ladies in their circle cleared her throat delicately. 'If you will excuse us, Your Grace, I promised Lady Neville I would say hello to her before the night is over.' The other women made their excuses as well and then bade them goodbye.

Now that her mother and the Dowager were no longer surrounded by those haughty ladies, Maddie began to make her way to them.

'I'm so grateful to you, Your Grace,' Mama began. 'And you do your best to include my Madeline in your compliments.'

'She is well accomplished,' the Dowager replied. 'You should be proud of her.'

'I am, truly. Maddie is a wonderful girl.'

The compliment made Maddie's steps falter. Her mother was proud of her? *That was a first.* It wasn't that she thought her mother to be a heartless harpy, but it was always evident that Mama favoured Caroline, even while growing up. Maddie didn't give a care because her father doted enough attention on her.

'But I must face reality,' her mother continued, seemingly unaware that Maddie was right behind her. 'Maddie is two and twenty—far too old to be making a spectacular match. Not to mention, her other...attributes...ward away any eligible gentlemen.'

The Dowager caught Maddie's gaze and panic crossed over her usually unflappable face. 'Um, perhaps you shouldn't discount Maddie quite so soon. She may yet surprise you.'

Mama waved a hand. 'You are very kind, Your Grace. I've done my best to mitigate her stature, but no gentleman would want such a physically imposing wife. He would be the laughing stock wherever he went.' She tsked. 'No, I've resigned myself to such a fate for her. And as long as Caroline marries a lord, Maddie can be a spinster. Cornelius has made our family wealthy enough that she need not worry when we meet our timely demise. She shall be well taken care of. And if I may say so, it might be nice to have a companion in my old age.'

And that minuscule hope that had been building inside Maddie shrivelled away. It was one thing to hear the words from others, but from her own mother, it hurt. Hunching her shoulders over, she hurried away to the first set of doors she came upon. The gust of fresh air she inhaled as soon as she exited told her she was in the Worthingtons' terrace gardens.

Thankfully, it was well lit, and a small group of ladies occupied the benches near the door, which meant it was safe for Maddie to be there. Miss Merton had warned her and Caroline many times about venturing off alone during balls lest they find themselves unchaperoned with a man. A scandal could ruin their prospects.

*Not that anything scandalous would ever happen to me.* Even if Maddie and some man were to be found alone in a darkened garden, no one would believe they were in a passionate embrace. *Everyone would think I was helping him pluck a fruit from a high branch.*

She nodded to the ladies, made her way to the edge of the terrace, and pretended to admire the various plants and shrubberies blooming and the flowers scenting the air with sweetness. Maddie was sure they were lovely, but she could hardly concentrate on them, not when her mother's words occupied her mind.

*No gentleman would want such a physically imposing wife...*

*Laughing stock...*

*Spinster.*

She had come out in society five years ago, and except for a few notorious fortune hunters, no one had made an offer for her hand. In truth, Maddie had resigned herself some time ago to a life of spinsterhood. She had her work at the furnace to occupy her, after all. While many men would have scoffed at the idea of a woman learning science, the eccentric Cornelius DeVries held no such prejudices, especially when it came to his eldest daughter. She'd been going to the forge with him ever since she could remember, and because he had no son, he passed his knowledge on to her.

Indeed, she had thought it wouldn't be so terrible, especially since Papa had made it clear the company could be hers someday, should she want it.

But that was before they'd come to England. Before she'd realised that it was possible to have everything one desired—a fulfilling life with one's passion *and* a husband and family—when her good friend Kate Mason married her duke and became the current Duchess of Mabury.

A few days before her wedding, Kate had confessed to Maddie that, though at first they had agreed on the betrothal as a business arrangement, she and the Duke had somehow fallen madly in love in the process. Not only that, but Mabury was building a train engine factory just for her so she could pursue her dreams of designing her own locomotive. And soon, Kate would undoubtedly also start producing a different kind of creation—an heir to the Mabury dukedom.

She truly was happy for her friend; Kate deserved it. But it only made Maddie want all that for herself, too. She'd been in denial because she never thought it possible, that she could only ever be tall, shy Maddie who hid behind her books and her work and never thought to ask or dream of more.

But perhaps she was fooling herself. Kate finding the love of her life who supported her in all her pursuits was a one-in-a-million chance.

And tonight was another reminder that it would be impossible for Maddie to have everything she wanted in life.

'Maddie?'

She spun around at the sound of the Dowager's voice. 'Your Grace.' Her cheeks warmed as the Duchess obviously knew Maddie had overheard her conversation with Eliza.

'I hope the fresh air has done you some good?'

'Yes,' she lied, not knowing what else to say.

'Excellent.' The older woman drew closer to her. 'I told your mother and father that I was feeling faint, so I'd like to retire early. I said I would require assistance and hoped you could accompany me back to Mabury

Hall. Would you be amenable to leaving now and skipping the rest of the ball?'

Would she be amenable to leaving this boring ball and avoiding all the gapes and whispers from the haughty guests as she passed by?

*Was the sky blue?*

'Yes,' she said. Realising she was too enthusiastic, she added, 'I mean, of course, Your Grace. If it pleases you, I would be happy to assist you.'

'Good. I've already bade goodbye to our host and hostess, and the carriage should be coming round any moment.'

Relief poured through her as she followed the Dowager back inside and then outside to the street at the front.

Soon, they were pulling up to Mabury Hall, the Wakefields' fashionable town house in Mayfair.

'By the way,' the Dowager began as they alighted from the carriage. 'I wanted to let you know that I'm expecting a guest tonight. The daughter of a dear friend who unfortunately passed away some time ago.'

'My condolences for your loss, Your Grace.'

'Thank you, dear.' She paused, smiling sadly. 'Her brother wrote to me, and I agreed to sponsor Lady Persephone for the season.'

'Lady Persephone?'

The Dowager chuckled. 'Yes. Elaine did have a wicked sense of humour. Anyway, Lady Persephone has travelled quite far—all the way from Scotland. Her journey will not have been easy, which is why I instructed her to make haste and arrive at any time. A letter came today telling me to expect her later this evening. I'll welcome her properly in the morning and will introduce her to everyone.'

'Will she need help when she arrives? I'm more than happy to assist her.'

'There's no need for you to wait up, Maddie,' the Dowager said as the butler opened the door for them. 'The household staff will have everything ready. I am going to retire to my room, but I wanted to be here just in case. You should head to bed and get some rest.'

Maddie stifled a yawn. 'Thank you, Your Grace. I believe I shall.'

Her maid, Betsy, was already waiting for her in her room by the time she entered, and she helped Maddie get undressed and washed up for bed. When she slipped between the silky covers, she nearly fell asleep, but the sound of neighing horses and the rolling wheels of a carriage jolted her awake.

*That must be the Dowager's guest.*

Curious about what a girl named Persephone would look like, Maddie hauled herself out of bed and strode to her window, which had a view of the street.

Sure enough, a coach piled high with luggage stopped just outside the townhouse. A footman opened the door, and as a boot landed on the step, the carriage dipped low.

Maddie let out an audible gasp as the passenger fully alighted. This definitely wasn't what she had been expecting when she'd run up to the window for a glance at Lady Persephone.

For one thing, the person who hopped out of the carriage was decidedly not female. For another? This male person was a giant.

Even from the second level of the house, she could tell that he was almost as tall as the carriage itself. His hulking shoulders were covered by a travelling cloak and his face obscured by a hat, so she couldn't quite be sure of the man's age. Perhaps he was Lady Persephone's father, who had accompanied her on this journey?

As if sensing her spying, the man turned his head

upward—right at Maddie. Her hand flew to her mouth, then she quickly shuttled backwards. She didn't know why, but her heart pounded like mad against her chest. Still, she wanted to peer outside again so she could see the stranger's face.

*I can't risk it.*

Surely he had seen her or, at the very least, seen someone spying from the window. It would be embarrassing if anyone had caught her like some peeping Tom. Perhaps tomorrow she'd be introduced to him and that would quell her curiosity.

Shaking all thoughts of the man from her head, she slipped back into bed.

Lord Cameron MacGregor, Earl of Balfour, couldn't help but feel like he was being watched. So, he glanced up at the lofty town house and spied a flash of a figure from a window. Said figure quickly disappeared from view, but at least now he knew he wasn't imagining it.

But this was London, after all. Crowded, hot, and full of eyes everywhere. With each visit, his impression of the city did not waver.

'My lord?' the footman asked with a delicate cough and a nod towards the inside of the carriage.

*Right.*

'Seph?' he called to his sister. 'We're here. Are you awake?'

A loud yawn sounded from the darkness, and after a quick shuffling of fabric and paper, a small, pretty face emerged from the carriage. Large, owlish eyes blinked sleepily from behind the lens of gold-rimmed glasses. 'Have we arrived in London, Cam?'

'Aye.'

A gloved hand darted out, grasping for the handle on

the side of the door but missing it completely. 'Careful, Seph.' Cam caught her hand before she fell out of the carriage.

'Sorry. I'm just so tired.'

'All right, easy there.' He guided her down the step. 'That's it.'

Persephone wavered as both feet landed on the ground. 'It's as if the world under me is still rocking to and fro.' She took a deep breath and steadied herself before looking up at the grand town house before them. 'Is this Mabury Hall?'

'I hope so,' he said with a chuckle. 'Otherwise, whichever fancy lord or lady we're disturbing in the middle of the night won't be happy to have a pair of Scots at their door.'

'Do you suppose—'

The front door opened and a tall, white-haired man in a dark suit appeared. 'Lord Balfour? Lady Persephone?' Despite his quiet, deferential tone, his accent was recognisably from London.

Cam answered with a quick nod. 'Aye.'

'Good evening, my lord, my lady.' His polished shoes clacked audibly on the stone steps as he hurried to them. 'Welcome to Mabury Hall. I am Eames, the butler. Her Grace, the Dowager Duchess of Mabury, asked me to welcome you and ensure you are settled in for the evening.' He motioned to the door. 'If you please.'

'Thank you, Eames.' Tucking Persephone's arm into his, Cam climbed up the front steps and into the house.

Eames slipped in behind them, then nodded to a woman dressed in a maid's black-and-white uniform who stood by the staircase. 'Your valet and Lady Persephone's maid should already be in your rooms unpacking. Allow us to lead you there.'

They trailed behind the butler as he climbed up the stairs. When they reached the top, he directed Persephone to follow the maid down the long hallway on the left. 'Lady Persephone will be staying next to the other young ladies in this wing, along with Mr and Mrs DeVries. Lord Balfour, I'll show you your room in the other wing.'

Persephone's eyebrows knitted together. 'Is that all right, Cam?'

''Tis fine, Seph.' He kissed her temple. 'Get some sleep. I'll see you in the morning.'

He watched as Persephone followed the maid down the hallway and disappear as they turned a corner, then Eames walked him in the opposite direction. They arrived in his rooms, where his valet, Murray, was already unpacking his trunks.

'If you need anything at all, my lord,' the butler said, 'just pull the bell and someone will be right up.'

'Thank you, Eames.'

'You're welcome, my lord.' With that, Eames bowed and left.

'Would you like a bath prepared, my lord?' Murray asked.

'It's much too late. I'm about ready to keel over.'

Murray pointed to the washstand. 'There's fresh water in the jug for ye to wash up, my lord. I'll prepare yer clothes.'

'Thank you, Murray.' Cam cleaned himself with the water and washcloth as best he could as Murray assisted him with his nightclothes.

He was looking forward to sleeping in a proper bed tonight. Exhaustion had him ready to collapse, as he hadn't had a decent night of rest in the last few days. He had to protect his sister, after all. They travelled with enough servants to watch over them, but there could never be enough eyes on her, not with her...peculiar nature.

Persephone tended to be clumsy and was near-blind without her spectacles, but more than that, she was absent-minded, especially when she was in deep thought, which was nearly all the time. She was so much like their mother in that way.

And that was the other reason Cam couldn't sleep.

*I promise, Ma,* he said silently. *I'll take good care of her. Just like you and Da woulda wanted.* He owed it to his departed parents.

Elaine MacGregor had died of a lingering illness seven years ago, and their father, Niall, a few months after. One day, his valet had found him in bed, unmoving, his body already cold. The doctor said Niall had had a heart condition and if he had been feeling unwell, he had kept it from them.

Fitting, really, that his father died of a broken heart. Though Niall had tried to remain strong for his children, he had confessed to Cam how much he missed his wife. *'She was the love of my life, my boy,'* he told him one night when he was in his cups. *'I can't tell you what that's like, but perhaps someday you'll understand.'*

*Not likely*, Cam snorted. He'd would never again allow anyone such power over him. Once was enough, thank you very much.

Besides, they didn't come all the way to England to find him a wife. They were here for Persephone and to fulfil the promise he, his brothers, and his father had made to his mother as she lay dying.

*Persephone... I was so looking forward to her season in England. I would have ensured she would make a good match. I want her to have her choice of husbands, whoever and wherever that may be.*

Elaine MacGregor was not wrong; while Niall's earldom should have been enough of an enticement for a respectable match for Persephone, it had been obtained purely by chance, from a distant relative who'd had no sons of his own. Before that, they had been farmers, then whisky distillers. The Glenbaire Whisky Distillery had been in the MacGregor family for many generations, certainly longer than the earldom his father had inherited.

They were trapped between two worlds—too high for the merchants and too low for the aristocrats. An English season, however, would help signal that the MacGregors were taking their place in society and Persephone would be available to a wider range of potential suitors. Thus, Elaine had been planning it ever since Persephone was born.

*I have no regrets,* she had told her husband and sons. *Being with you, my love, and raising our children has been the best part of my life. But Persephone... I would hold off Death if I could and make a bargain with the Devil himself if I could be there for her a little longer. So please, give her the season that I wished I could give her.*

Persephone had been so young when Ma died. *She's still too young now,* he thought with a mental shake of his head. Well, nineteen wasn't young for a lass to be married, but Persephone was special. She was already more sheltered than any of the debutantes on the marriage mart, and then there were peculiarities. Still, he would do as his dear mother asked, which would also help Persephone gain some exposure to polite society. But if he were truly honest with himself, he would not be broken-hearted if she didn't immediately find a match.

Murray's voice broke into his thoughts. 'My lord, if there is anything else...'

He shook his head. 'Thank you, Murray. Get to bed.

I'll see you in the morning.' With that, Cam slipped into bed and fell asleep.

The following day, Cam woke up, if a little later than usual, feeling refreshed and clear-headed. When he arrived a few minutes after Cam rang for him, Murray informed him that it was already half past nine.

'Her Grace instructed us not to disturb you, my lord. I've brought you some food.' He set the tray down on the table next to the bed.

'And my sister?'

'I believe she woke up early and headed to breakfast, along with the other guests. They are likely in the parlour.'

Cam didn't like that Persephone was meeting other people without him. He had hoped to speak to the Dowager in private and explain a few things, mostly about Persephone. She had to understand, after all, what she was getting herself into when she offered to sponsor his sister. And if the Dowager thought the task was much too difficult, he would understand and find another way to fulfil his promise to his mother.

After he finished dressing and eating, Cam went downstairs to meet his hostess. Eames informed him that the Dowager was already expecting him and led him to her private sitting room. Cam took a deep breath and prepared himself for the meeting. English people could be quite fussy, after all, but he was well versed in dealing with them.

Once Cam had become of age, Niall had begun to bring Cam with him to his business trips in England, and now that he had taken over running the business, Cam came at least once a year to check in with his man of business, George Atwell, and visit their most profitable customers.

While many of the English looked down on the Scottish, most of them, especially the gentlemen, were happy enough to consume their fine whisky, a fact that the MacGregors had exploited since they'd started exporting their product to England.

His father had a natural charisma, something Cam was happy to have inherited and found useful when dealing with people. *'That's the ol' MacGregor charm,'* his father would always say. *'Works on anyone, especially females under the age of one hundred.'*

And thanks to his English mother's lessons on the proper graces and manner, Cam knew how to act around the higher classes. Indeed, on his trips to London, he would often get comments on his manners. 'You're so civilised!' some of these fops would say, thinking it was a compliment to a Scot like him. But he ignored such words and continued to fawn and flatter their customers on their excellent taste and tough negotiating skills, but privately, he laughed all the way back home with more profit with each trip.

'His Lordship the Earl of Balfour,' Eames announced.

The dark-haired woman sitting in the brightly lit sitting room placed her book down and rose from her chair. 'Welcome, Lord Balfour,' she greeted as she glided towards him. 'Oh, my.' She craned her neck up at him, her dark eyes widening in surprise. 'I didn't realise you'd be so tall.'

Cam was used to such reactions; after all, his height was unusual. 'Your Grace.' He bowed, which did not even put them at eye level. He was about to reply with a witty compliment, something along the lines of not expecting her to be as bonny as a spring day, but stopped short when he looked down to observe her face. The Dowager Duchess was much younger than Cam had imagined, though he should not have been surprised, as she was the same age as his mother would have been.

His chest constricted at another reminder of his ma. While he had managed the grief well, the small reminders of her absence did not fail to cause a reaction in him.

When the Dowager's eyes narrowed, he put those thoughts aside. Clearing his throat, he slipped on the mask he always used around the quality. 'Please forgive my lateness in arising this morning and not properly presenting myself and my sister.'

'There is nothing to forgive. You've had a long journey.' She gestured to the empty chair in front of her. 'Please, have a seat.'

He did as she bade and exchanged a few pleasantries with her, relying on the MacGregor charm to get through the necessary ritual the upper classes insisted on performing. His impatient nature, however, longed to get straight to the point of why they were here, but he allowed Her Grace to lead the conversation as she was his hostess.

'Lord Balfour, though I have expressed it in my letter to you, allow me to offer you my condolences for the loss of your mother and father,' the Dowager finally said.

'Thank you, ma'am.'

'I'm not sure if your mother ever spoke of me, but we were dear friends for many years.' A wistful smile touched her lips. 'She and I married the same year. We even discovered that we were with child at the same time. We wrote each other frequently those first few years. But as these things go, we both became busy with our lives and our letters waned. I only regret…' She sniffed and dabbed at the corner of her eye with a handkerchief.

'Thank you for answering my letters, even though I hadn't thought to write to her in years.'

'You're very welcome. And thank you for your generous offer to sponsor Persephone.'

Cam had been surprised to receive the very late letter of condolence to their family a few months ago. He had written back to thank Her Grace, then she'd written again asking about him and his brothers and sister. It was his youngest brother, Liam, who was the most intelligent of them all, who had given Cam the idea to ask the Dowager for help in giving their sister the season their mother would have wanted, since none of them had the faintest idea about balls and invitations and gowns.

To his surprise, the Duchess had agreed to sponsor Persephone in London. Since Cam was the Earl and he frequented London, he decided to accompany her. Besides, there was always Glenbaire business he could attend to and customers he could visit. In fact, he needed to meet with a potential customer, one of the largest gentlemen's clubs in the city.

Cam usually had his man of business in London, George Atwell, conduct all of the initial introductions and presentations when it came to deals in England. However, the owner himself insisted that he would consider stocking Glenbaire in his club only if Cam himself came to town. While other men would have been insulted, Cam was intrigued. Indeed, it was how Niall had done business himself before he'd become the Earl and he'd had to delegate such tasks.

'It seems you have something else on your mind, Lord Balfour.' The Dowager's dark eyes trained on him, the intelligence in them unmistakable. It rather reminded

Cam of his mother's when she'd tried to suss out secrets from him 'Why don't you tell me what it is?'

'Er... Yes, about that.' But how was he to explain about Persephone? 'You see, my sister—'

'I've met her this morning,' the Dowager interrupted. 'What a delightful young woman.'

Delightful? Had she really met Persephone? Most people would not use that word in describing his sister, unless they were mocking her. However, there was no hint of malice in the Dowager's tone of voice.

'She is already with another of my guests. I think they're getting along quite well, too,' she continued.

'Other guests?' Cam didn't realise there would be other people staying there as well.

'Yes. Along with Persephone, I'm also sponsoring two girls from America for the season. Anyway, you were saying, my—'

Before she could continue, the door to the sitting room burst open. 'Cam! Eames told me you were here.'

Cam groaned inwardly as his sister flounced into the sitting room. 'Forgive my sister, Your Grace. She is—'

'You must meet my new friend,' Persephone interrupted.

*A friend?*

The fact that Persephone would consider anyone a friend boggled Cam enough to forget propriety. He gave an apologetic glance to the Dowager, who only returned it with a cryptic smile.

'Come in, Maddie,' Persephone called, then reached beyond the doorway, pulling out first an arm, then a person attached to said arm. 'This is Miss Madeline DeVries.'

Cam was halfway to rising when he locked eyes with his sister's new friend.

*Mother of Mercy.*

It was as if he'd been punched in the gut, for he found himself unable to look away from mesmerising eyes the colour of the clear blue sky. The rest of her face was quite arresting, with her clear milky skin, high cheekbones, and those plump pink lips that begged to be kissed.

Sheer force of attraction walloped him, and his throat was too dry to say anything. However, as she came closer and he rose to full height, something else caught him off guard. He didn't have to bend low to meet her eyes. In fact, the top of her head came to just about the tip of his nose.

Cam wasn't sure if it was astonishment, or the instant attraction to the woman, or if he were still disoriented from the trip that scrambled his mind—or all three—but all he could do was stare at her.

'Cam?' Persephone's voice cut through the daze. 'Please forgive my brother. He's usually much more affable.' She turned to him. 'Well? Say something.'

A woman had never rendered him speechless before. But yes, he definitely should say something instead of just staring at her.

*Turn on the ol' MacGregor charm*, his pa would have said if he were here.

Cam wanted to tell her that she was a stunning, mighty goddess. Like Athena or Queen Hippolyte, from the Greek myths of old. However, his addled mind somehow came up with something else.

'Holy mackerel, you're a great big Amazon!'

The room turned silent as a tomb and realisation struck Cam like a bolt of lightning.

*Hell's bells.*

But before he could apologise, Miss DeVries's pretty

face scrunched up and she burst into tears, then dashed out of the room.

'Oh, for goodness' sake!' Persephone smacked him on the arm. 'What were you thinking, saying that to her?'

Cam could live to a hundred years and never know the answer.

# Chapter Two

As soon as the Duchess had introduced them in the parlour that morning after breakfast, Maddie instantly liked Lady Persephone MacGregor. The pretty red-headed Scotswoman was vibrant and chatty and, much to Maddie's delight, interested in her work at the furnace. In fact, she mentioned that she herself took part in her family's business, but before Lady Persephone could elaborate, she'd stopped and slapped her hand on her forehead as if she'd just remembered something, then dragged Maddie out of the parlour before barging into the Dowager's private sitting room.

And then disaster had struck.

Maddie ran, not caring if it was discourteous to the Dowager, as long as she was far away from that—that *lout*. Besides, he had been rude to her first.

*A great big Amazon*, he'd called her.

Just when she thought she'd heard every insult possible, there were, apparently, more barbs and gibes out there in the world, waiting to be sprung on her.

But she'd never had them spoken so directly to her face, and not from such a handsome man.

So, the man she'd seen outside the window last night

was the Earl, but she should have guessed. When their gazes had met across the room, the strangest sensation had pooled in her belly. It had been warm, not like drinking a hot cup of tea on a chilly day but, rather, something much more intense.

Surprise and delight had filled her when, for once in her life, she had to look up at a gentleman. While insignificant to anyone else, to Maddie, it was as if everything was right in the world and her confidence had soared.

Then he'd said those hurtful words and shattered it again.

Tears blurred her vision, but she found her way to a place where she could seek solace. After staying at Mabury Hall before going to London, she already knew the house and made her way to the library. Slamming the door behind her, she strode to the wing-back chair by the window and plopped down.

'Er, Miss DeVries? Are you here?'

The lilting feminine tone told Maddie it was Lady Persephone.

'There you are,' the Scot said as she walked towards her. 'I'm so sorry my brother's a dimwit.'

Maddie flashed her a weak smile. 'It's not your fault.'

She sat down on the chair opposite her. 'Ma would be so disappointed in him. She taught us better than that.' Her eyes blinked behind her gold-rimmed spectacles. 'He's usually so pleasant, especially when around women.'

A twinge plucked at Maddie's chest at the mention of other women. Of course he would attract a lot of female attention; he was handsome, after all, and she'd noticed many ladies didn't seem to care what a gentleman said so long as they were rich and attractive.

'I'll make sure he apologises to you, Miss DeVries.'

The thought of seeing him again after the morning made Maddie's stomach churn. 'Oh, no. Please... I can't possibly...' She buried her face in her hands. 'It's so embarrassing.'

'Maybe he meant it as a...compliment?' Lady Persephone offered. 'You know, Amazon women are fierce warriors—'

'Who match men in their abilities,' Maddie finished. Oh, she knew exactly what he meant. 'There have been many insults about my height thrown at me, but none have every compared my stature to that of a man's.' And perhaps that's what had hurt the most. To have been so stripped of her femininity with just one sentence.

'I know my brother, and he didn't mean to insult you.'

'Can we speak of something else, please, Lady Persephone?' If she had to think about the Earl any more, she would surely expire from mortification.

'Of course. But please, do call me Persephone, at least when it's just us.'

'And you must call me Maddie,' she replied, then took a deep breath. 'Do you really consider me your friend? We just met this morning.'

'Does England have friendship rules that I didn't know about? I'm growing quite weary of them.'

'If there are, I wouldn't be aware of them.' The corner of Maddie's mouth quirked up. 'As you know, I'm American.'

'Then we can make up our own rules.' Persephone reached over and patted her hand. 'And if I say we're friends, then we're friends.'

'I'd very much like that.' It was too bad her brother was nothing like Persephone. Perhaps they weren't blood related. 'And seeing as we're friends, maybe you could continue what you were telling me earlier? About working with your family?'

'Ah yes.' Persephone's eyes lit up as she leaned forward and adjusted her spectacles. 'Do you know anything about whisky?'

Maddie spent the rest of the morning with Persephone, and for the first time in a while, she felt at ease. It had been so long since she'd had a genuine friend to talk to like this—not since before Kate had married.

Persephone was a breath of fresh air, and it was such a delight to be friends with another like-minded person. However, they were opposites in some ways. While Maddie was reserved and shy, Persephone never seemed to stop talking, especially about her scientific pursuits. Like Maddie, she'd been taught by her father everything about distilling whisky, though her interests spanned an array of subjects from Greek philosophy to astronomy. By the time they were called for luncheon, Maddie felt at ease around the Scotswoman.

Of course, Maddie's mother and sister weren't quite as welcoming. Both women had a lot to say when Maddie mentioned that she and Persephone had become friends.

'Friends?' Caroline sounded aghast. 'She is not a friend. She's a rival.'

The Dowager had left before the meal was over as she had a last-minute fitting at the modiste, while Lady Persephone had retired to her room as she still felt weary from their long journey. So, the three DeVries women finished dessert and coffee on their own.

'Not that she's much competition,' Mama added in a haughty tone. 'That red hair? Freckled complexion? How unfashionable.'

Caroline's eyes gleamed. 'I heard from my maid that she arrived with her young, handsome brother. An earl!'

Mama turned to Maddie. 'If this Lady Penelope—'

'Persephone,' she corrected.

Mama snorted impatiently. 'If this Lady Priscilla is your friend, then perhaps we can use your connection to her to our advantage.'

'*Persephone*,' she reiterated. 'And that's not what friendship is about.' For some reason, that twinge in her chest returned at the idea of the Earl with her sister. 'If you'll both excuse me, I must fetch some ink and paper from Eames so I can reply to Kate's letter.'

'Don't wander off now. We must get ready for the Gardiner ball tonight,' Mama called after her.

'Yes, Mama.' *Not another dreadful ball* But at least Persephone would be there. It would be nice to have someone to talk to, although considering Persephone's beauty and delicate stature, Maddie predicted she would once again be alone for the evening. And of course, she assumed the Earl would be there to escort her.

Her stomach knotted at the thought of seeing him. Though Persephone had assured her numerous times her brother 'just wasn't like that,' Maddie did not want to ever encounter him again. Which was impossible if she wanted to remain friends with Persephone. That, and if Mama and Caroline had plans for him…

She shut those thoughts out of her head. Being a guest of the Dowager's, at some point she was going to cross paths with the Earl again. His barb was not the first she'd heard and certainly not the last she would ever hear. *You must toughen up, Maddie*, she told herself. Develop a thicker skin, as they say.

After obtaining the writing materials from Eames, Maddie went up to her room and finished her correspondences. By the time she was done, Betsy had arrived to help her bathe and prepare for the ball.

'Oh, heavens.' Maddie winced as she saw the gown Betsy was holding up. 'Yellow,' she moaned. If it wasn't pink, it was *yellow*. The lace cuffs and white satin rosettes down the full skirt did not do the dress any favours. It reminded her of a cake she had once seen in a baker's shop window. How did her mother manage to find the most hideous dresses in London?

With a deep sigh, she allowed Betsy to dress her in the monstrosity. When the maid showed her the curling tongs, she blew out a breath. Mama always wanted her hair in tight sausage curls, as if she were a child's doll. Everyone else at these balls had elegant waves piled on top of their heads, held together with sparkling hairpins and combs.

'All right,' she said, resigned. 'Let's get on with it.'

After what seemed like forever, she was done preparing for the evening. 'No, thank you.' She waved away Betsy's offer of a mirror to examine her work. It didn't matter anyway. After dismissing Betsy with a grateful nod, she gathered her reticule before leaving her room. As she made her way downstairs, Caroline's nasal voice reverberated up the stairwell.

'My lord, if you don't mind my saying, you are absolutely hilarious!'

*My lord?* As far as Maddie knew, there was only one person in residence who could be called that. *Maybe Caroline was talking to someone else*, she assured herself as she reached the bottom of the stairs.

'I don't mind at all you saying that, Miss DeVries. And if you don't mind my saying, you do look bonny tonight.'

Maddie's heart sank at the sound of the familiar voice. Was it too late to go back and hide in her room?

'Bonny?' Caroline giggled. 'You, my lord, are a flatterer.'

'Aye, but I only pay compliments where they're warranted.'

Her stomach churned, and Maddie gripped the banister, readying herself to turn back. Unfortunately, Persephone, who stood right beside her brother, spotted her.

'Maddie. Oh, thank goodness you're here.' Persephone hurried towards her, then dragged her to where Maddie's parents, Caroline, and the Earl were waiting. She sent a pointed look to her brother. 'Allow me to present Miss Madeline DeVries. Miss DeVries, this is my brother, the Earl of Balfour.'

The Earl's face betrayed nothing of what had happened that morning. 'Good evening, Miss DeVries.'

'My lord.' Though her head turned in his direction, she focused on the wood panelling behind him, not daring to look up into his eyes.

'His Lordship was just telling us a funny story about their journey here,' Caroline interjected.

'The most amusing tale,' Mama added. 'You are such a talented storyteller, my lord.'

Maddie pressed her lips together. But it should not surprise her that her mother and sister fawned over him. He was unmarried and possessed a title, after all.

'I'm more interested in his whisky,' Papa chuckled.

'I have a few bottles with me, and I'd be honoured to share some with you,' the Earl said. 'Her Grace has told me all about your ventures back in America and now here in London, Mr DeVries. I respect a self-made man.'

Maddie could only stare as her father preened at the Earl's compliments. Since he was a shrewd businessman, she thought he'd be immune to flattery.

'Tell me, my lord,' Papa began. 'How did an Earl become a whisky maker?'

'Da wasn't always an Earl.' It was Persephone who answered. 'He was a distiller first. In fact, the MacGregors have been distilling whisky since the seventeen-sixties. Of course, we started as an illegal—'

The Earl coughed. 'Perhaps it's not that much of a fascinating story. Oh, here comes the Dowager now.' He nodded towards the stairs. 'Your Grace.'

Everyone curtseyed or bowed as the Dowager made her way to them. 'Ah, I see we're all here. Now, we don't want to be late. Let's move along, shall we?'

Persephone and her brother took their own carriage, while Maddie and her family rode with the Dowager.

While Mama, Papa, and Caroline spoke of how pleasant the Earl was, Maddie fumed. Who was that man she'd just met? Where was this charming angel this morning, who said all the right things? Did the Earl have an evil twin lurking about, insulting women?

Thankfully, the ride wasn't too long, and soon they were being announced as they entered the Gardiner ballroom. As usual, Caroline's admirers flocked to her and were already lining up to write their names on her dance card. The Dowager made the rounds, introducing the Earl and Persephone to her friends, and as she always did, Maddie stood off to the sides, watching the dancers.

In the beginning, Maddie had attempted to hide from the other guests or blend in with the walls. Both had been impossible, given her height and garish dress. In any case, the barbs and gibes found her anyway, wherever she went. But, as she did at every ball and gathering, she ignored them and concentrated on watching the elegant couples twirling across the floor.

'Miss DeVries.'

Maddie froze at the sound of the Earl's voice. It took all her strength not to turn to him as he came up beside her. 'I find myself feeling faint.' She sidestepped away from him. 'If you'll excuse me, my lord—'

A hand came to rest on her upper arm, on the exposed skin just above her gloves. The touch made her snap her head up. A jolt struck her when she met his intense stare. Up close, she realised that his eyes were green, like bright twin emeralds.

'Miss DeVries, please don't leave.'

She ignored the warmth that spread through her despite the fact only his gloves separated their bare skin. 'My lord, this isn't proper.'

The guests around didn't seem to pay them any mind, but if just one person saw him touching her with such familiarity... Well, that would certainly send tongues wagging.

'Maddie. Here you are,' Persephone said as she came up to her from behind. 'I need you—' She took in a sharp intake of breath. 'Cam.' Her teeth chewed at her bottom lip, like a child caught stealing sweets.

'Seph?' He drew his hand away from Maddie's arm. 'Where have you been? I've been searching all over for you.'

'You have?' she said innocently.

'Ever since I saw you running from Lord Kinsley like the devil himself was on your heels.'

'Nonsense.' She forced out a laugh. 'Er, I just remembered... I had to powder my nose.'

His eyebrows knit together. 'He was about to add his name to your dance card, too.'

Colour drained from Persephone's pretty face. 'I—'

The butler announcing the next dance interrupted her. 'Miss DeVries would love to dance.'

'I beg your pardon?' Maddie cried as she felt a hand push her forward—straight towards the Earl.

'Go on, now,' Persephone said. 'The music's about to start.'

Maddie stiffened as the Earl's arms came around her. Before she could protest, he pulled her into the sea of dancers.

'M-my lord,' she stammered. 'Please release me.'

'Thanks to my sister, it's far too late for that.' The way he rolled his *R*s sent shivers across her skin. She gasped, heat creeping up her cheeks.

'Miss DeVries?'

'Y-yes?' She looked up at him. A terrible mistake, as those green eyes mesmerised her, making it impossible to turn away.

'Your hands?'

'W-what about them?'

The music played, and so he took her hands and placed one on his shoulder, then slipped the other into his. His other hand landed on her waist. Before she knew it, they were swaying to the music. A waltz.

She was dancing.

And floating, too, as her heart soared in happiness. She almost forgot who she was dancing with. *A handsome partner*, she told herself, without thinking about who he was and what he had said to her. All that mattered was that after weeks of watching the beautiful couples from the sidelines, she was one of them. Delight filled her as they twirled about, and just for that one dance, she could imagine herself a dainty and delicate lady.

Lost in the moment, she allowed herself to glance up at him. Her breath caught in her throat when those intense eyes stared back at her. There was something about the way he gazed at her that sent a pleasant thrill through her, starting from somewhere deep in her belly and spreading throughout her body. The sensation distracted her so much that she didn't notice that the music had stopped and they were no longer spinning around the ballroom. The dance was over, and so was the fantasy.

She curtseyed to him as he bowed, but as she made a motion to walk away, he quickly crowded her off to the side. She barely had time to resist. 'My lord? Wh-where are you taking me?'

'I'm not stealing you away. I just want to have a wee chat,' he chuckled. 'Now, don't you run off like a timid little rabbit again.'

Perhaps it was the months of being ridiculed and laughed at, or maybe it was the way he acted around her family, or that he had once again ruined a wonderful moment for her, but something snapped inside Maddie.

'Little rabbit?' she hissed. 'Are you mocking me, my lord?'

'That's not what I meant,' he sputtered.

'Am I an Amazon or timid rabbit?' she interrupted. 'Both cannot be true at the same time.'

He slapped a hand on his forehead. 'Why are you being contrary? Just let me apologise so I can be done with you.'

*Be done with her?*

Like she was an obligation?

'If you're attempting to apologise, I regret to inform you that you are doing a poor job of it.' Maddie gasped at the audaciousness of her words, and her heart drummed madly against her chest. But it was as if a spirit had taken over her body, and there was no stopping it, nor the outrage that had built up inside her and was now overflowing.

He let out a frustrated sound and ran his fingers

through his blond locks. 'What is it about you that I can't put two words together correctly? I was trying to compliment you this morning.'

'By implying that I was...was...' She grasped for the right word. 'Mannish?'

'Mannish?'

'Yes.' That was a word, right? 'Like a man.'

'Yes—er, no! I meant to say you were impressive as a...er... I mean, Ama—'

She put a hand up. 'Say no more, my lord. Lest you dig yourself into a deeper hole.' There were too many people around them, and most of them were beginning to stare. 'That was a lovely dance, my lord,' she said in a loud tone so they could hear her. 'Thank you, and I look forward to another one.'

*In a hundred years, when I've turned into dust.*

With a respectful nod, she walked away in the opposite direction. Pretending she knew where she was going, she smiled at the ladies and gentlemen she passed. She'd nearly circumnavigated the room when she spied Persephone next to some sculpted potted topiary.

*Oh, thank heavens.*

'Persephone,' she called to her friend. 'Shall we go— wait, are you hiding?'

The Scotswoman popped out from between the two shrubs and glanced around, eyes darting left and right. 'N-nay,' she denied, but shrank back behind the branches.

'You *are* hiding,' Maddie said firmly. 'From what?'

'Not what. Who.'

'And who are you hiding from?'

'Them.' She pointed out into the ballroom. 'The men.'

'Which man?'

'All of them,' she said, exasperated.

Maddie frowned. 'Why?'

'Because they will want to dance. And I... I can't dance,' she confessed.

'You've never been taught?' Maddie asked. 'You should have said something. I'm sure the Dowager—'

'I have been taught, but I just can't do it.' Her lower lip trembled. 'I'm very clumsy, and no matter what I do, I can't count correctly or remember the steps.' She sighed. 'I can tell you how many casks of whisky we'll be producing each year just by looking at the barley harvest, but for the life of me, I always forget which way to turn for the quadrille and what foot goes out first for the waltz. I'm hopeless.'

'I'm sure that's not true. Perhaps we can—'

Persephone let out a squeak and hid behind her. 'They've found me.'

'Found you—oh.' Persephone twisted her around. Sure enough, two gentlemen were approaching them. 'Lord Wembley. Mr Carter.' Maddie had been introduced to them a few weeks ago when they'd attended an event at Highfield Park, the Duke of Mabury's country home, and had spied them at a few events in town.

'Miss DeVries,' Lord Wembley greeted her. 'Good evening. I was, uh, wondering if perhaps you would like to dance?'

Maddie blinked. 'M-me?'

'Yes. I'm hoping your dance card is not full yet?'

'It is not.' In fact, it was woefully empty.

'In that case, I would like the dance after,' Mr Carter interjected.

A heartbeat passed as she stared at the two men. She wondered if someone was playing a trick on her.

'Miss DeVries?' Lord Wembley repeated, offering his hand. 'If you please?'

Maddie placed her hand in his and followed him to the

middle of the ballroom. Unease settled in as she felt eyes on them—after all, they must have made quite a comical couple, with Lord Wembley's eye level at her chin.

However, when the lively music began and the couples started the quadrille, Maddie launched into the dance without a care in the world. In fact, with the quick steps and whirling about, she hardly gave a thought to the difference in their stature. And when they finished, giddiness coursed through her as Lord Wembley flashed her a smile as he bowed. If people were staring at them, she was too overjoyed to notice.

As she promised, she joined Mr Carter for the gallop, and after that, another gentleman, Lord Porter, asked to partner with her for the cotillion. By the end of that third dance, however, Maddie was weary, and so after thanking Lord Porter, she shuffled off towards the retiring room.

*'Psst!'*

Maddie stopped and glanced around.

'Maddie!' came the disembodied voice.

*Was that...?* 'Persephone?'

'Aye.' Scooting out from behind a pillar, her friend let out a long breath. 'Thank goodness those gentlemen asked you to dance.'

'I'm glad, too.' She smiled at her weakly. 'I never usually dance so much at a ball.'

'And why not? You do it so well.'

'Because no man wants me,' she stated.

'They did tonight,' Persephone pointed out. 'In fact, three of them did.'

The turn of events still boggled Maddie. 'No one asks me to dance at balls because they're all intimidated by my height. I have no idea why those three gentlemen asked me tonight.'

'Curious.' She tapped her fingers on her chin. 'So, you've never danced before?'

'Well…there was this one time…' She relayed to Persephone what had happened during Kate's engagement ball, when the Duke of Mabury had danced with her and then more men came forward to ask her. But since then, at every ball they'd attended in London, Maddie had been relegated to the sidelines. 'Maybe it was because we were out in the country, and men are different here in town.'

'These silly Englishmen.' Persephone shook her head in disgust. 'But then again, they are not like they are back home. In fact—' She inhaled a sharp breath. 'Maddie, you said that after your dance with the Duke, more gentlemen came forward to ask you?'

'Why, yes.' She pursed her lips. 'Do you think those men were attempting to curry favour with him?'

'Perhaps, but let's examine the chain of events. You danced with the Duke, and right after, you were flooded with invitations to dance. And tonight, after you danced with Cam, three gentlemen approached you.' She snapped her fingers. 'Therefore, we can conclude that after a man of high rank shows interest in you, other gentlemen follow in his wake.'

'Shows interest in me?' That made her laugh. 'The Duke is like…like a brother to me.' And he was thoroughly in love with Kate.

'And what about my brother?'

She wasn't sure what the Earl was to her, but the emotions he brought out certainly were far from brotherly. 'Need I remind you, *you* pushed me into dancing with him.'

'But the results are the same, are they not?' Persephone smirked at her. 'Men love a challenge. They can't resist it. When they see another man pursuing something, then it becomes an object of desire, and so, they must triumph over their competition to win said object.' She patted Maddie on the arm before she could refute her statement. 'Trust me. I grew up with five older brothers.'

Maddie had never thought of it that way, but she supposed it was a logical conclusion. Not that it made her feel any better.

'What's wrong? We've just solved your dancing problem.'

'My dancing problem?'

'You obviously love it but never get a chance to do it. I've watched you looking so enviously at the dancing couples all evening. But now you know how to entice these gentlemen into asking you, and you can dance at every ball.'

'So in order to get invitations to dance, someone must first dance with me.' She shrugged. 'Oh, never mind. I'll never get to dance, which means no man will ever court me or ask me to marry them.'

Persephone frowned. 'Marriage is your end goal?'

'Isn't it yours? That's why the Dowager is sponsoring you, is it not?' It was then Maddie realised that while she had spent hours talking to Persephone that morning, they'd touched little about her family or why she had come to England.

Persephone's nose wrinkled. 'I suppose. But we're not talking about me. Maddie, you're brilliant and wealthy. You don't need a husband to provide or protect you. You have your father's business to run.'

'I know, but…' She sighed. 'I still… I still want a family. Why can't I have that and still pursue my interests?'

'Of course you can, if that's what you want.' Persephone's eyebrows furrowed together. 'I have an idea.'

'An idea?'

'Yes. A plan, if you will. So you can get everything you want. But first, you must stay here.'

Before she could ask further questions, Persephone darted away.

What on earth did she mean by *plan*? Maddie was tempted to leave, but Persephone's words intrigued her. A few minutes later, her friend returned, but she was not alone. No—she was dragging someone along with her. A very tall, familiar someone.

'Slow down, Seph, before you trip—' The Earl's mouth clamped shut when their gazes met.

Her heart leapt to her throat, and she forced herself to turn away from those emerald orbs. 'What is the meaning of this, Persephone?'

She motioned to her brother with her hands. 'My plan.'

He raised a blond eyebrow. 'And what have you two been cooking up, now?'

'I haven't been cooking anything,' Maddie retorted.

'Just listen to me, will you?' Persephone clucked her tongue. 'Cam, we need your help.'

'Do you, now?' He crossed his arms over his chest.

'Well, Maddie does.'

'What do you mean, I need help?' Maddie cried. 'And why him?'

'Remember what I said earlier? About men and competition?'

It took a moment for Persephone's words and what her friend had in mind to sink in. She couldn't possibly think that... 'Oh, no.'

Persephone waggled her eyebrows. 'Oh, yes.'

Maddie wanted nothing more than to evaporate off the face of the earth at that moment.

Cam blew out an exasperated breath. 'For goodness' sake, will one of you explain to me what's going on?'

'Cam, you have to dance with Maddie at the beginning of every ball,' Persephone declared.

'Have to dance? Why?'

'So that other men will dance with her, of course.'

His head swayed back and forth from Persephone to Maddie and back to Persephone again. 'Why do you need me to dance with her?'

'Because if you do, other men will want to as well. And that will bring her closer to her goal.'

'Which is?'

'Why, marriage, of course.'

Silence hung in the air for a heartbeat before the Earl spoke again.

'Absolutely not.'

## Chapter Three

'Absolutely not.'

Cam knew there were very few absolutes in the world. But when Persephone said he needed to dance with Miss Madeline DeVries so she could find some milksop Englishman to marry her, he knew that was *absolutely* something he could not take part in.

'Whyever not?' Persephone asked.

A bitter taste crept into his mouth as he recalled watching Miss DeVries with those other men.

Cam couldn't do it—not if their first dance was any indication of what would happen each time he did. He thought the initial pull of attraction he felt upon meeting her was just a normal male reaction to a beautiful woman. He'd even tried to ignore her as she'd descended the stairs at Mabury Hall like some ethereal goddess earlier that evening, though his heart had thumped like mad. *Once the novelty of her wears off, I'll stop feeling this way*, he had assured himself.

But the moment he'd taken her in her arms for that waltz, he'd been enraptured by her. How could he not react to her, with the way her sky blue eyes sparkled and her skin glowed under the light of a hundred candles. Not even her hideous gown could detract from her beauty.

His attraction had intensified with every second he'd held her.

Which was why he'd done what he always did: defused the situation with humour.

He hadn't meant to offend her once again when he'd attempted to apologise. Persephone had berated him that afternoon over his appalling words and threatened to never speak to him again if he did not make things right with Miss DeVries. Of course, Cam wanted to apologise, if only to be done with her so he could stop this torture of being around her and not being able to have her.

Because he knew that pursuing her would only lead to disaster.

'Need I remind you, we are not here for me. I am not in search of a wife.'

'I'm not asking you to marry Maddie, only to help her. It's only one dance, Cam,' his sister pointed out when he didn't answer.

'At every ball?'

Persephone clapped her palms together. 'Exactly. Maddie, these gentlemen won't be able to ignore you any longer, and you'll be married soon enough.'

Cam chewed on his inner cheek. *If none of these English men want her, then they are damned fools.* Still, the very idea of having her in his arms again and then watching someone else dance with her after soured his gut, never mind the thought of her belonging to another…

'I said no,' he repeated. *Absolutely, definitely not.*

'Cam, it's just until she finds enough candidates to choose a husband from. It's just one dance.'

*One dance?* He had barely controlled himself during that first one. Sweat built up on his palms at the thought of being so close to her, touching her. No, he would never again act on his attraction to someone he wanted so badly.

And he wanted Miss Madeline DeVries so badly, he'd forget his own name.

'There is no need for you to trouble yourself, my lord,' Miss DeVries bristled. 'I am perfectly capable of finding my own suitors.'

'See, Seph? She doesn't want me.' That should have given him relief, but why did his chest tighten at the words? 'Now, if you ladies will excuse me.' With a nod, he turned on his heel and strode off. *I need air.* And he needed to think.

He made his way to one of the balconies and closed the door behind him. Leaning forward over the side, he took in a breath. The breeze helped, but it wasn't quite like it was back home, where scents of pine, peat, and malt tinged the fresh air.

He was eager to go back, to be far away from this place. But Niall, Cam, and the rest of his brothers had a promise to keep.

Nay. He was keen to go back home because he needed to get far, far away from *her.*

Miss Madeline DeVries.

'Maddie.' He would never allow himself to call her by her given name, so what was the harm in whispering it to the wind? Still, the name on his lips felt entirely intimate. But it would not be his to say. Someone else would call her that. Her husband. On their wedding night.

He released the balustrade, as his knuckles had gone white from gripping it too tightly. Would Scotland be far away enough for him to forget her? It would have to be, because he could not risk being a slave to his passions again.

It had cost too much the first time.

Cam had been an eager, randy lad of just nineteen

when he'd first laid eyes on Jenny Gordon in the village. He'd gone there with his best friend, Kirk, when he'd seen her walking to the tea shop. The attraction had been instant and intense, and she'd enchanted him with her beauty. At that moment, he'd vowed to make her his and set out to woo her, turning on the old MacGregor charm every chance he could. He'd been a man in love and he'd been obsessed with making her his.

His ma and da had warned him many times and tried to get him to temper his passion throughout the courtship. It wasn't that his parents had been against the match or had any objections against Jenny herself; but they'd said he was too young to settle down; or perhaps they had recognised that what Cam had felt was not love. But he'd been too captivated with Jenny to listen to their advice, and soon, he'd got his wish—they were betrothed.

As the wedding had drawn closer, however, he'd noticed Jenny acting strangely. She had become withdrawn from him and distant. He'd chalked that up to the wedding planning, as even he had been caught up in all the details.

However, the day before the ceremony, his entire world had shattered. Jenny and Kirk had come to him and told him she could not marry Cam—they had fallen in love with each other!

*'You were so charming and persistent, I was flattered with the attention,'* she had confessed. *'My ma and da begged me to accept your proposal even though I hardly knew you. And then everyone around me was expecting so much of me because I was to be a countess. I thought it was what I wanted. The wedding, the balls, the parties—it was too much. I—I had my doubts. I asked Kirk for advice, and eventually he guessed I was having sec-*

*ond thoughts. He was wonderful and patient with me and I couldn't help myself.'*

'But you said you love me,' he had accused.

*'I—I thought I did, Cam. I really thought I did. I just needed more.'*

'I love her, Cam,' Kirk had said sheepishly. 'And I'm sorry.'

*'You would make someone a wonderful husband, Cam,'* Jenny had added, as if that would soothe his broken heart. *'Just not mine.'*

Cam had wanted to lash out at them but just couldn't bring himself to do it. Kirk had been his best friend since they were in short pants, and he was one of the finest men he knew, tempering Cam's impulsive nature with his mature, calm presence. Indeed, Cam had got into only half the scraps he had because Kirk had been there to cool him down. He was the opposite of Cam—strong, intelligent, patient, and kind—and it was no wonder Jenny had fallen in love with him.

She'd needed more. More than what Cam could give her. His good looks, charm, and title were not enough for her.

They'd left that same day and eloped, then moved away, perhaps to spare Cam the humiliation. That had been nearly a decade ago, and though Jenny's face had nearly faded from his memory, the lesson from that time had not. He vowed to never be swept away by passion and attraction ever again.

Of course, he'd discreetly bedded many an eager lass since that time, but never more than once, and while most of them had been beautiful, he swore to never allow his feelings to grow for a woman. While he knew his duty as the Earl of Balfour meant he needed to produce an heir, there was time enough for that. Perhaps in the future he might find some comely, respectable lass to marry, one who wouldn't inspire such an obsession in him. If not, he had three younger brothers who could step into the role. As such, women and marriage were far from his mind at the moment.

Well, he'd thought that they were far from his mind, but then again, he hadn't met another woman who sparked such an instant, fervent attraction.

Until Miss Madeline DeVries.

'Bollocks,' he bit out. After tonight, he needn't worry about her, not after he'd mucked things up, as it was obvious she did not want him. He would do everything in his power to stop this instant attraction before it transformed into something deeper.

Ignoring the tightening in his chest, he headed back inside the ballroom. These events usually had a card room set up for the gentlemen, so he decided to seek it out. He was also in town for business, after all, and perhaps he could make some connections there. As he waded through the sea of people, a snippet of conversation caught his attention.

'...must be useful. I bet her family doesn't even need any ladders in their home. They simply ask her to pluck things off top shelves!'

He normally wasn't one for gossip, but he knew who they were referring to.

'And she can predict the weather before everyone else!' quipped another.

A barrage of sniggers and sneers met the jests—all of them women.

*Damned foolish people.*

He was about to walk away when he heard something that made him halt.

'I do feel sorry your mother and father have to be burdened so, Miss DeVries.'

'Thank you, Lady Gertrude,' Caroline DeVries sighed. 'My mother does fret about her finding a match. But I think the spinster life will suit Maddie. Perhaps she's even looking forward to it. I mean, can you imagine her, a lady of a household? She is not only ungainly, but also so terribly shy and awkward. How would she entertain? It's no wonder she doesn't have any suitors.'

'But then, why did Lord Porter dance with her?' someone asked.

'And Mr Carter and Lord Wembley,' another voice added.

Caroline harrumphed. 'Who knows? Perhaps the gentlemen had some kind of bet.' She chuckled. 'Which of them could survive dancing with my sister?'

A peal of laughter from the group. 'You are so right, Miss DeVries.'

Cam gritted his teeth as anger rose in him. How could her own sister talk of Maddie in such a manner? She sounded like she even encouraged it.

When he had met the younger Miss DeVries earlier, he'd thought her pretty enough, if a little flighty, but that was much expected from girls her age. But now, he had an inkling of what she was really like. He guessed that if Maddie was indeed 'shy and awkward,' her sister had had a hand in making her so.

Hands balled into fists at his sides, Cam marched away from the group, his eyes scanning the room. Once he found his target, he strode towards her, the crowd of people between them parting like the Red Sea.

'Miss DeVries.'

'Cam?' Persephone, who stood right next to Maddie, asked, her head cocking to the side.

Ignoring his sister, he said to Maddie, 'May I have this next dance?'

Maddie's head turned towards him, her eyes widening like an animal trapped by its prey. 'M-my lord?'

'A dance,' he repeated, then leaned closer to her ear. 'If you still want to continue this plan, this is your last chance.'

Her nose wrinkled. 'I told you, it is not my plan.'

'Just go,' Persephone urged. 'Do it.'

Though she hesitated, Maddie took his offered hand. 'I would love to, my lord.'

Their second was a livelier dance, though Maddie managed it well. Cam, too, found himself enjoying it, if only because he saw how happy it made her. The dance was over much too soon for Cam's liking, and once they stopped, he could feel all the eyes on them.

'Why are they staring?' Maddie asked.

'Looks like you've got your wish.' He nodded to the gentlemen on their right, who stood there like predators ready to pounce the moment Cam let go.

He'd never wanted to punch strangers so badly in his life.

'My wish?'

'To have more suitors.' The very words left a bitter taste in his mouth, and Cam knew he had to do something. So, he deposited her back at Persephone's side. 'There. I hope that was satisfactory?'

'Aye. And my plan is working.' His sister nodded behind him, and when he craned his neck back, he saw a handsome, dark-haired man approach them.

'Lord Balfour,' he greeted. 'Have you been enjoying your evening so far?'

Cam searched his memory for the man's name. 'Mr Baine.' Edward Baine was the son of a viscount, if he recalled. They'd been introduced earlier in the evening by their host and hostess. 'And yes, I have.'

Baine turned to the women. 'Lady Persephone. And Miss DeVries. I haven't seen you since the Chatsworth ball.'

Maddie blinked. 'That was months ago, my lord.'

'Was it? If so, then it has been remiss of me not to have furthered our acquaintance sooner.' He grinned sheepishly at her. 'I was wondering if I could have your next dance? Unless you are already spoken for.'

'Not at all,' she replied and took his offered hand.

When Maddie and Baine were out of earshot, Persephone nudged him. 'See? I told you this would work. I'm a genius,' she tittered. 'Now, all we have to do is repeat it at the next few balls, and soon Maddie will have her pick of suitors.' Her face lit up like an excited child's. 'Thank you for agreeing to do this, Cam.'

'You're welcome.' Cam blew out a breath. He just hoped he wouldn't regret it.

# Chapter Four

Maddie told herself she was not disappointed when the Earl did not show up for breakfast that morning. The Dowager had said he had urgent matters to attend to with his man of business in London, who had arrived earlier that day. However, she was thankful he wasn't there, as her mother and Caroline were especially insufferable this morning.

'Oh, did you see that dashing Mr Baine?' Mama tittered as the footman refilled her teacup. 'The two of you looked wonderful on the ballroom floor.'

'I agree,' Papa said. 'Although I don't know much about dancing.'

'And he was only two inches shorter than you,' Caroline added with a sneer.

Maddie took a sip of her tea. 'He danced well.'

'I'm so happy to hear this, Maddie,' said Miss Merton, who sat across from Maddie at the breakfast table. Originally, the Honourable Harriet Merton had been hired as a chaperone for Maddie, Caroline, and Kate Mason to help the American misses navigate the perilous London season. However, it had been her idea to ask the Dowager for help and act as sponsor for the girls. Many weeks ago, before they'd headed to London, her sister had taken ill, and so she'd gone to stay with her in Bath until she recovered. She had arrived late last night and thus was able to see them only this morning.

'Of course, the Earl danced with you twice,' Mama pointed out, as if Maddie couldn't remember it herself. 'Is twice too much? Cornelius, should you be having a word with His Lordship—'

'Mama.' She sent a pleading look to her father.

Cornelius cleared his throat. 'Eliza, dear, perhaps you should—'

'Oh!' Mama's eyes sparkled. 'An earl...'

'Your Grace, may I be excused? I must prepare for my gentlemen callers.' Caroline's gaze flitted towards Maddie. 'It's so tedious, but I can't turn away any of them lest I be accused of favouritism. Be glad you don't have that problem, Maddie.'

The jab hit its mark, like an arrow straight into Maddie's chest. While dancing was an enjoyable form of entertainment at balls, it was not an indication of a gentleman's interests in a young lady. Gifts and calls the following day were the real test, proof that they were willing to go beyond the ballroom dance-floor in their pursuit. While Caroline had entertained regularly these last few weeks, Maddie still had not received even one caller.

'Of course, Caroline,' the Dowager said.

Caroline gave Maddie one last smirk before she got up and walked out of the breakfast room. Maddie sighed with relief as the atmosphere became much lighter without her sister, with the conversation topics focusing less on Caroline.

After breakfast, Persephone took her aside. 'If you're not busy, let's head to the library.'

'I'm never busy,' she sighed. 'But I'm so glad I have you now, at least.'

Persephone smiled at her. 'Me, too.' Arm in arm, they walked towards the other wing of the town house. 'I've never had sisters before. Or close female friends. My ma died a few years ago. She was probably the closest thing I've had to any feminine influence.'

'I'm so sorry, Persephone.' Although Eliza could be vexing most of the time, Maddie knew she was lucky to have her mother.

'Well, here we are—oh, no.' She ran her hands down her dress and into the pockets. 'I've lost my spectacles!'

'You're wearing them,' Maddie pointed out.

'I know that.' The Scotswoman straightened the glasses perched on her nose. 'I mean my spare ones.'

'Spare ones?'

'Yes. You never know what can happen. Sometimes they'll just fly off my face for no reason, so I always carry a spare.' Her lips twisted. 'I must have dropped them somewhere between my room and the breakfast room. I should retrace my steps.'

'Do you need help?'

'Don't be silly.' She waved Maddie away. 'Stay here. I'll be right back.' Whirling around, she left the library.

Maddie entered the library by herself and headed to the row of shelves near the back of the room. She had finished the last book she'd borrowed, so she decided to search for the next volume in the series.

'Hmm.' As she glanced at the titles and volumes, it seemed that they were not in order and a few were missing, including the one right after the book she had just finished. She checked the lower shelves first, then craned her neck back. A dark brown book caught her eye, and she squinted at the spine.

'Volume three. There you are.' But why in the world was it all the way up there? She would have to stretch all the way up to reach it. *Perhaps I can find a ladder.* Seemed like such a bother for just one book.

Shrugging, she got on her tiptoes and extended her arm all the way over her head. 'Come on…' Her fingers barely brushed the leather-bound book.

'What the devil are you doing?'

The lilting burr made her heart leap into her throat and she lost her balance, sending her falling back. 'Oh!' Her body crashed into the opposite bookcase, which was mercifully sturdy, though the impact left her breathless.

'Maddie!' The Earl was beside her in an instant, hauling her to her feet. 'Are you all right, darlin'? Are you hurt?'

His strong, warm hand wrapped around her upper arm sent a strange zing straight down to her belly. 'I… I'm fine, my lord. Just a little shaken.'

'Should I call a doctor?'

'A doctor?' She shook her head. 'I told you, I'm fine.'

Emerald eyes searched her face. 'Did you hit your head?'

Having him so completely focused on her frazzled her nerves, sending her heart hammering. 'N-no, my lord.' She glanced down at his hand, which was still clutching her.

He quickly dropped his arm to his side. 'What were you doing, anyway?'

'Just trying to reach for a book.' She forced out a laugh, trying to cover up the drumming of her heartbeat. 'I'm afraid I'm not used to having things out of my reach.'

Frowning, he glanced up at the shelf. 'Which one?'

'I beg your pardon?'

'Which one did you want?'

'Th-that one. Volume three.'

He reached up and plucked it off with little effort. 'That's quite heavy reading.'

'I assure you, I can understand it perfectly well,' she rebutted. But then again, she didn't know any other young lady who would have chosen to read *Principles of Geology Volume III.*

'I mean, it's a weighty tome.' He bounced it up and down in his hand. 'You could have been hurt if it fell on your head.'

She pressed her lips together. 'I would have used a ladder, but I didn't see one.'

'Well, it's a good thing I was here then, isn't it?' He flashed her a smile.

Good Lord in heaven, her knees wobbled and she nearly fell back once more. 'Thank you.' She took the book from his hand and held it to her chest like a shield, though what she was protecting herself from, she wasn't sure. Perhaps his imposing presence, which seemed to fill the narrow space, making it difficult to breathe. 'If you'll excuse me…'

Maddie sidestepped to the left to pass him; however, he did the same, which meant he blocked her. When she moved right, so did he, and they ended up doing an awkward dance with neither of them getting past the other.

'Stop.'

She did, right in the middle of the aisle. Still, he was so wide that he didn't have any space on either side of him to let her through. This close, he loomed over her, and she couldn't help but stare up into those eyes, which were twinkling with amusement.

'If only there was music. We could probably coordinate our steps better.'

Heat crept up her cheeks at the reminder of their

dances last night. The awkwardness in the air was swiftly becoming unbearable. She wished she were somewhere other than this place. 'I should really leave, my lord. It's not proper for us to be here without a chaperone.'

'Aye,' he began. 'But then again, considering the plan you cooked up, aren't we past propriety at this point?'

Her face warmed even more, but not because of embarrassment. 'I told you, I didn't cook up anything. It was Persephone's idea.' She squared her shoulders. 'And you don't have to dance with me, my lord. Not anymore.'

'Ah, the suitors have been lining up outside, have they? Banging on the door?'

Now he was just plain insulting her. 'I would rather remain a wallflower than receive another pity dance from you. Now if you'll excuse me—' She once again attempted to move past him, but an arm shot out to block her way.

'Miss DeVries, wait. I swear to you, on my mother's soul, that I've not been raised in a barn. I don't know why…' He scrubbed a hand down his face. 'I can't seem to stop saying the wrong thing these days, but that has absolutely nothing to do with you. The fault is all mine. I am sorry for inadvertently insulting you. Forgive me for my thoughtlessness.'

The apology rendered her speechless. There was no excuse, no justification of his actions, just a sincere expression of regret for hurting her. 'I suppose…that you have had a long journey from Scotland. I know when we came from America, I was out of sorts for a few days and not myself.' Yes, maybe that was why he had insulted her that first time.

'Perhaps, but it is not an excuse. Therefore, I would appreciate your forgiveness.'

'You have it, my lord.' She could not help but see the sincerity in his face.

'Thank you.'

'But you are not incorrect.'

'I beg your pardon?'

Sighing, she turned to the shelf on her left and ran her fingers across the spines of the books. 'Despite our "efforts" last night, no gentleman has come knocking on the door, no gifts have been sent, or even requests for calls.' Her arm dropped to her side. 'My sister, meanwhile, never has an empty dance card and has more suitors than she knows what to do with. So, perhaps dancing with me is a waste of your time and I am simply not a desirable candidate for a wife.'

He muttered something under his breath, but exactly what, she couldn't comprehend.

'I beg your pardon, my lord?'

He spoke up. 'I think we should make a plan.'

'A plan?'

'Aye.' He crossed his arms over his chest. 'We can't just charge in and hope for the best. That's what my da always said.'

'I never thought of it that way.' Her father was the same, especially when it came to their furnace. They didn't exactly just mix rocks together and fire them up. No, they had to measure and weigh the minerals, then they went through the smelting process step by step. 'But what else must I do?'

He paused for a moment. 'I think there is more to it than simply dancing.'

'There is? But what else could there be, aside from the fact that I am simply not as desirable as Car—'

'There is more,' he interrupted through gritted teeth.

'The dancing is just part of it. For this plan to work, we must do more.'

'More?' she echoed. 'What more could we possibly do?'

'It's simple, isn't? When I dance with you, other men want to dance with you as well. Therefore, if you want gentlemen to come courting, I must court you as well.'

For a brief moment, Maddie wondered if *Principles of Geology Volume III* had indeed dropped on her head and she was in a dream conjured in a comatose state.

'It would be pretend, of course,' he added quickly.

'Pretend.' Still, heat gathered around the suddenly constricting neck of her collar. What did she think he meant, anyway? That he would court her for real?

'So, what do you say, Miss DeVries? Do we have an agreement?'

Part of her wanted to say yes—it would not be a real courtship. But a different part of her told her to proceed with caution. 'You can't possibly be serious.' She shook her head. 'Dancing is one thing, but to pretend to court me—it's simply…*mad.*'

'What's mad?'

Maddie nearly jumped out of her skin, then let out a breath of relief when she realised it was Persephone.

The Earl clasped his hands behind his back. 'Ah, here you are, Seph. Glad you're here and you can be a witness to our agreement.'

The Scotswoman placed her hands on her hips. 'What agreement?'

'Your little plan,' he said.

'But I thought you already agreed to dance with Maddie at every ball?'

'Yes, but we decided it's not enough. For Miss DeVries

to receive any kind of male attention beyond the ballroom floor, I must also pretend to court her.'

Maddie looked at Persephone sheepishly, who blinked back at her, then looked at her brother, and then back at Maddie, owlish eyes growing wide. *Oh, Lord. Even she thinks it's a stupid idea.*

'It's brilliant, absolutely brilliant.' She clasped her hands together. 'I'd been thinking about it all morning, actually.'

'You have?' Maddie asked.

'Yes, when Caroline mentioned all her suitors. Oh, you were so brave putting on that front whenever she needled you, Maddie. But I knew her words wounded you.'

'Wounded you?' the Earl repeated. 'What exactly did she say?'

'That Maddie should be glad she didn't have any suitors—'

'She didn't mean it that way.' Maddie's cheeks puffed out in defence. Oh, Lord, how much more embarrassment could she take this morning? Persephone didn't do it on purpose, of course, but to have her shortcomings laid out in front of the Earl was too much.

Persephone wasn't derailed and forged on. 'Cam, this idea of yours… It might actually work. If you court Maddie, then other men will follow in your wake.'

'Pretend to court her,' he qualified.

'Yes, yes.' Persephone rolled her eyes. 'But oh, this is exciting, indeed.'

'This can't be proper,' Maddie protested. 'What if our deceit was exposed?'

'By whom?' Persephone clucked her tongue. 'As long as this stays between the three of us, no one will know. Besides, once other men begin courting you and you choose a suitor other than Cam, it will not matter. It happens all the time.'

She supposed Persephone was right. A young woman could choose only one, and it wasn't like the Earl's reputation would suffer from a rejection from an American heiress with no title. *And it's a pretend courtship.* She couldn't hurt his feelings, because he had none for her in the first place. The thought sent something wilting inside of her, but she ignored it.

'How exciting,' Persephone tittered. 'I can't wait to see this all unfold.'

'But let's not forget why you are here in England, Seph.' The Earl raised a blond eyebrow at her. 'Ma wanted you to have this season. You should at least dance once tonight. I've actually been approached by at least two young men asking for an introduction.'

'Oh, dear, I've lost my spectacles,' Persephone burst out.

'They're on your face, lass,' the Earl pointed out.

'I mean my spare ones.'

Maddie frowned. 'I thought you already went to look for them?'

'I d-dropped them again…somewhere.' She backed away. 'I'll see you later then, Cam. Maddie.' She turned tail and hurried away from them.

The Earl's lips pressed together and a line appeared between his eyebrows. 'I should go speak with her. But before that, do we have an agreement, Miss DeVries?'

Doubt still crept in her mind, so she shot him back a question. 'Why would you do this?'

He seemed taken aback but quickly recovered. 'I have made a promise to my sister to help you in this endeavour, and I'm afraid I cannot back out on my promise,' he countered. 'She has very few friends— nay, she has no friends at all. But she has obviously taken a liking to you. Coming to England has not been easy for her. I appreciate that you have made her feel less alone in such a strange place, in what must be a confusing time for her. So please, allow me to do this one thing to thank you. For her.'

Maddie could only stare at him, stunned. It was not at all the reason she'd expected. 'I… Yes.'

Oh, Lord, she was really doing this.


*He was really doing this.*

Cam stared down into those beautiful sky blue eyes, wondering what in God's name he was thinking.

What was it about Madeline DeVries that he just could not resist? She'd already given him a way out of that silly plan, and he should have taken that gift she'd offered. But no, he'd had to entangle himself further, suggesting this ridiculous pretend courtship that would surely lead to disaster.

Dancing with her was one thing, but courting her was another. That would involve spending more time together. *I should have left well enough alone.*

Still, seeing her so forlorn had sparked something in him—not to mention, that brat of a sister of hers had only fuelled his outrage. Why anyone would think Maddie was inferior to Caroline—including Maddie herself— was a mystery to him.

*I cannot do this.*

He reminded himself of the last time he'd acted on his impulses, envisioning Jenny and Kirk that morning they'd come to tell him the news.

*Never again.*

He would have to stop this madness before he completely lost himself. But how?

An idea sprung up in his mind: have her married as fast as possible, ensuring that she was out of his reach before this attraction turned into an obsession.

Aye, that was the answer.

This was a ruse, a ploy, and nothing more. Though he still needed to take precautions.

Clearing his throat, he began, 'Now that we are in agreement, perhaps we can lay down some rules.'

Her expression turned serious. 'Rules?'

'Yes. If we are to achieve your goal, then we must do so methodically. We must have a strategy, along with some rules. To protect all parties.' *Mainly, myself.*

She seemed to mull his words over. 'All right, my lord. And what are these rules?'

Cam blurted out the first thing he could think of. 'We must only dance once per ball.'

'Once?' She sounded disappointed. 'But we've already danced twice in the same evening.'

And Cam would never forget it. How she'd felt in his arms and the way her face had lit up with excitement both times. Maddie simply standing and doing nothing was enough of a temptation, but when she was dancing, she was like a living goddess. He wouldn't be able to resist her if he had to do that more than once a night.

'Two dances with the same partner is usually acceptable at any event,' he began. 'But if you show me too much favour, other gentlemen might infer that your mind is already made up, and they may decide it is not worth the effort to court you.'

'That makes sense,' she relented. 'What else?'

He thought back to his time with Jenny and how he'd wooed her. She'd often loved getting presents from him and he had given her plenty. 'I'll not shower you with gifts,' he stated in the coolest manner he could muster.

'I must decline them anyway,' she pointed out. 'Miss Merton says young ladies can only accept gifts from their fiancé.'

'Fair enough.' There would be no trouble there, then. 'Next, we spend minimal time together.' When he was trying to win Jenny, he'd often found ways to run into her in the village or show up at her father's home. No, he could not be around Maddie constantly. She was far too tempting.

'What do you mean by minimal?'

'I do not actually need to court you but, rather, put on an illusion of it.'

'And how would you do that, my lord?'

'Tonight, after our dance, I will ask your father for permission to call on you.' Even though they were staying in the same house, he would still have to do things properly. 'I will do this in front of other guests, and hopefully let the gossips of the ton do their work, and I won't need to actually pay you a call. We need not spend any more time together outside balls or during mealtimes at the Dowager's home.' And he planned to miss as many of those as possible without offending their host. 'And we will especially never find ourselves alone. That's our fourth rule.'

Her brows wrinkled. 'Whyever would we need to be alone? And it's not like we would have a chance.'

'*Ahem.*' He gestured around them with his hands.

'Oh. Right.' Her cheeks pinked. 'But what should I do about other suitors?'

'I'm sure your mama will know how to handle them.' He ignored the tightening in his chest. 'That's the fifth rule, by the way. I won't meddle in your affairs.'

'Y-you won't?'

'Of course not. It's your decision, after all.'

'Ah, of c-course,' she stammered. 'I did not mean to imply that I would need your assistance on such matters. Any more rules I should know about?'

'I shall let you know if I think of anything else to-night.' He bowed his head, then turned on his heel.

As he left the library, he blew out a breath, hoping to ease the tightening in his chest. He could not take any chances. He needed to keep her at arm's length, and these ground rules would ensure he would never make the same mistake again.

# Chapter Five

Cam surveyed the Earl of Hartnell's ballroom, where the elite of London's society gathered, and laughed, and revelled as if all was well and normal.

But nothing about Cam's life seemed normal—at least not since he'd met Miss Madeline DeVries. His instinct to stay as far away as possible from her was the correct reaction.

And yet, now he was in much deeper, and it was all his doing.

It wasn't too late yet. He could tell her he'd changed his mind. Maybe he could leave now and he wouldn't have to dance with her.

'Cam, we're here,' Persephone said, seemingly popping out of nowhere. His sister had insisted they go to the Hartnell ball earlier than the Dowager and the DeVrieses. 'It will allow Maddie to have a more dramatic entrance, as she'll always be announced after us,' she had explained.

However, when it was time to go, Persephone had conveniently torn her dress and then bade him to head to the ball in their carriage first and that she would ride to the ball with the Dowager.

'Glad to see you've arrived.' Persephone had been acting oddly since they'd arrived in London— well, odd even for her, he supposed. 'Disaster was averted with your dress, I presume?'

'My what—oh, yes.' She fiddled with a bit of lace on her dress. 'Anyway, we're here. You should ask Maddie to dance now.' She nodded towards the other end of the room, where Maddie, her sister, and her parents were walking towards the refreshment table. They barely had time to accept the glasses of lemonade offered by the footman when two gentlemen came swooping in.

'Perhaps Miss DeVries doesn't need my assistance after all.' Cam gnashed his teeth.

'Maybe.' Persephone's lips puckered like she'd eaten a lemon when both men wrote their names on Caroline's card but completely ignored Maddie. 'Just look at how sad she is.'

Though fleeting, Cam clearly saw the disappointment on Maddie's pretty face. Irrational anger bubbled through him. Even dressed in that ridiculous ruffled green-orange gown that washed out her complexion, Maddie was still far lovelier than her insipid sister.

'Now's your chance to help poor Maddie so she can find a husband and have the family she's always wanted.'

His chest tightened at Persephone's words. Yet, he himself had reached that conclusion this morning. Pretending to court Maddie now might be the only way to ensure her marriage. Then he would not be able to act on his obsession.

'Well?' Persephone demanded. 'What are you going to do? They just announced the next dance.'

Cam didn't reply to Persephone but instead snatched a flute of champagne from a passing waiter, then downed it in one gulp and handed the empty glass to his sister before marching across the room.

Maddie must have felt his eyes on her, as she turned her head to face him. Her plump lips parted as their gazes met, and that attraction once again tugged at his gut. She quickly turned away, and a thought surfaced in his mind: Did Maddie even feel anything at all towards him? Perhaps the real reason she'd tried to dissuade him from this pretend courtship was that she was repulsed by him.

It was, however, too late to back out now, because as soon as Maddie's mother saw him approach, she nodded and waved at him. Ignoring her now would amount to a cut.

'My lord,' Eliza DeVries greeted him breathlessly, her excitement barely contained. 'How lovely to see you. We were told you had gone ahead of us.'

'Mrs DeVries,' he murmured, then turned to Maddie's father. 'Mr DeVries. I was wondering if I may have the honour of dancing with your daughter?' When Caroline smiled at him and took a step forward, he added, 'Miss Madeline.'

Eliza let out a squeak and covered her mouth with her hand, while Caroline's jaw dropped.

'Of course, my lord,' Cornelius replied with a chuckle. 'Though you should really be asking my daughter.'

He offered his hand to her, ignoring the viperous stare from Caroline. 'Miss DeVries? May I have this dance?'

'My lord.' She took it, and he whisked her away. When they arrived at their position, she glanced around. 'People are staring at us again.'

'Good,' he bit out.

*This was why they were doing this, after all.*

An uncomfortable sensation settled in his stomach,

but he ignored it. He placed his hand on her waist while taking her other hand, then the music began to play.

Once again, Maddie's face brightened as they danced. She seemed transformed—much lighter, happier, and less nervous. She even smiled at him, a gesture that made his heart leap. He would never forget that moment or her pretty face, and so he filed it away, and perhaps one day, when he was old and grey, he could look back on this with fondness, knowing he'd done the right thing for her.

'You truly love to dance, don't you?' he observed.

'I do.'

'Why?'

She didn't have time to answer right away as they changed direction. Once she was back in his arms, she said, 'During my very first lesson, my dance master would constantly shout insults at me when I made mistakes.'

He ground his teeth together. 'And what insults would he hurl at you?'

'Nothing I could understand. He was Italian.' The slightest smile appeared on her lips. 'But, after that, I vowed to study hard and learn how to dance. And during those afternoon dance lessons, I concentrated so hard on getting the steps right that I couldn't think of anything else. It was as if my mind was so preoccupied with thoughts of turning the right way or holding my body up straight that I could forget everything outside that ballroom. And forget that I'm not as—' Her lips clamped shut and her eyes lowered.

'Not as what?'

'It— It's nothing, my lord.'

Cam suspected what she wanted to say. That she was not as pretty as her sister. *Bollocks*. 'And what happened after all that practice?'

That smile returned. 'Eventually the dance master told me that I was better than Caroline.'

'Maybe it was your handsome Italian dance master that inspired you,' he teased.

She laughed, throwing her head back and exposing her long, elegant neck. 'Signor Cavallini was nearly seventy years old and had ten children and six grandchildren.'

'He sounds quite energetic.'

'He was a dance master.'

Her cheeks puffed from exertion, giving them the prettiest blush, and once again he could not tear his eyes away from her. More than that, he could not help but admire her tenacity. Instead of whining or running away in tears, she'd faced the challenge and striven to become better.

Cam did not believe that women were weaker than or inferior to men. His own mother had proved that, and he had learned never to underestimate her. Elaine Mac-Gregor had had an inner strength that was understated. It had been unnoticeable, just beneath the surface, but it had been there.

Growing up, he'd wondered how an English lady like her had found her home in the Highlands. One day, when he was about sixteen, while they were taking a walk in the woods, he'd asked and she had answered, *'I fell in love with your father at first sight, and so how could I not love the place where he came from? And while life here is so different and much rougher than where I grew up, I had to learn to adapt. Look at the reeds in the river.'* She had pointed to tall, skinny stalks on the water. *'When the water rushes past them, do they break off? No, they bend and curve, and in doing so, they remain intact.'*

'My lord?' Maddie's words broke into his reverie. 'Are you all right?'

His heart stuttered in his chest as those luminous blue eyes stared up at him. 'Aye.'

Thankfully, the dance was nearly over. As soon as the music stopped and the dance finished, he escorted her back to her parents' side. Sure enough, three gentlemen were fast approaching them.

Cam fought the urge to scare them off. However, he had to play his part, if only to further their grand scheme so Maddie could be wed and out of his reach.

'Mr DeVries,' he began, loud enough for the other men to hear as they wrote their names on Maddie's dance card. 'I would like your permission to call upon Miss Madeline.' From the corner of his vision, he saw Maddie stiffen.

'Call upon her?' Mr DeVries chuckled. 'We are all staying at the Dowager's town house. You can see her anytime.'

His wife let out a squeak and gripped his arm. 'That's not what he means, Cornelius.' Her eyes sparkled as she choked out, 'My husband grants his permission. We will see you in the parlour at half past three tomorrow. Myself and Miss Merton will be there.'

Maddie looked at him helplessly, her hands writhing together. 'T-tomorrow? I mean. His Lordship did not s-specify when... He should really send you a card first—'

'Maddie, don't be silly,' Eliza hissed. 'Like your father said, we are all staying in the same house. A card would be a waste of good paper.' She let out a chuckle. 'We will see you tomorrow.'

'I look forward to it.' He glanced over at Maddie. 'Miss DeVries, thank you for the lovely dance.' His gaze flickered to the gentlemen, who all regarded him with the same expression. Cam recognised it, of course—any man would have. They were eyeing him, assessing him and his competitive position.

*Stupid fops*, he thought as he turned and walked away. They saw Maddie's value only because he wanted her, not for what she could offer. That she could be a good wife, a partner in life.

*Hell.*

He halted in his tracks and massaged his temple with his thumb and forefinger. How did he get manipulated into actually paying Maddie a call? This was against their rules.

*I have to stop this now.* This obsession was heading into dangerous territory. It seemed he needed to add one last rule.

*Do not fall in love.*

# Chapter Six

Maddie could not believe it. *She was dancing! At a ball!*

She should be happy. No—ecstatic. And part of her truly was elated that she was no longer a wallflower, wilting in the background while she watched others in their merriment.

Yet, the dancing left her wanting for more. Or rather, it wasn't the dancing but her partners. Or most of them, anyway. Her current partner included.

Lord Andrew Annesley was the second son of a marquess. Mama could hardly contain herself when he strode over to ask for her next dance. He was handsome and of a good pedigree. Why, he was even taller than most of the other men she partnered with, reaching nearly to her eye level.

However, there was just something about him that was…lacking.

'And so… I said, "Sir, I am no fool. That is…not a peacock…feather,"' Lord Annesley huffed as they returned to each other when it was their turn to perform the steps in the middle. When they'd begun the dance, he had been telling her a story about his trip to the milliner that afternoon. 'And I demanded…my money back.'

'How, er, tenacious of you, my lord.' Oh, heavens, the man never stopped talking. And maybe that was what bothered Maddie. Lord Annesley chattered on and on about everything and nothing at the same time.

In fact, that seemed to be the commonality among her dance partners tonight. They spoke only about themselves or gossiped among the ton or other inconsequential subjects. None of them even asked Maddie about her interests and thoughts. Well, none, except one.

*You truly love to dance, don't you?*

And as she did with each of her dance partners tonight, she kept comparing Lord Annesley to the Earl. Instead of talking about himself, the Earl had asked her why she loved to dance and even let her ramble on without interrupting. Dear Lord, and *how* she had rambled on about Signor Cavallini and her silly dance lessons! She winced with embarrassment at the memory.

'Miss DeVries?' Lord Annesley frowned at her disapprovingly. 'Are you listening—'

Maddie twirled around and skipped away from him to return to the opposite corner, blowing out a breath of relief. Why did quadrilles take so long? She glanced at the musicians, willing them to pick up the tempo. However, as she turned her head, she saw a glimpse of the Earl chatting casually with a small group of people. The fluttering in her stomach made her miss a step, but thankfully, no one noticed. What was it about him that made her so flustered? And why did her mind keep circling back to him?

It had been better when she'd thought him to be a boorish lout who insulted her. But in the span of one day, he'd managed to turn her opinion of him, first by apologising, then by showing how much he truly cared about Persephone. Her heart stirred at his thoughtfulness. Maddie knew most men would not care about their younger sister's feelings, but he clearly did.

*He's pretending to court you because of Persephone,* she reminded herself. *As thanks for being her friend.*

It was hard to not be disappointed by their first rule that they could only dance once per ball. But she understood that showing him more favour than her other suitors—well, potential suitors, at this point—would not bode well for their plan. She wanted to attract men, not scare them off.

'I thoroughly enjoyed our dance, Miss DeVries.'

Maddie secretly sighed in relief as she curtseyed. 'Thank you, my lord.'

'If you are not otherwise engaged,' he began as he led her back to her parents and sister, 'I would like to call on you this week.'

'I am not— I mean, of course.' One other dance partner—Mr James Davenport—had implied that he might pay her a call in the next day or so.

'Wonderful.'

She returned his smile, as it seemed like the right thing to do.

This was what she wanted, right?

'Oh, Maddie.' Her mother gripped her arm in excitement once Lord Annesley was halfway across the room. 'It looks like your fortunes have taken a turn. Lord Annesley's father has one of the oldest titles in England, I'm told.'

Maddie didn't even wonder where her mother had got that information, considering neither of them had even been introduced to Lord Annesley before this evening.

'We only spoke for a few minutes when we were introduced earlier,' Papa said. 'He was very, uh, enthusiastic and passionate with his words.'

*Especially when it came to fashion*, Maddie added silently.

'What else did you talk about?' Mama asked.

'He says he would like to pay me a call this week,' Maddie informed them.

'Oh, a call from a lord!' Mama flicked her fan open and waved it frantically. 'It must be your new gown. The seamstress fought me on the sunset and chartreuse, but I knew it was the right combination to draw attention to your features and away from your height. We must order new gowns in these colours for you immediately.'

Maddie groaned inwardly. 'I still have at least three gowns I haven't worn. I'm sure they're perfectly fine.'

'Nonsense. You will have *every* gown in that colour.'

'You seem overly excited, my dear,' Papa said gently. 'Caro, perhaps you could escort your mother to the retiring room? Be a dear and sit with her for a moment.'

Mama's fanning turned even more brisk. 'Excellent idea, Cornelius.'

'You can use the time to plan your shopping trip together.' Papa gave Caroline an encouraging nudge towards Mama. 'And you can visit that glove store you've been talking about all evening.'

'Oh, yes, a wonderful idea.' Caroline took their mother's elbow and guided her away. 'Come now, Mama. You need rest. I think I will need those kid gloves in….'

'Thank you, Papa,' Maddie said to her father once they were alone.

'Mr DeVries, Miss DeVries. Good evening.'

Maddie turned towards the gentleman who had approached them. 'Mr Wadsworth,' she greeted in return. Their hostess had introduced Mr George Wadsworth earlier in the evening, and he had immediately asked to write his name on her dance card.

'I would like to claim my dance,' he said, then added, 'If Mr DeVries wouldn't mind.'

'Of course not.' Papa gestured to her. 'Have a lovely time.' He winked at her.

'Thank you, Papa.' She allowed Mr Wadsworth to lead her away. However, even as she took her position on the ballroom floor, she could not help but search the room for the Earl's familiar, tall frame. It was usually easily easy to spot him, but it seemed as if he had all but disappeared.

*Why am I looking for him, anyway?*

All that mattered was that her dance card was filled, and perhaps, if their ploy worked, she would soon have at least one or two suitors to choose from. At the very least, if she did not have any suitors, she could still enjoy the dancing.

The next morning, as Maddie headed down to breakfast, she ran into Persephone at the top of the staircase.

'How was the rest of ball?' Persephone asked. 'From the smudges under your eyes, I can tell you were up all night. Tell me,' she tugged at Maddie's sleeve. 'Did you receive any proposals?'

Maddie chuckled. 'No proposals, but there were a few gentlemen who said they would pay me a call this week. But where did you go? I didn't see you all evening.'

'Where else?' Persephone puffed out a breath. 'Hiding in all the anterooms, which is why I didn't have a chance to watch you. The Countess of Hartnell should consider redecorating her home, as it is severely lacking in foliage or objects large enough to conceal oneself.'

'Oh, dear.' *Poor Persephone.* 'What can I do to help?'

Persephone linked their arms together as they descended the stairs. 'I'm afraid no one can help me. Besides, we need to concentrate on you.' She lowered her voice. 'And I cannot wait to see if this plan of yours will work. A pretend courtship. Why didn't I think of it?'

'We don't know yet if it will work.' Caroline's words from last night came back to her—telling her they would pay her a call was different from actually doing it.

'I'm sure it will,' Persephone assured her as they reached the bottom of the steps and made their way to the breakfast room.

Breakfast at Mabury Hall was an informal affair, where everyone came and went as they pleased. The Dowager, Miss Merton, Maddie's parents, and Caroline had already started, so the two girls took their places at the table. Once again, the Earl was not present, and Maddie bit her tongue to keep from asking where he was. Perhaps he was once again meeting with his man of business.

'Kate and Sebastian want to visit soon,' the Dowager had been telling them. 'I received a letter from her this morning, and she mentioned that they're nearly ready to break ground on the railway—'

'Your Grace,' Eames greeted as he entered the breakfast room.

'Good morning, Eames.' The Dowager eyed the two stacks of letters and cards on the silver tray the butler carried. 'We're quite popular this morning, aren't we?'

'Indeed, Your Grace.' He handed her the larger pile, then gave the rest to Maddie's parents.

Papa opened the card on top of the pile. 'Hmm.'

'Ooh, that card looks expensive.' Mama leaned over. 'Who is it from?'

'Lord Andrew Annesely,' Papa read aloud, then the next one. 'And this one's from a Mr Davenport.'

'That one says Sir Alfred Kensington!' Mama sputtered, pointing to the last card.

Caroline's delicate blond eyebrows drew together. 'I don't recognise those names.'

'They're all gentlemen Maddie danced with,' Mama announced.

Maddie couldn't move or say anything. She actually had callers after a ball. A soft nudge at her feet startled her, and she turned to Persephone, who smirked at her and mouthed, *See?*

'Are there any more?' Caroline enquired, her lips pursed together.

'A few,' Papa mumbled as he went through the stack. 'Mostly business acquaintances ah!' He handed one to his wife. 'I don't recognise this one.'

'Mr Garrison,' she read. 'Didn't you dance with him last night, Caroline?'

'One? That's it?' Caroline fumed. 'I only received one measly card?'

'Isn't your afternoon schedule for the rest of the week already full?' Miss Merton enquired. 'Why, if you had got more than one, you wouldn't have been able to meet them all.'

Caroline stood up so fast, the chair scraped loudly on the hardwood floor. 'Please excuse me, Your Grace. I've lost my appetite.' The Dowager barely had time to nod before she stomped out.

Mama didn't seem perturbed by Caroline's dramatic exit. 'Maddie, three gentlemen want to call on you. I can hardly believe it!'

She couldn't either.

And all because the Earl danced with her and asked permission from her father to call on her. Why, only two of the gentlemen had heard him, yet news of it had travelled quickly to the other men in the room. Kate often jested that if the ton's gossips could be harnessed into a form of communication device on the tracks, they could revolutionise the railroad industry.

'We must be ready for when they come calling,' Mama continued. 'Oh, we will head straight to the dress shop today. I only hope Mrs Ellesmore has more of the same fabrics from your gown last night.'

Maddie stifled the urge to scream and looked around helplessly, searching for someone—anyone—to save her from her mother's horrendous fashion sense.

'Eliza,' the Dowager began with a delicate clearing of her throat. 'I believe Miss Merton requires your assistance today.'

'I do?' Miss Merton asked. When the Dowager sent her a meaningful look, she quickly added, 'Yes, I do. For, er—'

'Sorting out and replying to our invitations,' the Dowager provided. 'I'm afraid I'm entirely too busy today.' She gestured to the stack of envelopes in front of her. 'I trust no one else but Miss Merton to sift through the pile and accept ones from the most prominent hostesses and exclusive events in London your daughters must attend.'

Miss Merton's head bobbed up and down. 'We must choose only the best balls and parties, after all. But I cannot do it alone.'

Mama gripped the edge of the table. 'That is important work, indeed. But what about Maddie's gowns?'

'I told you, Mama. I don't need any new gowns.'

'Nonsense. You must have them.'

'But—'

'I shall take her,' the Dowager suggested. 'That's one of my errands today, anyway. She may as well come with me.'

'It's not—'

'I *insist*,' she said with a cryptic smile.

'Don't be rude, Madeline,' Mama warned. 'She shall accompany you, Your Grace.'

'It's settled, then. Persephone, why don't you come along? We would love the company.'

'I'd be happy to.' However, Persephone's expression told Maddie she would rather do anything but that.

'You must be back as soon as possible, as the Earl will be paying you a call today.' Mama practically shook with excitement. 'Lady Persephone, where is your brother, by the way?'

'He's in a meeting, Mrs DeVries,' she replied. 'And asked not to be disturbed.'

'How unfortunate.' Mama tsked, then glanced down at Maddie's gown. 'But then again, perhaps it's better he wasn't at breakfast, seeing as you're in such a drab outfit.'

'If you'll excuse me.' The Dowager rose, and so did everyone. 'And we must move along. Ladies, I will see you in the hall at half past nine. Have a good day.'

Miss Merton picked up the stacks of cards the Dowager left behind. 'We should start on these right away, Mrs DeVries. If we do not answer them within the appropriate amount of time, the hostesses might think we are snubbing them.'

'We cannot have that,' Mama agreed.

'Let's head to the Dowager's sitting room then.' With that, the two women left.

'I shall begin my day as well,' Papa announced. 'By the way, Maddie, the architect said they'll be sending over the plans for the new forge on the Thames today.'

Though the DeVrieses had originally planned this sojourn to London to find husbands for Maddie and Caroline, somehow Cornelius had been convinced to open a London branch of his iron furnace to service the joint English railway venture between the owner of Mason

R&L, Arthur Mason, and his new son-in-law, the Duke of Mabury. 'I'll need you to help me look them over.'

'Of course, Papa.'

He nodded his goodbye to both of them before leaving.

'I detest going to the modiste,' Persephone sighed. 'I wish I were looking over plans for a forge, too.'

She smiled at her friend. 'Me, too. But I suppose we must endure this one morning at the dressmaker's. Besides, without Mama there, I might be able to persuade the Dowager that I don't need new gowns.' *And certainly not in those dreadful colours.*

'Before we go, we should tell Cam what a success his plan is,' Persephone suggested.

'W-what?' The idea of seeing the Earl this morning both thrilled and alarmed her. 'I don't—'

'Come on.' She hooked her hand into the crook of Maddie's elbow and dragged her along. 'I know he's not actually having a meeting. He's in the smoking room, having his morning coffee and reading the paper.' Her mouth twisted. 'He usually loves eating a hearty breakfast. I'm not sure why he'd skip it today to have coffee by himself.'

Maddie knew why, of course.

Their third rule.

He was avoiding her. 'Maybe it's not a good idea to disturb him.'

'Nonsense. He should know all about your suitors. After all, he came up with the plan.' Persephone's grip was surprisingly strong, and soon they were outside the smoking room. 'He's in there,' she said, pulling the door open. 'Go on.'

'What if he's—' She found herself staggering through the doorway, then heard the door slam shut behind her.

She spun around. 'Persephone?' *Did she just toss me in here and then leave?*

'What are you doing here?'

The Earl's familiar voice made her jump. 'Persephone... She said you were in here.' When she turned to face him, emerald-green eyes pinned her to the spot and made it hard to breathe.

'I asked her to meet me here after breakfast. Why are you here? And didn't we discuss this?' He prowled towards her, his long strides making quick work of the distance between them. 'Fourth rule. We cannot be alone.' He stopped halfway as his entire body tensed and his arms stiffened at his sides.

'I know, my lord. But she thought I should come see you first.'

*Drat! What was Persephone thinking, running off like that?*

'And why is that?'

'To tell you our plan is turning out well.'

'Is it now?' He cocked his head to the side.

'Y-yes.' Why was she acting like a scared mouse? She should be thankful to him. 'It seems I've at least three gentlemen coming to call this week. And it's all thanks to you.'

The Earl's expression remained impassive. 'Congratulations, then.'

'That may be premature,' she said with a forced laugh. 'They're only coming for fifteen minutes of boring conversation in front of a room full of chaperones.'

'Is that what you think this afternoon will be like when I come to pay my call to you, then?'

Oh, dear, had she forgotten her mother had strongarmed him into that? 'I'm so sorry for that, my lord. My mother can be tenacious. A-and we don't have to have our call today. I'm sure if you explain you were busy, she wouldn't mind delaying it.'

'Perhaps I will.'

The way he said it so casually made her chest tighten. 'We're agreed, then.'

'I can ask Persephone to relay the message of regret to your mama.'

'That would be wise.' Mama would have a conniption, but they had no choice.

'Then I will see you at our next dance.'

The words made her stomach—and other regions below that—flutter. 'I, uh, I should… I will definitely…' Flustered, she didn't bother completing the sentence and spun around, pushing on the door before scurrying out. She was so occupied with trying to get away from him that she didn't realise there was someone else coming down the opposite way.

'Maddie?'

Maddie jumped back before she crashed into the Dowager. 'Y-Your Grace.'

'Are you quite all right?' Knowing dark eyes peered at her. 'You look flushed.'

'I am fine, ma'am. If you'll excuse me, I need to dress for our outing.' After a quick curtsey, she slid past her and raced up to her room, then rang for her maid.

As Betsy helped her change, Maddie tried to focus on anything except the Earl. But of course, her mind kept wandering to him as it always did.

*I will see you at our next dance.*

Her heart hammered and her insides turned to the consistency of molten iron fresh from the furnace. But why did he affect her so?

This whole thing was a farce. A sham. A trick they

were playing on the aristocracy. He did not actually want to dance with her.

None of it was real.

'Miss? You're all ready.'

'Thank you, Betsy.'

Creeping out of her room, Maddie proceeded downstairs, praying that she wouldn't encounter the Earl. Lord, how was she to face him after this morning? *I shouldn't have run away.* She should have nodded coolly, then turned and left with her head held high. Or she could have laughed and said something witty.

By the time she reached the foyer, Persephone and the Dowager were already waiting for her. Her Grace's gaze narrowed at her, but she didn't say anything and nodded to Eames, who held the door open for them.

The Dowager's carriage took them to Bond Street to Mrs Helena Ellesmore's dress shop. She was the best dressmaker in London, and all the mamas and debutantes of the season clamoured to get an appointment with her and thus booked weeks in advance—except for the Dowager Duchess of Mabury, of course. The modiste had made Kate's wedding gown and trousseau when she'd married the Dowager's son, for which she'd not only charged an exorbitant amount because it had all had to be done in a month, but also received increased fame among the ton. It was no wonder that she would clear her schedule for her most important client.

'Welcome, Your Grace.' Mrs Ellesmore curtseyed low as they alighted from the carriage. 'Miss DeVries. How lovely to see you again.'

'Good morning, Mrs Ellesmore,' the Dowager began. 'This is Lady Persephone MacGregor.'

'An honour to meet you, my lady.' She eyed Persephone, perhaps assessing if she was to be another client she could add to her roster.

The Dowager gestured towards the shop. 'Let's go inside, shall we?'

'Now,' the seamstress asked as she led them into her shop. 'I've cancelled my appointments for the next few hours as per your request, Your Grace. How can I help you?'

'It's not me you can help.' She turned to Maddie. 'But, rather, Miss DeVries. She needs some new gowns.'

'Please, Your Grace, Mrs Ellesmore, if I may be, er, frank, I don't really need any new gowns. My mother insisted, but I do have a fair number I have yet to wear.'

'None that you would want to wear,' Persephone interjected. 'You hate those gowns. I can see how miserable you are when you wear them.'

'I— I don't… I mean, I wasn't…' She sent Mrs Ellesmore an apologetic look. 'I'm so sorry. They are very well made.' Too well made, in fact, as no matter how hard she tried, she couldn't tear or rip any of them as an excuse not to wear them.

To Maddie's surprise, the seamstress let out a chuckle. 'Oh, my dear, I'm glad I'm not the only one who thinks they are awful. Why, I often wonder why your mother chose those ghastly bright colours, as they don't become you.'

Maddie let out a breath of relief. Thank goodness Mrs Ellesmore was not offended. 'But why do you continue to make them for me?'

'Because she and the Dowager are my best clients, and I do what my clients tell me.' She tsked. 'Poor dear. I always felt so sorry for you, especially when she let your sister pick out her own fabrics and gowns.' She looked Maddie up and down. 'I've so many ideas for you. The

ing Elaine, she raised her children properly. But I'm not blind, nor will I turn a blind eye if he's somehow taking advantage of you.'

It took all of Maddie's might to suppress the urge to laugh at the ludicrous notion. The Earl taking advantage of her? If anything, she was the one exploiting him.

'He has not said or done anything to offend you?'

'I assure you, Your Grace, he's been a perfect gentleman.'

'Here we are.' Mrs Ellesmore returned, followed by a young woman who carried a pale peach gown. 'Gertie, please help Miss DeVries into the dress.' Gertie walked over to Maddie, then drew the curtain around them so she could undress her and assist her. Once she was laced up, Gertie pulled the curtain away.

'How lovely you look,' the Dowager exclaimed.

'Now, that suits you much better than chartreuse,' Persephone added.

Turning to face the mirror behind, Maddie couldn't help but gasp when she saw her reflection. The understated colours were muted further with a layer of delicate lace on top, and the only adornment on the dress was the cluster of white and peach roses on the neckline, which exposed her neck and upper chest.

'See?' Mrs Ellesmore said smugly. 'The right colour and cut only enhances your beauty and height. You are like a towering goddess from Mount Olympus.'

An anxious thought surfaced in her mind. 'Mama would never let me wear this to the garden party, would she?'

The Dowager clucked her tongue. 'Do not worry about your mama, dear. I will take care of her.'

'And I will not breathe a word, either,' Mrs Ellesmore promised. 'Now, how about—' She covered her mouth with her hands. 'Wait here. I have something special I've been saving in the other room. Gertie, please retrieve the new fabric that was delivered this morning.'

The young woman scurried off, then returned, carrying a bolt of fabric. It was an unusual shade of blue that shimmered under the light.

'Isn't it beautiful?' Mrs Ellesmore caught the loose end of the fabric and waved it with a flourish. 'And see how light it is? It will make you look as if you are flying when you dance the waltz.'

The Dowager's dark eyes widened. 'Mrs Ellesmore, you truly are a genius. That colour would look absolutely striking on her.'

*Mama would never approve of it*, Maddie thought. The fabric was too rich and bold. If Caroline were here, she would insist on buying the entire bolt to prevent anyone else from having it. *But neither of them were here now.*

'I must make you a gown with it. I insist,' Mrs Ellesmore said firmly. 'When is your next ball?'

'In three days' time. The Baybrook ball,' the Dowager answered. 'Can you have it ready by then?'

'For you? Of course, Your Grace.'

Maddie inhaled a sharp breath, her gaze still fixed on the beautiful fabric. Was this really happening? It was as if she was in some fairy tale and she had not one but two magical godmothers. 'How can I ever thank you?'

Mrs Ellesmore laughed. 'There is one thing you could do—never wear those awful gowns again.'

# Chapter Seven

'My lord?' George Atwell cleared his throat. 'Should I repeat those figures for you?'

Cam gripped the arms of the leather chair tightly. Ever since their encounter this morning, he could scarcely think of anything else but Maddie. He'd been caught by surprise when she'd come to him, and even more by her news.

*Our plan is turning out well.*

Bloody hell.

'Er, yes. Or, better yet, just write them down and I shall examine them later.'

Since Cam was also in London for Glenbaire business, the Dowager was kind enough to offer the smoking room in Mabury Hall as his temporary office. Cam was glad for the distraction of his work and that Atwell had arrived soon after Maddie had run off, which prevented him from doing something foolish.

Like chasing after her.

'There's one more thing we need to discuss before I go, my lord. The gentlemen's club whose owner insisted on meeting you.'

'Ah, yes. The Underworld.' Actually, the club's name

was legally Hale's, but everyone called it The Underworld. 'Do we have a place and time for this meeting?'

'No, but a boy from the club came to my office and gave me this.' Atwell retrieved a black calling card from the breast pocket of his vest. 'He said to put it directly in your hands.'

Cam took it and held it up to the light. There was no writing on the card, except for an embossed gold stamp of what appeared to be a coin. *Charon's Obol*. 'I'm guessing this is payment for the ferryman.'

'I beg your pardon, my lord?'

'It's nothing.' He tucked the card into his pocket. 'I'll take care of it.'

'If that is all, my lord, I must be off.' Atwell began to put away the papers and envelopes strewn about on the desk into his leather satchel. 'I'll be sure to post these letters for you right away. I shall see myself out.'

'Thank you, Atwell.'

Alone once again, the silence inside the room deafened Cam's ears. The door that led outside and connected to the rest of the house seemed far away. Or perhaps he was just too much of a coward to go out there where he could run into Maddie again.

*I am a grown man,* he scoffed to himself. *And she is just a silly girl.*

Yes, that's what Maddie was.

Just a silly girl, who wanted to fulfil her dream of finding a husband and raising a passel of children.

Nothing more.

Bolting from the chair, Cam marched out of the smoking room with a determined stride. It was half past two, and the house was unusually quiet. According to Murray, Persephone had left to accompany the Dowager and Maddie on an errand sometime after breakfast.

He puffed out an exasperated breath. *Persephone*. She was really the only female he should be worrying about. Maddie had distracted him from his real purpose in coming to London.

*Once Persephone returns from her outing, I'll sit her down to talk and get to the bottom of her disappearing acts.*

While he would never push her to choose a husband, she still needed to mingle among society so she could gain some maturity and lose some of her awkwardness.

Cam had been so distracted by his thoughts of the past that he must have taken a wrong turn. He'd meant to go back to his rooms but was now outside the library instead. The last time he'd been there, he'd wanted to borrow a book but had got distracted by Maddie.

Perhaps this time he could peruse the shelves in peace. However, when he heard muffled voices coming from the inside, he halted. Carefully, he opened the door a crack.

'I do like how they've expanded this west-facing wall. I wasn't satisfied with the first version and....'

Cam recognised the speaker as Cornelius DeVries, so he entered, thinking it was safe.

How wrong he was.

'But what about the space between the two furnaces and the stove?'

His heart jumped at the sound of Maddie's soft voice. *I should get out of here.*

But as always, when she was around, he was like a moth to a flame, and his feet would not move.

'What about them?' Cornelius asked.

'The furnaces are too far from the stove, which means we'll have to make the pipes longer,' she continued. 'We'll lose heat, especially since London has cooler temperatures throughout the year than Pennsylvania.'

'What—oh, yes, yes. Thank you, dear. I didn't think of that.'

*What in the world was going on?*

Curious, Cam crept closer. A bust of Aristotle sitting on top of a column blocked his view of her, so he peered around the marble figure.

Cornelius and Maddie were bent over one of the large tables in the middle of the room, poring over large sheets of paper spread out on the surface. Wanting to see what they were examining, he inched closer, gripping Aristotle's head for support. Unfortunately, the great philosopher wasn't affixed to the column as firmly as he'd thought, and it slipped from the pedestal, the weighty effigy crashing to the ground and rolling across the floor.

*Hellfire!*

Mercifully, the bust remained intact, but now two sets of sky blue eyes fixed on him as father and daughter lifted their heads towards him.

'Er…good afternoon, Mr DeVries.' Colour heightened Maddie's complexion in the most adorable way. 'Miss DeVries.'

'Lord Balfour, how nice to see you.' Cornelius glanced at the clock. 'Mercy me, you're supposed to call on my daughter this afternoon. Did I get the time wrong?'

Cam cursed silently. He was supposed to ask Persephone to relay his regrets to Mrs DeVries, but he wasn't sure if she'd arrived.

'The Earl decided to cancel,' Maddie explained. 'Persephone told me and I was just about to tell Mama after we finished here. He had, uh, a prior appointment at half past three.'

'An urgent business matter, I'm afraid,' Cam added. 'My sincerest apologies to you and your wife.'

'Oh, dear, your mother will be disappointed.' Cornelius's brows drew together. 'Well…do you have fifteen minutes now? You could join us.' He gestured to the other side of the table.

Maddie shook her head. 'Papa, this isn't how it's done.'

'Isn't it? Fifteen minutes of conversation in a room with a chaperone? I'm your father. I don't think there is a more appropriate guardian for your virtue than me,' he said with a chuckle. 'My lord? What do you say?'

What could he say? 'If you approve, then I have no objections.'

Cam already knew this was a mistake, but as was the case when it involved Miss Madeline DeVries, he might as well toss that mistake over his shoulder and add it to the growing pile behind him. Besides, his curiosity was already stoked given what he'd overheard. Clasping his hands behind him, he strode over to them.

'What would you like to discuss, my lord? The weather?'

'It seems I was interrupting you, Mr DeVries.' He nodded at the papers on the table. 'Perhaps you should finish your discussion with Miss DeVries first? Again, my apologies for the intrusion.'

*Or, rather, being caught spying on you and your daughter.*

'Not at all, my lord. Actually, it's a good thing you did arrive, as Maddie and I often get caught up whenever we discuss business and end up losing track of time.'

'Business?' He couldn't help but glance over at Maddie, who was staring at the floor as if she suddenly found her shoes interesting. 'You discuss your business with Miss DeVries?'

'Of course,' he said matter-of-factly. 'She's been by my side at the furnace since she was in pigtails. I've taught her everything she knows. One day she may even take over for me.'

*Take over?*

'Anyway, my dear,' Cornelius said, turning back to Maddie. 'You were pointing to the river before His Lordship arrived. Did you have a problem with the site?'

Maddie hesitated. 'Perhaps now is not the time—'

'Please.' Cam waved a hand. 'Do not mind me. I can wait.' And, only the heavens knew why, he wanted to hear Maddie talk more about furnaces and stoves.

She pursed her plump pink lips. 'They're building too close to the edge of the river.' A finger tapped on the drawing—which looked like building plans—on the table. 'We must consider soil erosion in the next few decades, or else our furnace may someday end up in the Thames.'

'Doesn't erosion take millions of years?' Cam interrupted. 'It doesn't sound like that's something you have to worry about now.'

'Normally, yes.' Maddie traced her fingers along the wavy line that was meant to represent the riverbank. 'However, any type of waterway that has a large volume of traffic will likely erode faster. We have three rivers back in Pittsburgh, and though we cannot see the effects of commerce and increased traffic yet, I cannot help but think this progress has a price.'

'We must be ready.' Cornelius's voice took on a serious tone. 'As I always say, if you fail to prepare—'

'—then prepare to fail,' Maddie finished with a grin.

Cornelius beamed at his daughter, the pride in his eyes evident.

And Cam didn't blame him, because right now, he, too, felt all sorts of emotions for the woman standing before him. Most of them he couldn't say in polite company.

Maddie didn't seem to notice the change in Cam's

countenance or how his entire body tensed as she continued on. They seemingly spoke an entirely different language as they launched into some kind of debate. Words Cam had never heard before were thrown about, like *ash content* and *carbon oxide*. As he watched her, one thought popped into his head.

*Yes, please. Tell me more about carbon and coke.*

He wanted to hear what she had to say about erosion and piping.

Perhaps while he was unrolling one of her silk stockings and—

'You look like you're lost in thought,' Cornelius said. 'Or are we boring you to death? What's on your mind, my lord?'

Cam nearly choked at the thought of revealing to the man what was currently occupying his thoughts. 'I… uh… No, please. I am not bored at all. I'm quite fascinated by your spirited discussion. In fact, it reminds me of the time when my father was alive and my brothers and I would talk business.'

'Ah, your whisky business.' Cornelius stroked his chin. 'I'm afraid I don't know anything about whisky. You and your brothers must know everything about production, then, if you learned from your father.'

'From growing the crops all the way to bottling,' he said proudly. 'Learned everything from Da, and he learned it from his father. The knowledge has been passed on from father to son for generations.'

'Isn't Lady Persephone part of the business too?' Maddie piped in.

Now Cornelius looked intrigued. 'Tell us more.'

'There isn't much to tell, really,' he said with a shrug. 'When Ma and Da died, we all felt…lost. Most of the responsibilities of the distillery and the tenants and lands of the Earldom had fallen on my shoulders. My younger brothers, therefore, took on the rest, including raising Persephone, who was only thirteen at the time. Lachlan, Finley, and Liam, bless their hearts, had stepped up in caring for her.' He chewed on his lip. 'Though looking back, I'm not sure that was good idea.'

'And why not?' Cornelius asked.

'Lachlan and Finley had been working on the production side of Glenbaire, while Liam was a genius when it came to developing and refining distilling techniques, as well as blending and growing crops. Thus, Persephone had practically grown up in the distillery, following us around and soaking up every bit of knowledge she could. By the time she was fifteen, she could change a faulty discharge line and regulate a pot still's temperature by looking at the foam through the sight glass.' She had obviously inherited her intelligence from their mother, who Cam suspected had been somewhat of a bluestocking. *Your ma's the smart one, boy*, Da had always said.

'Why, that's wonderful!' Cornelius exclaimed. Maddie, meanwhile, gave him the oddest look.

'But now, I wonder if I'd done Persephone a disservice by letting her run wild in the distillery.' He winced. 'She is…very different from what a lady should be, and my ma might not be happy with me for how she turned out.'

Cornelius harrumphed. 'Nonsense. It's in her blood as much as it is in yours. Just like my Mad—'

*Bong! Bong! Bong!*

'Oh, dear!' Cornelius exclaimed as the clock struck the hour. 'My lord, it looks like we've wasted your allotted fifteen minutes. Forgive me.'

'Do not trouble yourself, Mr DeVries. I'll pay Miss DeVries a call at another time.'

What was a good day to arouse himself so thoroughly to the point of pain, Wednesday or Friday?

'I'll tell Mrs DeVries. She'll be thrilled.'

'If you excuse me, I'm late for my appointment.' He gave Maddie a quick glance—any more and he might embarrass himself. Thank God Murray had selected a long frock coat for him to wear this morning that covered his nether regions.

Swiftly, he turned around and marched out of the library, counting each step until he was safely outside. He expelled the breath he'd been holding with a loud huff.

*Silly girl, my arse.*

Who was that woman in there? How had he not known this side of Maddie existed? He'd been so spellbound by his initial attraction to her that he'd never bothered to find out more about her. She was not only so damned beautiful, but now he'd discovered her to be brilliant as well.

And since when had he ever found intellect arousing?

He groaned. As if he wasn't already captivated by her, he now also had to deal with full-blown lust.

This was precisely the reason why he tried to stay away from her and build up sky-high walls around himself to keep her out.

*Focus on her flaws,* he urged himself.

What flaws?

Not even her hideous outfits could deter her appeal. That particular shade of green she'd worn last night reminded him of the regurgitated contents of his stomach after a night of drinking back when he was younger and couldn't hold his liquor. Then there were those ridiculous hairstyles that made her look like a child's porcelain doll.

*Yes, think of that.* Vomit and children's toys. If he could focus on those aspects, perhaps he'd finally succeed in ridding himself of this infernal obsession with Miss Madeline DeVries.

## Chapter Eight

Maddie wrung her hands together as Betsy put on the final touches on her hair. 'Are you sure it looks all right?'

The maid grinned at her. 'You look beautiful, Miss Maddie.'

Instead of the usual torture with the curling tongs, tonight Betsy had pinned up her locks into elaborate curls around her head. Then, she'd added small pins decorated with silk roses to match the ones on her dress.

'Thank you so much, Betsy. I know you're disobeying Mama's orders and risking your job over a silly hairstyle.'

'Think nothing of it, Miss.' Betsy's face turned sour. 'If I may speak frankly, I always hated those outdated styles Mrs DeVries had me do for you. Your hair's so beautiful, and I've been wantin' to do something more to yer likin' but I've been afraid of yer ma. But Her Grace said if I got in trouble, she'd hire me or find me a position somewhere else.'

It seemed the Dowager had thought of everything. Indeed, she'd even come up with a plan to ensure Mama didn't see her until it was too late. Right before their set time to leave for the Houghton garden party, the Dowager would make an excuse to delay her departure, and

Persephone—who had heartily agreed to participate—would invite Mama, Papa, and Caroline to ride in their carriage. Meanwhile, Maddie and Miss Merton would offer to stay behind to accompany the Dowager. Once Mama was safely out of the house, Maddie would change into her new gown.

'Are you ready, miss?'

'I suppose.' Maddie accepted the matching reticule Betsy handed her and offered her thanks once again before heading downstairs.

'Madeline, I hardly recognised you!' Miss Merton exclaimed when she saw Maddie coming down the stairs. 'That dress is gorgeous—and so are you.'

'Thank you, Miss Merton.' She turned to the Dowager, who beamed at her. 'Do I look all right?'

'I concur with Miss Merton—you do, indeed, look gorgeous. Now, let's run along.'

The Earl and Countess of Houghton lived in a grand home in Hanover Square. The butler welcomed them inside, and then they were ushered out to the magnificent gardens. There was no doubt that Houghton House had one of the largest and most beautiful gardens in London, a fact that the Earl never made anyone forget. It had a wide array of plants and flowers, but its crowning glory was the white marble fountain in the middle. Guests were scattered about, admiring the garden's lovely flora or chatting and socialising in small groups as liveried footmen roamed about, offering tasty morsels of food and glasses of champagne.

Maddie glanced around nervously, wondering where her mother was as the Dowager led them towards their hostess.

'Lady Houghton, thank you for the invitation.'

The Countess of Houghton curtseyed. 'Welcome to

Houghton House, Your Grace. I'm so thrilled you are here. I have not seen you since the Duke's wedding.'

'I wouldn't miss it for the world, Lady Houghton. The gardens are looking especially lovely this year. You must be so proud.'

'Oh, I am, Your Grace.'

'You remember my guests?'

'Why, yes, of course.' The Countess nodded at Miss Merton in greeting. 'Miss Merton.' She turned to Maddie, head craning back. 'And... Miss...?'

'DeVries, Your Ladyship. Madeline DeVries.'

'W-why, you're... I didn't...' she spluttered. 'Why, I hardly recognised you, Miss Madeline.'

*Probably because you didn't spot me from a mile away in my hideous dress*, Maddie thought wryly.

'It's wondrous how a new gown can truly transform a woman, isn't it?' the Dowager commented. 'Mrs Ellesmore is a genius when it comes to cuts and selection of fabrics.'

'She's as pretty as a peach.'

'Indeed,' Miss Merton agreed. 'If you don't mind my saying, Lady Houghton, your roses have fierce competition this afternoon.'

'Your Grace, you've arrived!'

*Oh, no.*

Mama.

Her mood plummeted like a rock kicked over the side of a cliff. Sure enough, Mama was fast approaching, Papa and Caroline trailing closely behind.

'Have you seen Maddie?' Mama asked.

'Eliza, dear.' Papa struggled to keep a straight face. 'Maddie is right here.'

'What?' Mama placed a hand on her heart as pure

shock registered on her face. 'Madeline, what are you wearing?'

Maddie opened her mouth, but the Dowager managed to speak first. 'I'm afraid it's all my fault, Mrs DeVries. I spilled some ink on poor Maddie's dress and there was nothing clean for her to change into. Thankfully, I had this old dress in the closet. We only had to let out the hem a few inches. My deepest apologies for ruining Maddie's gown with my carelessness, Mrs DeVries. But I think she looks beautiful in this one,' the Dowager said. 'Don't you agree? Like a spring goddess.'

'You're too kind, Your Grace.' Mama's cheeks puffed up. 'And do not fret over the ink. Accidents happen, right?'

'Yes. Happy accidents.' The Dowager flashed Maddie a grin.

'If you'll excuse me,' Caroline interjected with a sneer. 'I'm feeling rather faint. I think I shall take a rest in the retiring rooms.' She marched off without another word.

The Dowager cleared her throat delicately. 'Now, Lady Houghton, I don't want to monopolise all your time, especially with so many guests here. Would you excuse us? I would like to introduce the DeVrieses to a few more acquaintances.'

'By all means, Your Grace.'

'I think we may have a new sensation of the season,' Miss Merton stage-whispered to Maddie as they followed behind the Dowager. 'They say a late-blooming flower is the prettiest.'

'Whatever do you mean, Miss Merton?'

A twinkle appeared in her companion's eye. 'You, my dear.' She gripped Maddie's hand. 'Everyone is looking at you. I predict you're going to be a sensation for the rest of the season.'

Despite feeling the stares on her, Maddie didn't want to raise her hopes. 'I think you overestimate this dress, Miss Merton.'

'We'll see.'

'Your Grace, Miss Merton,' the older gentleman who approached them greeted them as he bowed low. 'Pardon the intrusion, but I had to come over and pay my respects.'

'Sir Allendale,' the Dowager greeted. 'How lovely to see you in town. How is your son, Walter?'

'He's doing well, thank you. Just finished his last year at Eton. In fact that's why I came over.' Lord Allendale signalled to someone behind them. 'Here he is. My pride and joy, Walter.'

A young man, tall and reed-thin with a mop of unruly blond hair, hurried over. 'Y-Your Grace.'

Sir Allendale touched his shoulder. 'He begged me to be introduced to you and your, uh, lovely guests.'

'*Father.*' Walter's face was completely scarlet as he glanced down at the ground, but not before his eyes flickered to Maddie.

'I would be glad to make the introductions,' the Dowager said. 'Sir Allendale, Mr Allendale, you already know Miss Merton, but this is Mr Cornelius DeVries, Mrs DeVries and their daughter, Miss Madeline DeVries. This is Sir Wilbur Allendale and his son, Mr Walter Allendale.'

'A pleasure,' Sir Allendale greeted them, then nudged his son forward with an encouraging pat on the back.

'Honoured—' Walter cleared his throat as the word came out like a squeak. 'Honoured to make your acquaintance, Mr and Mrs DeVries. Miss M-Madeline.' He turned even redder.

They exchanged a few more pleasantries for a few

minutes—except for Walter, who remained mute—until the Dowager declared she *had* to say hello to another friend over by the buffet table.

'We hope to see you again, Your Grace.' Sir Allendale bowed. 'And your guests.'

'That would be lovely.'

As they walked away, Maddie's ear caught the older Allendale scoff at his son, '…you wanted the introduction. Why did you just stare at her like a ninny?'

'I tried, Papa, but my tongue would not untangle itself, and then I forgot to breathe…'

'This is the masquerade ball over again,' the old man moaned.

Miss Merton, who obviously heard the exchange as well, let out a giggle. 'Poor boy. He's painfully shy, you know. Lost his mother at a young age, and so his father dotes on him.' She tsked. 'He's a bit young, but he's a good prospect.'

'Prospect for what?' Maddie asked.

'For marriage.' Her companion chuckled. 'I think the lad's halfway in love with you.'

'M-me? But he hardly spoke a word. Couldn't even look at me.'

'Last year, it was rumoured he was deeply enamoured with Miss Georgina Miller. He was so nervous, he passed out while dancing with her at the Earl of Crainbourne's masquerade ball.' Miss Merton's eyes narrowed thoughtfully. 'On second thought, you wouldn't want a fiancé who keeled over each time he saw you. I think Mr Allendale is like young wine—he could do with a few more years of maturing.' That twinkle in her eyes returned as she smiled wryly at Maddie. 'But I suspect you may soon have your choice of vintage.'

Maddie was sceptical of Miss Merton's words—except that they had yet to reach their destination and already two acquaintances of the Dowager's had requested an introduction to them.

'See?' Miss Merton said. 'I told you.'

'Lord Lambert is old enough to be my father,' Maddie pointed out. 'Perhaps he merely wanted to make his acquaintance with Papa since there are few gentlemen of his age here.'

'Pish-posh, dear. Just enjoy the attention.' Miss Merton handed her a glass of chilled lemonade as they had finally reached the refreshment table.

'Your Grace. Mr DeVries. Mrs DeVries.' It was Lady Houghton once again, but this time, she was not alone. She came with a young gentleman in tow. 'Forgive the intrusion.'

'Not at all,' Papa said. 'We are always happy to see our generous hostess. You honour us with your attention.'

The countess smiled. 'Excellent. I was making the rounds when I realised I was remiss in not making an introduction. Your Grace, may I present my nephew, Desmond, Viscount Palmer, who also happens to be co-hosting this party with me since the Earl is indisposed at our Hampshire estate.'

The young man stepped forward and bowed deeply. 'Your Grace.'

'And this is Miss Harriet Merton, Mr and Mrs Cornelius DeVries, and their daughter, Miss Madeline, from America.'

'Lovely to meet you,' Viscount Palmer said, his cool blue eyes regarding everyone.

'You have such a dashing nephew,' Mama commented. 'Why have we never seen you until now? Your aunt has been to most of the events of the season, and we were here for her ball a few months ago.'

'I'm afraid my father has been ill, and I've been watching over him,' Palmer replied. 'The Earl has been languishing for some time, so I haven't been to town at all.'

'I'm so dreadfully sorry to hear that,' the Dowager said. 'Please relay my regards next time you see him, and I wish him well.'

'What a wonderful son you are,' Mama exclaimed. 'Does your Viscountess not mind being in the country during the season?'

'I'm afraid I've not been blessed with a wife, Mrs DeVries.'

Mama looked to Maddie conspiratorially. 'Interesting.'

Maddie kept her lips pressed tight but groaned inwardly.

'I do hope we see more of you,' Mama continued. 'Will you be at the Baybrook ball?'

'I plan to be, unless I am called back to Chester Manor.'

'So will we. With Maddie, of course.'

Cool blue eyes turned to Maddie. 'Perhaps Miss Madeline can save space on her dance card for me.'

'She will,' Mama answered.

'I look forward to it. If you'll excuse me,' the Viscount began. 'I believe I see some old friends arriving. I should welcome them. Your Grace.' He bowed to the Dowager and nodded to the rest of them before striding away.

Miss Merton sent her a knowing grin and mouthed, *See?*

Maddie smiled back. Viscount Palmer initially seemed cold, but she had to admit there was something about his aloofness that piqued her curiosity.

*Perhaps this dress had some kind of magic.*

Because for the first time in her life, Maddie felt like

she was being seen. Not stared or gawked or gaped at. But people were truly looking at her with interest.

'I shall see to my guests as well. Do enjoy yourselves. We have games out on the lawn, if you are so inclined, and other amusements inside the house, including a quartet playing in the music room.' She curtseyed to the Dowager before she, too, headed off.

'Oh, Maddie.' Mama looked ready to burst, her cheeks pink and puffy. 'I wasn't keen on garden parties—after all, who would want to stand under the sun all afternoon? But I have a very good feeling you may meet more eligible lords here. If only there were dancing, then it would be acceptable for them to call on you. Oh, and that Viscount Palmer! He's so handsome, and the heir to an Earldom.'

Maddie's eyes slid heavenwards. Mama was probably already planning what to wear to the old Earl's funeral.

'Aren't you glad I convinced you to come, dear?' Papa said to Mama, and Maddie gave him a smile of thanks for changing the subject.

'Yes, and I almost forgive you for leaving me out of the Earl's call to Maddie yesterday.'

Blood rushed to Maddie's ears at the reminder. She'd been so caught up in the plan to conceal her new gown from Mama that she'd nearly forgotten about the Earl. She took a generous sip of the lemonade, though it did nothing to cool the embarrassment rising up her neck. Oh, why did he even come into the library yesterday?

Though Maddie had heard some of the story from Persephone, she didn't know Cam's perspective. *Oh, Cam.* He had to shoulder all that responsibility, not to mention take care of his brothers and sister. How could he even think he did Persephone a disservice when she'd obviously grown up to be an intelligent and kind person, worth ten times any other debutante she'd met? She couldn't help but admire him.

*Oh, stop!*

They were supposed to pretend to court, but somehow they'd once again broken one of the rules of their scheme.

*The Earl was being polite,* she reasoned. And it was her father who had asked him to stay.

Besides, it had been an excellent way to maintain their deception, though her stomach soured at the thought that her father had to be involved in their deceit, even if it was unwittingly so. But then the Earl had left so abruptly, as if he could not stand to be with her another minute.

*Do not think about him.*

But it was no use. He was like a tune or an idea buried in her head. The moment she started thinking of him, she could not stop.

*Think of something else. Anything. Something completely unrelated to the Earl.*

So, she began reciting Steno's principles to herself.

*The Principle of Superposition. Principle of Initial Horizontality. Principle of Strata Continuity. Law of Constancy of Interfacial Angles.*

The Earl's handsome face and all its angles came to her mind. Would he like this dress she was wearing?

*Drat.*

Maybe thinking of Steno was too ambitious. Maybe she needed something more Earl-adjacent.

*How about Persephone?*

Maddie frowned. Her friend was nowhere in sight. *Again.* But where could she be hiding? And why? There was no dancing here, after all. 'Has anyone seen Lady Persephone?'

Mama shrugged. 'She hurried off as soon as we arrived. Who knows where she could be by now?'

Handing her empty glass to a waiting footman, she announced, 'I'll go search for her, then. She might have got lost.' Unfortunately, with the Houghton gardens being so extensive and having a vast array of greenery and statues to hide behind, locating her friend might be an impossible task.

*I'll begin with the hedges.*

She headed towards the east side of the garden, entering the first row. Finding it empty, she turned a corner and continue to zigzag her way through the rest of the hedges.

*Oh, dear. This will take far too long.*

She had to move faster if she wanted to find her friend soon. With a determined snort, she straightened her shoulders and dashed out from the hedges—only to bump into someone walking along the path.

'I beg your pardon!' she exclaimed and staggered back. A pair of strong hands encircled her upper arms, preventing her from completely falling over. 'I—'

'Maddie?'

The low burr never failed to make heat coil in her belly. 'You— I mean, my lord.' *Do not look up. Whatever you do. Do. Not. Look—*

Too late. Maddie found herself mesmerised by emerald-green eyes. 'W-why are you here?'

'I was invited,' he said. 'I came with Persephone and your parents, but it seems my sister has once again disappeared. Have you—' He sucked in a breath. 'What the devil are you wearing?'

'A gown?'

His gaze dropped low, and his eyes reminded Maddie of molten iron. 'That is not green.'

'I beg your pardon?'

'Your gown. What happened to the green one?'

'I don't know.' Perhaps Betsy was burning it in the hearth as they spoke. 'And it was not green, it was chartreuse.' This was a ridiculous conversation—not to mention, they were alone and he was holding her with a familiarity that was unseemly.

Well, it would be unseemly if someone else were around....

*Oh, heaven help me.*

'My lord, please release me.'

His hands immediately dropped to his sides. 'I was only holding you to prevent you from falling over. And may I remind you, you were the one who jumped out from behind that bush into me.'

She dusted her hands on the delicate lace of her skirts. 'How was I supposed to see you coming around the corner?'

'Does your father know you're wearing that?'

What was with him and the blasted gown? *He probably hates it.* 'Yes, my father does know, thank you very much.'

He gnashed his teeth so hard Maddie could hear them scraping together. 'Well, never wear it again.'

Now, that was taking his hatred of the gown much too far. 'This was a gift from the Dowager, and I will wear it when I please.'

'Not if you want all of London staring at you,' he retorted with another scrutinising look at her neckline.

Shock at his words made her entire body go rigid.

*How dare he?*

But she would not cry. Not in this dress that made her feel like she was worthy of attention. And certainly not because this boorish oaf implied she was displaying her wares like a seaside doxy. And so, she channelled her emotions elsewhere and allowed anger to rise in her until she was ready to explode. 'You—'

'Miss DeVries, are you lost?' came a cool voice from behind her.

Turning around, she saw Viscount Palmer standing a few feet away from them.

'The gardens have many winding paths.' The Viscount closed the distance between them easily. 'So it's easy to find oneself—' he turned to the Earl '—led astray.'

The Earl's nostrils flared. 'Why, you young pup—'

'My lord,' Maddie interrupted. 'Thank you for finding me. I did get lost.'

'Lord Balfour,' the Viscount acknowledged. 'May I show you the way back to the party, as well?'

'No, thank you,' the Earl said brusquely. 'I'll be finding my own way.'

'As you wish.' Palmer offered her his arm. 'Miss DeVries?'

Maddie didn't dare sneak a glance at the Earl, no matter how much she was tempted. 'Thank you, my lord.' Gingerly, she placed a hand on his arm and allowed him to lead her away, which Maddie was immensely grateful for, because her thoughts were scattered like marbles spilled across the floor. If she'd attempted to walk away on her own, she probably would have wound up in the Thames.

'Here you are.' The Viscount lowered his arm, so Maddie dropped her hand to her side. 'I have delivered you safely back to you parents.'

'Maddie?' Mama's eyes widened.

'My dear, you look flushed.' Papa's brows knitted together. 'Did you find Lady Persephone?'

'I did not.' She forced out a chuckle. 'I got lost instead. But the Viscount found me.'

'Oh, we owe you a great debt,' Mama said dramatically. 'Who knows where she could have ended up?'

'Calm yourself, dear.' Papa patted her hand. 'But thank you, my lord, for assisting my daughter.'

'My pleasure.' He tipped his hat. 'If you'll excuse me, I must return to my duties as host.'

Mama looked ready to faint from happiness. 'I… I…'

'What a polite young man, that Viscount Palmer,' Papa remarked.

Caroline—Maddie had failed to notice she had returned—sniggered. 'He's only a viscount?'

'And an heir to an earldom,' Miss Merton said.

Her sister's lips pulled back tight. 'Aren't you lucky? And this one isn't nose-to-bosom with you.'

The remark about her bosom reminded Maddie of the Earl's words.

*The neckline isn't even that low.*

Indeed, it was appropriate, especially for a warm day like today. Why he had such a conniption about it, she didn't know.

'He's looking back at you,' Miss Merton whispered.

Maddie tilted her head up, and sure enough, from across the garden, the Viscount caught her gaze. He cocked his head to the side before turning away and continuing to speak with another guest.

'How did the Viscount find you?' Miss Merton enquired. 'I thought you were searching for Lady Persephone?'

'Looking for me? Why?'

Maddie's heart leapt out of her chest as the lady in question appeared from nowhere. 'Dear Lord, you scared me.'

'Scared you?' Persephone tilted her head to the side. 'How did I do that?'

'I thought you were hi—never mind.' *Why didn't you tell me your brother was here?* But Maddie supposed she should have guessed. He always accompanied Persephone to parties. 'So, where have you been?' she asked in a low whisper.

'Hiding where no man would dare come near.' She nodded to the tables and chairs set under a canopy, where a few older women were drinking tea and eating cakes. 'In plain sight, by the ton's most notorious gossips.'

She laughed, her spirits lifting. Despite her close connection to a certain *Man-Who-Must-Not-Be-Thought-Of*, Maddie hoped she and Persephone would remain friends.

# Chapter Nine

Cam wondered what the consequences of punching an English viscount in the face would be.

Because whatever they were, it was probably worth it. Especially the face that belonged to that smug, meddling Palmer.

*I should not have come here.*

As he watched the Viscount disappear around the corner with Maddie, Cam's fury grew. He had thought he'd be safe from his growing lust for Maddie at this garden party; after all, there would be no dancing here. Besides, Persephone had been eager to come, and Cam was happy to indulge his sister. He didn't even mind that the De-Vrieses had ridden with them, as he always found Cornelius's company amiable enough that he could tolerate his wife and younger daughter.

Though arriving together, they'd gone their separate ways as Cornelius had been pulled away by some acquaintances, and Cam had struck up a conversation with the Earl of Kerrigan, whom he had met on his last trip to London. At some point, however, Persephone had slipped away so Cam went in search of her.

Why was it that each time he went in search of his wayward sister, he managed to find Maddie instead?

Mother of mercy, she looked magnificent today. The dress enhanced all her best features—not to mention, the silk flowers on the neckline drew attention to her creamy, rosy skin and elegant neck. All he wanted to do was fix his lips on the spot where her shoulder met her neck, then move lower and lick his tongue under the silky fabric.

Which was why he'd lashed out at her, hoping to push her away.

*Maybe I overreacted.*

Where the hell was the old MacGregor charm? Once again, not only had he succeeded in insulting her, but this time, he had managed to anger her as well. She'd looked ready to unleash the fires of hell on him.

But more than that, he'd seen something else in her face that had made him feel like the worst cad in existence—hurt. He'd actually wounded her. Now all he wanted to do was get down on his knees and beg for forgiveness. He almost had, until Palmer had interrupted them.

*Damned prick.*

Earlier, he and Kerrigan had been introduced to Palmer by another mutual acquaintance, as he was apparently taking the place of Houghton as host today. Cam wasn't sure why, but he disliked Palmer from the beginning. He did not miss the Viscount's thinly veiled animosity directed towards them. Was it due to the fact that Cam was Scottish and Kerrigan was Irish?

Watching him walk away with Maddie certainly did not help endear him to Cam. More than that, an uneasy sensation pricked at his gut because he'd pegged Palmer for what he was—rich, titled, connected, and raised in this society that seemed determined to keep upstarts like him and Kerrigan out. A lump grew in his throat as he admitted to himself that Palmer was exactly the kind of husband Maddie was looking for.

Hands clenched into fists at his sides, he marched back towards the middle of the gardens, where the guests were gathered. His eyes searched among the throng and found Persephone with Miss Merton…and Maddie. Even from afar, her loveliness arrested him, making his chest ache fiercely with wanting.

*At least that damned Palmer wasn't sniffing about like a dog looking for its next meal.*

Cam knew he should go over there and attempt to apologise. But as he saw Maddie laugh at something Persephone said, he froze. He did not want to further cause her pain, so instead, he shoved his hands in his pockets and trudged towards the house. The Houghtons' butler stopped him as he was about to exit.

'Shall I send for your carriage, my lord?'

He shook his head. 'No. But please relay the message to my coachman that he should wait for my sister, Lady Persephone, instead.'

'Of course, my lord.' He frowned. 'Did you want me to call a hackney cab?'

'No, I shall walk.'

Cam didn't wait for the bewildered butler to object as he made a hasty exit out into the stylish streets of Hanover Square. Without a destination in mind, he picked a direction and walked as he attempted to distract himself from further thoughts of a certain maddening American miss. However, all he could think about was the pain he'd caused Maddie. In the previous instance that he'd inadvertently insulted her, she'd forgiven him, but he doubted she would be so easily swayed this time. No, he would have to find another way to tell her how sorry he was.

He continued strolling along the neighbourhood, past the elegant town houses, until he found himself on a busy shopping street. *A gift*. He would find her a gift to mend the rift between them.

*An apology gift*, he clarified firmly. It would not be a courting gift and, therefore, would not violate any of their rules.

His mind made up, he strolled down the street, searching the various window displays of the shops he passed by.

Milliner. Glove shop. Tailor. Confectioner. Perfumery.

He shook his head mentally. Maddie would not be swayed by such trinkets.

As he continued down the street, his prospects for an apology gift for Maddie dwindled as he reached the less fashionable area of the neighbourhood, with only businesses like grocers and tatters and cobblers. He was about to retreat when the display window of the last establishment he passed by caught his eye. It featured an array of old knick-knacks and bric-a-brac, from raggedy dolls to rusted instruments to old clocks. The faded sign above the window read Carson's Curiosities.

Having no more prospects for a present, Cam pushed the door open, a bell jangling overhead as he entered the threshold.

'Good day, sir,' the white-haired man behind the counter greeted. 'How may I assist you?'

'I'm just browsing.'

'Of course. Please feel free to look around. I'll be here if you need me.'

'Thank you.'

A stuffed falcon on Cam's left watched him with its eerie glass eyes as he walked by, while on his other side, a stack of old books occupied a marble table. He paused to look at the books, thinking of Maddie, but upon further inspection he saw they were in some kind of language he didn't understand, so he moved on, proceeding deeper into the shop.

In the corner, he spied a display case with various objects protected behind the glass. He drew closer to the cabinet, peering through the window at the jumble of items inside. There seemed to be no rhyme or reason to the collection—a pair of scissors, a figurine of a cat, a miniature portrait of a boy and girl—though most of the things he could not even identify. The middle shelf held medical instruments, perhaps, as he saw some ominous-looking tongs that were about the length of his arm, pincers, a file, and a hammer.

'I believe those are blacksmiths' tools.'

Cam's head whipped back to the old man, who had seemingly appeared from nowhere to pop up behind him.

'Pardon me, sir. I didn't want you to get lost back here.' The old man grinned. 'Are you interested in antique tools?'

'I thought they were medical tools. Or torture devices.'

The old man laughed. 'I have some of those, too, from the medieval period. But these—' he gestured to the blacksmith tools '—are only about…oh, two hundred years old. We don't rely on blacksmiths nearly as much today, with those humungous furnaces that produce iron by the ton.'

The mention of furnaces had him thinking of Maddie immediately. 'May I see them please, Mr…?'

'Carson.' He retrieved a key from his pocket, opened the case, then stepped back.

Cam leaned forward and examined the iron tongs, not really sure why he wanted to see them. They were inappropriate gifts for any occasion. He was about to pick up the hammer but paused when he saw the small object next to it.

'Huh.'

It was brass pipe of some sort, about the size of a small spoon but tapered at the end. 'What was this for?'

Carson took the object from the shelf and examined it up close. 'Hmm… It looks to be a blacksmith's blow-pipe, but it's much too small to be part of this set. So, I can't be certain what it is.'

'I may know someone who does.' The pipe was small enough that he could easily conceal it. That, and no one would ever mistake it for a courting gift. 'I'll take it.'

If Mr Carson thought it was strange Cam wanted to buy a spoon, he didn't show it. Instead he happily wrapped up the item and took Cam's money.

Leaving the shop, Cam found himself strolling back up the street, towards Hanover Square, the package wrapped in brown paper in his inner coat pocket. He wasn't certain when he would give it her. Or if he would even get the chance to approach her, given her fury this afternoon. He would stay clear of her for now and pray that the distance would soften her anger.

Avoiding Maddie had been excruciating, but it had to be done. It was especially hard, as she'd had a few gentlemen callers the next day. Cam feared she wouldn't even dance with him now that she had men clamouring for her attention.

'Do you need anything else, milord?' Murray asked as he brushed some lint from Cam's coat.

'No, thank you, Murray.' He nodded at the valet to dismiss him. When he was out the door, Cam retrieved the package wrapped in brown paper from his trunk and slipped it into his coat pocket. He wasn't sure when he'd get a chance to give it to Maddie, but he'd been carrying it around with him, the weight soothing against his chest.

Hurrying downstairs, he cursed softly as he saw everyone was already in the foyer.

'Apologies, everyone, I—'

*Good God in Heaven.*

Everyone in the room—hell, the room itself—melted away, and his focus pinpointed to Maddie. She was like a shimmering star in her blue dress, eclipsing all other heavenly beings. Silver diamond pins winked in her golden hair, and the low neckline of the dress showed off even more of her rosy complexion, as well as the swell of her generous breasts.

'Cam? Cam!' Persephone tapped him on the shoulder, bringing him out of his reverie. 'We are already late. We should run along.'

He cleared his throat. 'Er, right.' Coming to his senses, he led Persephone outside to their waiting carriage.

'You know what you have to do, right?' Persephone said once they were alone.

'What?'

His sister tsked. 'The first dance. With Maddie.'

How could he forget? 'Of course. I shall whisk her away the moment we arrive.' *Assuming she doesn't cut me directly for implying she was a strumpet.*

'I'm so very glad you're doing this for her, Cam.' She sighed. 'Maddie has such a good heart. She deserves someone who can appreciate what she has to offer. I think she just lacked confidence—and having that dreadful woman for a sister didn't help. Maddie thinks she's lesser and doesn't deserve to be cherished because she doesn't fit the mould of what society dictates is a proper young woman.' Her nose wrinkled. 'But I've seen her slowly gaining that self-confidence, especially after you danced with her. So, thank you for agreeing to dance with her.'

The package wrapped in brown paper weighed heavily against his chest. 'My pleasure,' he bit out.

The rest of the short ride continued in silence, and soon they were alighting out of the carriage and being announced as they entered the Duke of Baybrook's sumptuous town house on Upper Brook Street.

'Cameron, Earl of Balfour! Lady Persephone MacGregor!'

Persephone tugged at his arm and they made their way across the room to where the DeVrieses were sitting. She sat on the empty chair next to Maddie, who was so deep in conversation with Miss Merton that she didn't notice them approach.

'Maddie!' she hissed, and then jabbed her in the back.

Maddie yelped and shot to her feet. 'What in heaven's— Persephone?'

His sister nudged him with her foot, then cocked her head to Maddie.

'Miss Madeline,' he began. 'May I have this dance?'

Unfortunately—or fortunately for Cam—everyone in the immediate vicinity had their attention on them. Though Maddie hesitated, she eventually acknowledged Cam. 'I would love to, my lord.'

Cam took the hand she offered and led her to the middle of the ballroom floor. He could scarcely breathe with her so close. 'You look lovely, Miss DeVries.'

She nodded politely but did not look him straight in the eye. In fact, throughout the dance, it was as if she did everything she could to look everywhere except at him. Though her head tilted to him, her eyes focused behind him, or on his forehead. The cool politeness she exuded made his gut twist. He almost preferred the rage she'd nearly shown at the Houghton garden party.

When the dance ended, Maddie rushed through her curtsey, her pretty lips twisting impatiently. Cam was tempted to delay her, but seeing as the other dancers were leaving the floor, he dutifully escorted her back to Miss Merton. Sure enough, there was already a gentleman waiting for Maddie.

'Miss DeVries, may I have this dance?' the man asked, his gaze drifting down to her chest briefly.

Maddie smiled at him. 'Of course, Mr Davenport.'

*Damn it all to hell.*

Cam's throat tightened as if he'd swallowed nails as he watched Maddie being led away by another man. But what was he supposed to do? Their one dance of the evening was done, a rule he'd insisted on.

He was about to turn away when he felt something bump against him.

'Oh!' came the feminine cry.

Being so tall, Cam was used to not seeing other people run into him, so his instinct and reflex made him reach out and grab the first thing he could—which turned out to be Miss Caroline DeVries.

*Double damn.*

'Forgive me, my lord. I'm so very clumsy.' She attempted to make her voice breathy and low, but it grated on Cam's nerves. 'Oh, my dance card is empty at the moment.' Grabbing his hand in hers, she pushed closer to him. 'I would love to dance.'

Her audacity was incredible. Cam wanted to push her away, but there was at least one group of matrons behind Miss DeVries that was already looking at them expectantly. He harrumphed and guided her towards the ballroom floor.

This was going to be a long and painful dance.

'My lord, it's such a sin we have never danced before.' Caroline curtseyed low—much lower than deemed appropriate, her bosom nearly spilling out of her daring low-cut pink gown.

'Indeed.' He averted his eyes as he bowed to her.

Cam was wrong. Dancing with Miss Caroline DeVries was not painful. It was excruciating. The polka was a lively dance which required the male to keep his partner close as they spun around, but she seemed to be taking liberties with the definition of 'close.' With every twist and turn, her torso pushed nearer and nearer until she was brushing against his chest.

Irritation got the best of him, and so he sent her a warning glare, to which she responded by batting her eyes at him as her left arm squeezed his shoulder tightly.

Fighting the urge to leave her, he instead looked over her head. Unfortunately, at that exact moment, Maddie and her partner sailed right across his line of sight, and Cam faltered when she threw her head back and laughed as Davenport whirled her around.

'My lord,' she hissed. 'You stepped on my foot.'

'Did I? Forgive me,' he said through gritted teeth, his gaze following Maddie like a hawk.

His patience grew thin as the dance progressed, and somehow, he managed to complete the dance without further incident or crushing his partner's toes. He bowed to Miss DeVries quickly. In that brief moment he took his eyes off her, Maddie disappeared.

Where was she?

One by one, he scanned each and every couple, but none of them were Maddie and Davenport. They had simply disappeared. A terrible feeling buried itself in his chest as he hurriedly escorted Miss DeVries back to her companion.

'My lord,' she said coquettishly. 'That was—'

'Have you seen Maddie—er, Miss Madeline?' he asked Miss Merton.

'She was dancing with Mr Davenport,' the companion replied. 'Are they on the other side of the room?'

'No, I didn't see them among the dancers.' He took a deep breath, trying to compose himself.

'I'm sure Maddie's all right.' Caroline laughed. 'Silly girl. She may have got lost again.'

Miss Merton rose to her feet. 'True, but her dance partner should have guided her back here to me.' Her shoulders straightened, and her expression turned serious.

Cam had never seen the normally cheerful Miss Merton looking so dour. She reminded him of a female hound watching protectively over her pups, ready to bare her teeth should any danger come to her young.

'I shall go search for her,' Miss Merton said.

'And I will assist you.' He barely spared Miss Caroline a glance as he hurried after Miss Merton. 'Where do you think they are?'

Miss Merton paused, her delicate eyebrows gathering together. 'Music room.'

'Music room? How do you know—' But Cam didn't finish his sentence as she darted off with the speed of a woman half her age. He rushed after her, catching up to her just outside the ballroom as she hurried towards what he assumed was the music room. Sure enough, he saw two figures making their way down the hallway.

'…and are these paintings special, Mr Davenport?' Maddie asked.

'Very special indeed, Miss DeVries.' Davenport's hand

gripped her elbow and continued to lead her away. 'I promise, you will find them amusing.'

Cam's blood boiled, and he flew after the couple. 'And just where do you think you're taking her?'

Maddie, too, stood still, her eyes flashing. 'You—'

Davenport froze, then dropped his hand to his side. 'I beg your pardon, sir?'

'It's Lord Balfour to you,' he corrected. 'And answer my question.'

To his credit, Davenport remained calm. 'I was merely assisting Miss DeVries.'

'Assisting in her ruination, maybe. You know better than to abscond a young miss away from her chaperone.' He gestured to Miss Merton, who had caught up to him.

'What is the meaning of this, Mr Davenport?' she demanded. 'Maddie, are you all right?'

'Yes, Miss Merton,' she assured the companion. 'I was dizzy and the ballroom was too stuffy. Mr Davenport said we should go to the music room where I could sit down and look at some paintings.'

'By yourselves?' Cam bit out.

'He said there would be other guests there and that Lord and Lady Baybrook always left the music room open for anyone to enjoy.' She looked at him meaningfully. 'Isn't that right, Mr Davenport?'

Davenport swallowed audibly. 'Uh…'

Miss Merton let out an indignant cry. 'Why, I never… Mr Davenport, I have been attending the Baybrook ball for years and they have never allowed guests in there. However, I do know that it is a popular room for couples to conduct trysts.'

All the colour drained from Maddie's face as the truth of what Davenport had planned for her sank in. 'Mr Davenport, is this true?'

He forced out a chuckle and scratched at his collar. 'This is all just a misunderstanding. We're all gentlemen and ladies here.'

'I can see only one gentleman here, Mr Davenport.' Miss Merton's eyes flashed with fury. 'And a good thing, too, that Lord Balfour was vigilant in watching over Miss DeVries and noticed she was gone.'

Davenport's expression turned unpleasant. 'She's such an awkward, naive fool,' he spat out. 'How you could possibly want her—'

Rage filled him as he reached down and grabbed Davenport by the collar. He pulled a fist back.

'Lord Balfour, no!' Miss Merton cried.

'What?' He blew out a breath. 'You know what he was planning to do. This blackguard doesn't deserve any mercy. I ought to beat him within an inch of his life.'

'My lord, think of the scandal,' she implored. 'Think of Maddie.'

He was thinking of Maddie. Didn't she see that?

'P-please, my lord.' It was Maddie who spoke this time. 'There's no need for violence.'

Reluctantly, he lowered his hand and released Davenport.

'Filthy scum,' Davenport sneered back. 'Just you wait! I will tell everyone what a violent beast you are. You best go back where you came from. And that little tart? She knew what she was doing! She wanted it.'

Anger reignited within Cam, and he lunged at the bastard again, but a hand on his arm stopped him.

'My lord, a moment,' Miss Merton began, giving him a gentle squeeze then stepping in front of him.

'Are you hiding behind an old lady now?' Davenport scoffed. 'Coward.'

'Young man, do you have any idea who I am?' Miss

Merton's spine turned rigid as her tone took on a firm yet refined quality. 'I've been moving in the upper echelons of the ton when you were but a mere child in the cradle. I've seen so many seasons and debutantes and fops like you. Do you not think I knew exactly what you were up to? Do you truly believe you are the first so-called gentleman to abscond with a young lady in her first season at this very ball?' Her gaze could have melted the flesh off Davenport's face. 'Leave and never speak of this again nor come near Miss Madeline. I don't want to see hide nor hair of you. If I do, I will spread rumours that will have ladies reaching for their smelling salts. Do you understand me?'

'Y-yes, ma'am,' Davenport sputtered.

'Go!'

Turning tail, Davenport scarpered out the door.

Cam stared at Miss Merton, slack-jawed. 'That was... incredible.'

Miss Merton's smile turned sweet, as if all was well and nothing had happened. 'We play to our strengths. Now,' she turned back to Maddie. 'Are you all right, my dear?'

'Y-yes.'

'There, there.' Miss Merton smoothed back a curl that had come loose from her coiffure. 'Everything will be all right.'

'I was just... We were dancing, and I felt dizzy. He said we could escape the stuffiness in the music room and there would be other guests there.' She worried at her lip. 'Mr Davenport was right. I am a fool.'

'No, you are not a fool, Maddie.' Miss Merton gripped her firmly by the shoulders. 'An innocent, but not a fool. You couldn't have known what Davenport had planned.

I'm just very glad for Lord Balfour's keen observation skills.'

Maddie's head whipped towards him, and she took in a quick breath. 'My lord, th-thank you. Who knows what could have happened had you not interfered.'

'This was not your fault, darling,' he responded. Miss Merton's eyebrow went all the way up to her hairline, but he continued on. 'Davenport's a despicable scoundrel. You've done nothing wrong.'

Maddie didn't look convinced, her shoulders sagging as her head lowered.

'Oh, dear me.' Miss Merton sighed. 'Maddie, would you like to go home? I'm sure we could leave quietly without anyone noticing. Perhaps a cup of tea and bed is what you need.'

'No, Maddie.' Cam gently touched her chin and tipped her face up. 'Do not run away. Not now.' He could see her confidence—the one she'd worked so hard on these past few days—seeping away. He would not let that happen.

'Dance with me, Maddie.'

# Chapter Ten

'D-dance with you?' Maddie thought she'd heard him wrong.

'Yes.' His tone was deadly serious.

'But, my lord,' she breathed. 'The rules. I thought we agreed on one—'

'Forgot the damned rules,' he muttered.

'A dance might help you calm your nerves,' Miss Merton suggested.

She winced inwardly, thinking of what a fool she was. Mr Davenport had paid her a call just yesterday. He'd been witty and charming, but also polite and well mannered. He'd done all the right things, spoken all the right words. Mama had been thrilled by his visit and she'd promised him a dance at the ball. Maddie had immediately decided that she no longer needed to dance with the Earl, but unfortunately, she had forgotten to inform Persephone that, and then it was too late.

After that awkward dance, she wanted to forget him, so she had been glad Mr Davenport was waiting for her. However, when she'd seen Caroline and the Earl dancing, a spark of an unknown emotion had lit inside her.

She didn't want to see him with his arms around another woman, and certainly not her sister.

Perhaps some part of her did know what Mr Davenport was up to but didn't care because she'd been so overcome by the sight of her sister and the Earl dancing.

'Maddie?' Miss Merton's soothing voice jolted her back to the present.

She looked up at the Earl. 'I'm not sure—'

'Please, Maddie.' Emerald eyes bore right into her. 'Just one more dance.'

A breath lodged in her throat. 'All right.'

He gently took her hand into his. From then on, everything was like a dream. She allowed him to lead her to the ballroom floor. Music played, his arms came around her, and once again, she lost herself in the dance. This time, though, she focused on him. Her feet knew the steps and her body moved to the rhythm, but her mind fixed on the man who held her close.

For a moment, it all felt real.

'Thank you for the dance, Miss DeVries.'

And then it was over. 'Thank you, my lord.'

He escorted her back to Miss Merton's side. 'Good evening, Miss Merton, Miss DeVries.' With a curt nod, he left.

Air rushed out of her, leaving Maddie feeling breathless as she watched his tall form walking away.

Miss Merton sidled up to her. 'Are you sure you would like to stay? I could feign a headache so you could escort me home.'

Maddie was sorely tempted; however, she saw Mama marching excitedly towards them and knew there was no escape.

'Maddie, did I see you dancing with the Earl again?' Her entire body practically vibrated with excitement.

'What did you talk about? Did he say anything about paying you another call?'

'Mama,' she said gently. 'It was just a dance.'

'A second dance,' she corrected. 'But I suppose you're right. Until he has asked to court you, you must keep your options open. Miss Merton, are you quite sure there aren't any other eligible dukes in the room?'

'I'm afraid not,' the companion replied.

Mama inhaled deeply. 'What rotten luck that the Duke of Mabury had to fall in love with Kate Mason.' She harrumphed. 'Do not worry my dear. With your newfound popularity, we'll find you someone.'

Maddie danced with a few more gentlemen, and while she did enjoy herself, she could not help but compare them all to the Earl.

*I should be thankful he offered a second dance, considering how rude I was to him during the first.*

Miss Merton had been right—the dance did calm her down after her encounter with Mr Davenport, but more than that, the self-doubts that had been building in her—wondering if she'd done anything wrong or if it was her fault she was nearly ruined—all but disappeared. Any other man would have coddled her or tucked her away like a fragile doll. But the Earl did the opposite.

'I am so glad you are finally meeting some eligible gentlemen,' Miss Merton remarked after her last partner escorted her back. 'You are such a graceful dancer.'

'Thank you, Miss Merton.' She sat down next to the companion. 'But dancing is far different from courting, is it not?'

'Be patient, dear.' She patted Maddie's hand. 'Your time will come too.'

Maddie glanced across the room where Caroline was surrounded by her usual gaggle of beaux. At some point, most of those men would pay her a call and eventually court her. Of course, her sister had no plan to actually accept any proposals from her current crop of suitors. She was waiting for a larger catch—no man lower than an earl or, if possible, a duke. She would relish the chance to have everyone curtseying to her and calling her 'Your Grace.'

'Do not compare yourself to your sister,' Miss Merton admonished, seemingly reading her mind. 'You are two different women, and—do not repeat this to your mother, but—some women are just born flirts.'

'I wish I knew how to flirt,' she murmured under her breath so Miss Merton could not hear her. It seemed to her that flirting was a necessity in navigating the season. She observed the other women in the room who were also surrounded by men, the way they would laugh at whatever the men said or bat their eyes coquettishly. She would look foolish if she tried that, especially as she would have to crane her neck down for them to even see her eyes. Could such things even be learned? Or, as Miss Merton said, did one have to be born with it?

Though she attempted to put the question out of her mind, it continued to plague her throughout the evening and even until she went home and was in bed. It was early morning when she came to the conclusion that while dancing was an excellent way to meet gentlemen, flirting could help her keep them interested in her and possibly receive a proposal.

*If flirting can be learned, how does one do it?*

Were there tutors for that? Or books? Whom would she practise with? What if she was terrible at it?

Betsy's arrival to wake her up and dress for the day was a welcome reprieve from her thoughts. She was glad to see Persephone at breakfast, because once again, she had been missing the entire evening of the ball.

'And where were you hiding this time?' she teased her friend. 'Behind those Italian sculptures Lady Baybrook seems to love displaying in every corner? That one of Achilles in the drawing room was quite wide and would have kept you well concealed.'

'Ah, why didn't I think of that?' Persephone tsked. 'As it was, I crept behind Venus at first, but all the men kept staring at her, so I had to duck behind Athena.'

'A wise choice,' Maddie quipped.

'But how was your evening?' Persephone asked. 'No, wait. Tell me about it after breakfast so we can speak privately. We can go to the garden.'

Mabury Hall's garden was not as grand as the Houghton's, but it was still sizeable enough. Maddie quite enjoyed taking a stroll on the meandering paths through the lavender, foxgloves, wisteria, and hollyhocks.

'So,' Persephone began. 'Tell me all about the ball. Did you have gentlemen clamouring after you? How many times did you dance?'

Maddie paused, unsure what to tell her friend. 'Something…happened.' And so she told her about the incident with Mr Davenport and intervention from the Earl and Miss Merton.

'I had no idea Miss Merton could be so fierce,' Persephone exclaimed. 'When I first met her a few days ago, I thought her to be a sweet and shy spinster.'

'You're thinking of me,' Maddie joked, though it wasn't quite funny to her. 'I don't know if this plan is going to work. Perhaps I'm only going to attract the wrong kind of attention. Maybe Mr Davenport was right.'

'No, no.' Persephone halted and faced her. 'Don't say that. You've had three callers this week.'

'I'm still so shy and I never know what to say around

gentlemen except for discussions on weather. I'm hope-less.'

'No, you are not.'

'I've been thinking,' Maddie began. 'About…flirting.'

'With whom?'

'No, I mean I've been thinking of it. That perhaps I need to learn how to do it.' She told Persephone of her observations of the night before.

'Hmm.' Persephone's mouth pursed. 'I suppose you are not wrong. But how are you to learn? Are there books on the subject?'

'If there are, I've yet to come across them.'

'Perhaps all you need— Cam, how lovely to see you outside.'

A small flutter tickled Maddie's belly at the Earl's name. As he came closer and she locked eyes with him, that flutter turned frantic as a bee's wings. The morning sunshine glinted off his golden hair and the light hit his face at all the right angles to show off his handsome features.

'Good morning, Seph. Miss DeVries.'

'My lord, good morning,' she greeted, glad that her voice did not shake.

'Glad to see you aren't hiding in your office,' Persephone laughed.

'Aye, I thought I'd enjoy the fresh air.' He smoothed a hand down the left side of his chest. 'Seph, I'd like to speak to Miss DeVries for a moment. Would you mind giving us a few minutes of privacy?'

'Of course,' she said cheerfully. 'I shall…go and smell some of the hydrangeas.'

Maddie nearly grabbed Persephone's sleeve to stop her from leaving, but her friend was too quick and scampered away. Swallowing hard, she turned to the Earl. 'What can I do for you, my lord?'

'How are you this morning, Miss DeVries?'

'I'm quite well, thank you for asking.' Oh, Lord, she really was awkward.

'I trust last night has not soured your taste for balls and dancing?'

Did he have to bring that up? 'No, of course not.' She bit her lip. 'And once again, thank you for your assistance.'

'Think nothing of it.' He paused, once again patting a hand over his heart. 'I meant what I said, earlier,' he said in a low voice. 'You did nothing to deserve that. He acted of his own accord, and that has nothing to do with you or what you were wearing.'

'What I'm wearing? Why—oh.' He was speaking of the last words he'd said to her at the Houghton garden party.

'What I said to you was entirely out of line. It seems I'm forever asking for your forgiveness for the things I say,' he said sheepishly. 'But I hope you could find it in your heart to forgive me. Again.'

She'd been fuming mad in the garden—had it only been three days since? It seemed like forever ago. 'You prevented my ruination. Of course I can forgive you.'

He let out a breath. 'Thank you.'

'Is there anything else, my lord?'

'I—' He cleared his throat as his hand reached inside his coat pocket and pulled something out. 'I wanted to give you something.'

'Give me something?'

'Aye.' He handed her a package wrapped in wrinkled brown paper.

She tested its weight, trying to guess its contents. 'What is it?'

'Open it.'

Carefully, she unwrapped the package, revealing an object that looked like a pipe. Maddie immediately recognised it. 'Hmm.' Lifting it high, she turned it in her hand.

'I thought maybe you would appreciate it,' he said. 'I was told it's part of a blacksmith's set of tools.'

'Not quite. It's much too small, and blacksmiths' tools are made of a heartier material than brass.'

'Then what is it?'

He didn't know? Why did he buy it, then? 'It's an assayer's blowpipe.' When he gave her a blank look, she continued, 'While it is very similar to the blacksmith's blowpipe, it's much smaller because it's only used to test the proportions of precious metals in ores.'

He leaned over. 'How does it work?'

'The assayer mixes a sample of the ore, along with some other chemicals. Then, he lights a flame using a lamp or candle, then uses the pipe to direct the flame and increase its temperature.' To demonstrate, she placed her lips on the mouthpiece and blew out. 'See?'

The Earl's eyes widened to the size of saucers. 'I, uh...' he sputtered then coughed.

'Are you all right, my lord?'

'Er...yes—yes.' He raked his fingers through his hair.

Maddie frowned. Why would he give her such an object? And more importantly, why did her give her anything at all?

'It's not a courting gift,' he said quickly.

'Of course not.' Maddie would never mistake it for such, anyway. 'And thank you.'

'You're welcome. Now, if you'll excuse me, I must take my leave. Good day, Miss DeVries.'

Maddie watched him as he strode away from her, still

confused by the gift, the brass warm in her palm. More
questions assaulted her mind. Why did he choose this
not-courting gift for her? If he were truly sorry, then he
might have picked something that most; if not all, females might expect, like flowers or ribbons or other such
trivial trinkets. Instead, the Earl had found something he
thought she would like, based on her interests.

*I didn't even realise he'd been listening to Papa and
I going on about the furnace.*

He'd actually paid attention to what she was saying
and acknowledged it with this gift.

It made her stomach flutter.

Wrapping her fingers around the blowpipe, she called
to him, 'Wait, my lord.'

He halted, body going stiff. 'Aye?'

Scrounging up all her courage, she sauntered after
him and sidestepping his large frame so they were face
to face. 'My lord, I was wondering if you could…assist
me further?'

'Assist you?' A blond eyebrow rose up. 'In what way?
Are you in trouble, lass?'

'No, no. Not at all. I need further help with our plan.'

'Did you want me to dance more with you?' He tsked.
'I can only dance with you so much—you know that.'

'It's not that. See…your attentions have been effec-
tive so far,' she began. 'But there is one other thing you
could help me with.'

'Of course, what is it?'

'Well…uh…' How did one ask this question? She supposed one just *asked*. 'I was wondering…if you could
teach me how to flirt?'

'I beg your pardon?' Cam wondered if arousal from
Maddie's earlier demonstration with the blowpipe had
truly addled his brain. 'Teach you to flirt?'

'Yes. I don't know how, you see.' Her fingers played with the blowpipe in her hand, and Cam wished to God he'd never set eyes on the damned thing. 'It seems to me that flirting is a necessary part of the courtship ritual.' A furrow appeared between her eyebrows. 'No wonder Mr Davenport thought me to be a naive fool.'

'Never say his name again.' Cam's mood darkened at the sound of it. 'Don't believe anything he said about you, Maddie. You're not a fool.'

'But I am naive,' she pointed out. 'I have no experience with men. Oh, how could I even think I could be like her?'

'Like who?'

'Caroline. She has so many prospects, and I'm still middling about.'

Cam's anger rose further. How he hated it when she compared herself to her sister. 'I'm sure the right gentleman will come along and sweep you off your feet.' His stomach soured at the thought, but he continued on. 'And why would you think I would be a suitable tutor for such a venture?'

'You're a man.'

'Aye.' The insistent twitch in his cock confirmed it.

'And you have had…experience with women?'

'Aye,' he answered again, but did not like where this line of questioning was going.

'Which means you know how men and women flirt ~ach other. I don't know who else to ask. Please? There is no one else to teach me. I doubt my parents or Miss Merton would assist me. And I certainly can't ask my sister. Or yours.'

Cam's gaze drifted towards Persephone, who stood on the opposite end of the hedges, bent over a geranium bush. An idea came to him. 'If I agree, you must do me a favour as well.'

'Anything.'

'At the next ball, you must ensure Persephone does not disappear again.'

'Whatever do you mean, my lord?'

Though he admired her loyalty to his sister, he would not let them play him for a fool. 'Do not act innocent with me now, Miss DeVries. You know about my sister's antics.' The sheepish smile on her face confirmed as much. 'At the next ball, you will take Persephone in hand so that I may at least introduce her to a few gentlemen.'

She paused, as if weighing her options. 'I... All right. We have a deal, my lord.'

'One more thing.' He lifted a finger in the air. 'If we are to proceed with such an undertaking, then I insist you call me by my given name.'

'Your name, my lord?'

'Aye.'

'Why?'

Cam's mind blanked for a moment. Why did he say that? 'Because...because in order to flirt effectively, you must be at ease. All this *my lord* and *Your Lordship* will only hinder the learning process.'

'All right.' She paused. 'Does this mean you must call me by my name, as well?'

'Aye. But this is only when no one else is around.'

'No one else is around?' she echoed.

'Of course. How else am I to teach you? In the parlour with Miss Merton and your mother looking on?'

'I thought perhaps you could give me instructions and I could test them out on other gentlemen.'

The thought of her 'testing' anything out on any other man made him want to punch something.

'But I suppose you are correct,' she added. 'It would make sense if you teach me how to flirt and then I could practise with you first. I would not want to embarrass myself in public.'

'It's only practical.' God in heaven, what was he saying? Had he really offered to teach her to flirt and then have her try it out on him?

'And I promise, I shall not let Persephone run away,' she said with a determined nod. 'You have my word.'

'Excellent.'

'When shall we have our first lesson, my lo— Cam?'

His heart gave a little jolt at the way she said his name. Cam couldn't recall how many times he'd wondered how it would sound like from her lips. It was much better than he'd imagined. 'How about now? Meet me in the smoking room.'

'Right here? What if we are caught alone?'

'I shall inform Eames that I am headed to Mr Atwell's office, then send my coach off. But I will slip back inside the house and meet you there in—' he checked his pocket watch ' half an hour.'

'I understand,' she said. 'I shall see you there then.'

His throat had gone dry, so he managed only a nod.

This was preposterous. Ludicrous. All-out crazy. But he just could not say no to her. Besides, who knows what other scheme she or his sister might come up with? Better that he keep watch on her and stay close, or they might find someone else to rope into their plans.

*You're doing this for Persephone*, he told himself. He was determined to give her the season Ma had wanted for her. And she would get it, if only she would stay still and let him.

But now, he was once again caught up further into this scheme with Maddie. Teach her to flirt? He did not know the first thing about how to teach a lady to flirt. He knew *how*, of course, but it came naturally to him, with the old MacGregor charm. How could he instruct someone else—a woman, at that—on such matters?

Or maybe he didn't have to teach her.

Not exactly.

As he gathered his thoughts, he did exactly what he told Maddie he would do with Eames and his coachman. To his surprise, Maddie was already in the smoking room when he arrived, sitting on the leather chair opposite the one he usually occupied.

'Papa left for a business meeting and Mama and Caroline went for a stroll in the park,' she said. 'I thought it best to slip away as soon as possible while there was no one around.'

'And Persephone?'

'With the Dowager and Miss Merton. I told them I had a headache and was upstairs in my room.' Blue eyes stared up at him expectantly. 'Shall we begin, my lord?'

'Of course.' He strode over to her and sat down. 'First, we—what is that?'

Maddie had retrieved something from her skirts and placed it on her lap. 'A notebook and pencil,' she said matter-of-factly. 'I'm taking down notes. It's the best way to remember things and ideas.'

'Right. Now…' He smoothed his hands down his thighs. 'What is flirting?' Maddie's pencil *scritch-scratched* across the page of her notebook, and Cam found himself transported back to his days in the schoolroom. 'Flirting is the act of signalling one's interest to attract a potential mate.'

*Scritch-scratch.*

'Many species of animal, for example, engage in a type of flirting. It varies from species to species.…' Cam

things I could come up with, especially with your colouring and height. No man would be able to turn away from you.'

'Mrs Ellesmore, now's your chance,' the Dowager declared with a beaming smile. 'Mrs DeVries is occupied for the day, so you may do as you wish.'

'Do as you wish?' Maddie echoed.

The Dowager continued, 'If Mrs DeVries complains, I shall tell her everything was my idea and you may send me the bill instead.'

Mrs Ellesmore clapped her hands together. 'Wonderful.' She dragged Maddie to the dais in the corner of the room before she could protest. 'My mind is swirling with ideas... Blue will suit you because of your eyes. With the right shade, we can even make them appear violet. And your neckline! Low, to expose your décolletage and long neck. You will look graceful as a swan.' She rounded the dais, muttering to herself. 'Four—no, five gowns. And one ball gown, at least.'

'Is there any way we can have at least one ready for tomorrow?' the Dowager asked. 'The Countess of Houghton is hosting her garden party in the afternoon.'

'Hmm, I might have something that would suit her that is ready. Thank goodness I haven't cut the hem yet. But Your Grace, Lady Danville will be most disappointed...'

'I'm sure you can find a way to appease her. Why not give her a discount on her next gown, and whatever the difference, consider it a rush fee for Miss DeVries's dresses?'

'A generous and kind offer. I'll fetch the dress and have Miss DeVries try it on immediately.' She hurried away into the other room.

Maddie fiddled her fingers together. 'Your Grace, it's not that I'm not grateful... But you don't have to do this for me. And even if Mama does complain, I'm sure I can convince Papa to pay for the dress.'

'Maddie, please allow me to do this.' The Dowager smiled weakly at her. 'I must confess, I share Mrs Ellesmore's opinion, but I did not want to say anything to your mother for fear of offending her.'

She doubted her Grace could offend Mama; if the Dowager told her to dance the jig in the middle of Covent Garden, Eliza would do it to keep their sponsor happy if only to keep their family circulating within the upper social circles of the ton.

'But then, I thought perhaps if I could…remove her influence for a few hours, I could help your wardrobe. The colours and styles she chooses do you no favour.'

'She thinks those colours and styles give me a more "delicate" look.' Maddie's shoulders slumped. 'And distract from my flaws.'

Persephone guffawed. 'That is one way to state it.'

'Flaws?' The Dowager shook her head. 'My dear, your height and figure are nothing to hide. I believe with the right gown you will be stunning.'

'You are too kind, Your Grace.'

'One more thing.' The Dowager glanced around, looking over at Persephone, who was occupied with examining a dress form on the other side of the room. 'I do not mean to pry, but you should know that after I ran into you in the hallway, I saw the Earl leaving the smoking room.'

*Oh, Lord.*

Her heart thudded in her chest. Maddie was, unfortunately, a terrible liar. Besides, how could she lie to this woman who'd opened up her home to them and so obviously cared for her well-being? 'Nothing happened, Your Grace.'

'The Earl is the son of my good friend, and know-

close enough that Cam swore he could smell her flowery perfume.

He gulped. 'Er, yes.'

'Seems silly.' She shrugged. 'What else?'

'The next step is letting the gentleman know you have been listening to him. So, you must say things like, *Oh, yes, my lord* or *I agree, my lord*.'

'But what if I don't agree?'

'It doesn't matter,' he stated. 'You must agree. With absolutely everything.'

She sighed. 'All right. Is there anything else I must do?'

'Laugh, too, at their jokes. Even if you do not find them funny.'

'Laugh—' Her lips pressed together. 'Fine. I'll do it.'

*Fine?* Cam let out a huff. He expected her to complain. Or give up and realise it was not worth flirting with these milksop aristocrats. He would have to find a different tactic to sway her from this ridiculous notion. 'All right, our lesson is over for now.'

'So soon?' She sounded almost disappointed.

'Why? Is there anything else?'

'Well, there is one more question I had.'

Cam supposed he might as well get all her questions out of the way. 'Tell me, then.' She didn't answer, but instead, her face turned bright red. 'What is it?'

She licked her lips. 'It's about…kissing.'

Cam's entire being froze. This did not bode well.

He should ignore her question and send her packing. 'What about kissing?'

*Cameron MacGregor, you utter and complete fool.*

'H-how do I know if a man wants to kiss me?'

*Think, think!* Cam wasn't sure how to answer that, exactly, as all sense seemed to be leaving his head and going…much lower. 'So you may prevent it, correct? Because as you know, kissing is something reserved for husbands and wives.'

She didn't look convinced but said, 'Of course.'

'Of course. Has anyone ever tried to kiss you?'

She nodded. 'Back in Pittsburgh. He was one of my father's apprentices, and his name was—'

'I don't need details,' he interrupted. 'Did he succeed?'

'No.'

His tightening in his chest eased. 'Good.'

'He was too short,' Maddie continued. 'He couldn't reach my lips.'

'Truly?'

'Yes. He asked me to wait so he could fetch a box!' She burst into laughter. 'Then I left. It—it was really the f-first time I was glad I'm so tall.' She wiped the corners of her eyes with her fingers. 'I didn't even know he wanted to kiss me. We were just alone and he tried it.'

'Well, that's your first mistake,' he said. 'Being alone with a man.'

Something sparked in her eyes—something dangerous. 'Is it?'

*Retreat!* his instinct screamed. But other parts of him said, *Full speed ahead!*

'Definitely.'

'And what other mistakes should I avoid?'

Cam's heart hammered in his chest. 'You let him get close enough.'

She took a step forward. 'Like this?'

'Aye. And then he may assess your interest in your gaze.' Her brilliant blue eyes bore right into him. 'And then he will lean down.' He bent his head closer. *This was a practical lesson, after all.* 'And you must not encourage him.'

'How do I do that?'

'By not touching him.' Surely, she wouldn't dare—

A hand landed over his heart. 'Like this?'

Oh, Lord God above, he was going to do it. He was going to kiss her.

And Cam couldn't quite bring himself to stop.

## Chapter Eleven

Oh, heavens, what was she thinking?

Well, perhaps for the first time in her life, Maddie was not thinking. No. This time, she let her instinct take over. Not just that—she let it run wild.

The first brush of his lips was shockingly gentle. She wasn't sure exactly what she was expecting, but it was not…that. They moved over hers in a light caress, as if testing her reaction. So, she slid her hand up to his shoulder, giving it an encouraging squeeze. She sighed against him and sidled closer.

'Maddie,' he groaned against her mouth before his fingers cupped her jaw, thumb stroking her chin. To her shock, he tugged at the corner of her mouth as he slipped his tongue over her parted lips. The intimate touch caused a shock in her, down low to the crevice between her legs. To her surprise, Maddie found herself opening to him further, his tongue sliding across hers, tasting her as if she were delicious treat.

A hand landed on her waist, moving to her bottom, cupping her through her layers of skirts. He pulled her close, their bodies pressing together tight in a motion that made Maddie's knees weak. A knee somehow slid between her legs, pushing up against her, and when she slid down, the most delicious shudder went through her.

'Hello? How are the lessons going?'

Cam's strong hands released her and Maddie leapt away from him. 'Persephone!' she cried as her friend entered the smoking room.

'What are you doing here, Seph?' Cam combed his fingers through his dishevelled hair.

Oh, dear, did she do that? She did remember feeling how soft it was. For some reason, she thought it would be rough and wiry. Not silky like a babe's downy hair.

'I wanted to see you how you were progressing with the flirting lessons,' she replied matter-of-factly.

'You told her?'

'Of—of course I did.' Knees still weak, Maddie staggered backwards but stopped herself before she fell any further.

'Even the part about where she cannot disappear at the next ball?'

Persephone nodded. 'I would do anything to help Maddie.'

'She's my friend. I can't lie to her.' Indeed, that had been Maddie's first instinct because of the bargain she had struck with Cam. But it wasn't right, exchanging Persephone for her personal gain. To her surprise, Persephone agreed.

'I even helped keep the Dowager and Miss Merton occupied so she may attend these lessons with you.' Persephone ambled over to them. 'So? How did it go?'

Maddie couldn't look him in the eye. Her mind was still all a-jumble from that kiss. 'It—it went well.'

'Indeed.' Cam tugged at his coat lapels with his hands. 'I was going through some practical lessons with Maddie.'

'What kind of practical lessons?' Persephone asked eagerly. 'Will they help her find a husband?'

Maddie nearly choked trying to stop the gasp from escaping her mouth.

'I've been teaching her what to do,' he said, a cool mask slipping over his face. 'And what not to do.'

*Oh, dear.*

She'd made a misstep.

*He didn't want to kiss me.*

Despite the bizarre start, she'd enjoyed his lesson. Talking to Cam was refreshing. Except for her father, men didn't generally talk to her so candidly, so she was disappointed when he'd ended their lesson so abruptly. She hadn't wanted them to end so soon, and so she'd asked about kissing. She'd been staring at his lips, wondering...

What happened could never happen again. She was the one who'd encouraged it—no, she'd practically mauled him. Mortification made her entire body grow hot.

'Thank you, m-my lord,' she stammered. 'It's been enlightening, to say the least. If you'll excuse me, I must run along.'

Maddie could not have left the room fast enough. She ran up to her rooms and closed the door behind her, bracing against the heavy wood as if she could keep the embarrassment from getting inside and catching up to her like an invader trying to storm a castle.

Cam's lips on hers.

His strong shoulders.

His hands on her bottom.

Heat coiled low in her belly. She was not ignorant of what happened between a man and a woman. Her mother had explained to her, in a roundabout way, about where children come from. Plus, she'd heard a conversation or two between the men at the furnace to fill in the gaps. However, aside from that, she had no experience at all and had never even been kissed.

Until now.

Her first kiss.

It hadn't even affected him, and why should it have? He was an experienced man. Perhaps he kissed women every day.

The thought of it made her cross and ate at her, like when she'd seen him dancing with Caroline. Though this was worse, because she was imagining him kissing another woman and not just waltzing.

*I must remain unaffected.*

'Yes,' she said aloud with a firm resolve. 'It didn't even affect him.' It was part of the lesson she'd practically begged him for. If he could manage to act like nothing had happened, then so could she.

Maddie was relieved that the next event was a dinner party the following day and it was to be at Mabury Hall. There would be no dancing here, and perhaps if she were lucky, no Cam, either. As was the case since he'd arrived, he hardly joined them for meals.

'Don't you look bonny,' Persephone remarked as they met in the hallway. 'Mrs Ellesmore is a genius.'

'Thank you.' Maddie normally hated the sight of a yellow gown, but when this one had arrived earlier that day, she had gasped aloud. The fabric was not the usual bright yellow her mother picked but a champagne gold that matched her hair. The ruffles were minimal, only on the bottom, and the dress had a fitted bodice and an open neckline that tapered to a V down her chest.

'Are you disappointed not to be dancing tonight?'

'Not at all. I'm glad to rest my feet.'

'Good, because I'm glad we won't be at a ball for a good while. That means I won't have to dance with anyone Cam introduces me to.'

Maddie's step nearly faltered at the name. 'Y-yes, I'm glad for you.' And for herself, because after yesterday's mortifying events, she didn't know how she could even look Cam in the eye. It was one thing for her to resolve to act like nothing had happened, but quite another in reality.

The thoughts of the kiss plagued her mind. She relived it in her mind over and over, unable to forget his lips and his hands and that delicious tingle between her legs. But she would get to the end of the memory and how they had been interrupted. Embarrassment flooded her once more, as if it had just happened.

'Where is your brother, by the way?' Maddie made her tone appear as casual as possible.

'Since he's the highest-ranking male in the house, he'll be escorting the Dowager to dinner,' Persephone said.

Maddie ignored that minuscule stab in her chest. 'Ah, of course.'

'Silly, isn't it?' Persephone blew out a breath. 'Just because some distant uncle on my father's side keeled over without any sons, my brother gets to walk ahead into the dining room ahead of us.'

Maddie chuckled. 'According to Miss Merton, the rest of the dinner won't be as formal, as they're seating us more casually in order to encourage conversation.'

The Dowager and Miss Merton had set up tonight's dinner party to further both Maddie's and Caroline's prospects with their most promising gentlemen callers. It would give them an opportunity to become more acquainted outside dancing at balls and the rigid morning-call ritual.

They'd narrowed the guest list down to two gentlemen each. For Maddie, they had invited Sir Alfred Kensington and Lord Andrew Annesley, and for Caroline, Lord George Butler and Jasper, Viscount Moseby. They had also planned to invite two other couples, but Miss Merton didn't disclose their names.

'We should make haste. Dinner's about to start,' Maddie said to Persephone.

The two girls made their way downstairs to the hall just outside the dining room, arriving just in time as the butler announced dinner. Persephone bade her a quick goodbye and dashed up front. Maddie was all the way in the rear with her parents and Caroline, and so she didn't get a chance to see the other guests.

The doors to the dining room opened, and they all filed in. Except for the part that she had to be in the same room with Cam, she was looking forward to this, as she wanted to put her flirting skills to test. At least she could put to use what she had learned from that disastrous day.

The moment she entered, however, her eyes immediately went to Cam. He was seated at one end of the table, opposite the Dowager. Maddie's heart did a funny little flip at the sight of him looking so impeccably handsome in his formal evening attire, his jaw freshly shaven and golden hair tamed back. The snowy white of his shirt contrasted with his golden skin, and Maddie once again found her gaze glued to those lips.

Mercifully, she had to turn the other way to reach her seat on the other side of the table. She said a little prayer asking the Good Lord that he hadn't caught her staring at him.

When she took her place, she saw Lord Annesely to her right and, to her surprise, Viscount Palmer on her left.

'My lord,' she greeted as they took their seats. 'I did not realise you'd been invited.'

'Miss DeVries,' he acknowledged. 'I'm afraid I am only a last-minute addition. My aunt and uncle asked me to come along.' He nodded to Lord and Lady Houghton, who were seated at the other end of the table on the Dowager's side, next to Mama and Papa and one other couple. 'Apparently, Sir Alfred Kensington was thrown off his horse this afternoon and so has taken abed.'

Maddie covered her mouth with her hand. 'Oh, heavens. I do hope he's all right.'

'It wasn't serious, at least from what my aunt heard.' He took the glass of wine one of the footmen had filled for him. 'Anyway, the Dowager asked her if I was still in town, and if so, could I possibly attend her dinner party tonight so we do not have an imbalance of guests.' He smiled warmly at her as he took a sip from his glass. 'I must admit, I've never been happier to fill an empty seat.'

Was he flirting with her? Maddie wasn't certain. When they'd first met, he'd been quite aloof, though by the end, after he'd returned her to her parents, she'd thought they'd made a connection—she couldn't have imagined that look they had exchanged. However, when he hadn't turned up at the Baybrook ball, she'd written him off.

'How fortuitous,' she replied, taking a sip from her own glass.

'Indeed. I was disappointed that I could not make it to the Baybrook ball for that dance you promised me. The Earl had taken a turn for the worse, and so I had to make haste back to Hampshire.'

'Is your father—'

'Fine.' He put the glass down. 'After getting him settled, I came back to town early today.'

'I'm so glad your father's condition did not worsen, my lord. And that—'

Their conversation was interrupted as the doors opened and the liveried footmen arrived to serve the first course. Meals at Mabury Hall and Highfield Park were always sumptuous affairs even on normal days, but on special occasions they were spectacular, thanks to the household's talented French chef, Monsieur Faucher. Tonight's first course was a delicious consommé of fresh vegetables. Maddie had been served the dish before, but it was never the same each time because Faucher used only the vegetables that were in season. Maddie's spoon was halfway to her mouth when she felt a prickle on the back of her neck. Immediately, her gaze lifted towards the head of the table, and sure enough, Cam was staring right at her.

He quickly turned away as Persephone, who sat to his right, spoke to him. Maddie returned to her food.

After that kiss, there was no way she could ever be near him again.

But then, she would miss talking with him and spending time with him. His candour, his wit, the way he talked to her as if she weren't just some silly little girl. Whenever she spoke, he had his full attention on her, like he actually cared about what she said. It showed, especially in his actions, like the not gift that was currently hidden underneath her pillow.

'Delicious, isn't it, Miss DeVries?' Lord Annesely remarked.

'I—yes.' She swallowed her spoonful and then wiped her mouth with her napkin. Remembering he was here because of her, she decided to begin putting yesterday's lessons into practice.

*It's not just about what you say, but what you don't say. When a man is speaking, you should look into his eyes.*

Placing her spoon down, she turned her head towards Annesely, hoping to catch his gaze. 'My lord, have you, um...' What were his interests? 'Seen any new fashions recently?' Oh, heavens, that sounded utterly vapid.

*You must appear that you are eager to hear anything they have to say.*

His eyes lit up and he put his spoon down. 'I'm glad you asked, Miss DeVries.' Sitting up straight, he parted his coat and gestured to his waistcoat. 'Isn't it divine? It's the latest fashion from Paris.'

'It's, uh...' She didn't know how to describe the shiny pink-and-green-striped monstrosity wrapped around his torso. Ugly? Eyesore? Blinding?

*You must agree. With absolutely everything.*

'Absolutely divine, my lord.'

Lord Annesely beamed at her. 'I'm glad you think so. You know, I've always thought French fashion was much more refined than English...'

Maddie kept her smile frozen on her face as she let Lord Annesely continue on his oral treatise of French versus English fashion, throwing in a 'yes, my lord' and 'how right you are, my lord' a few times for good measure. Her mind, however, drifted off, once again thinking back to that kiss yesterday.

Cam's soft lips.

His strong hands, cupping her bottom.

'Miss DeVries? What do you think?'

Lord Annesely's question jolted her back. 'Um, yes, my lord?'

'I knew you would understand my passion for cravats,' he said excitedly.

'Of course.' Mercifully, the footmen stepped forward to clear their plates, and Maddie was thankful for the reprieve.

'The French truly are a marvel,' Lord Annesely continued as they were served a delicious-smelling terrine. 'They just have that… I don't know what.' He barked out a laugh. 'Right? Because that's what the direct translation of *je ne sais quoi* is!'

A second ticked by before Maddie realised it was a joke. 'Oh, of course it is.' She let out a forced laugh. 'How clever you are, my lord.' Inside, however, Maddie was dying a slow death. *Only eight more courses to go.*

Course after course came, and Maddie continued to flirt with Lord Annesely, agreeing with everything he said and laughing at his terrible jokes, all the while trying to maintain eye contact. Frankly, it was exhausting, and when they finished dessert, she nearly wept in happiness.

'I quite enjoyed Lord Annesely's tirade against double-breasted coats,' Viscount Palmer quipped from her left. 'If he could speak with the same passion in Parliament, he could get a lot of laws passed.'

Maddie couldn't suppress the laugh bubbling inside her. 'My lord, you are incorrigible,' she whispered.

'Don't tell me you weren't swayed by his arguments for the abolition of top hats?' He winked at her.

'Did you say top hats?' Lord Annesely interrupted, his brows slashing down. 'I—'

'If everyone is finished,' the Dowager announced, 'let us head to the parlour.'

They all stood up and followed the Dowager over to the adjacent room, where the footmen served sherry for the ladies and brandy for the gentlemen.

'Miss DeVries, this was such an enjoyable dinner,' Lord Annesely began. 'I'm afraid I cannot stay for too long as I'm heading to our estate in the morning. But, I was wondering if you'd like to go on a carriage ride with me next week?'

Maddie couldn't believe what she was hearing. A carriage ride? 'That sounds lovely, my lord.'

'I shall be back in town Monday, so how about Tuesday?'

'I will tell my mother and Miss Merton to keep the afternoon free.'

'Excellent. If you'll excuse me, I must bid goodbye to the Dowager. Pleasant evening, Miss DeVries.'

'A pleasant evening to you, too, my lord.' As she watched him walk away, a single thought appeared in Maddie's mind.

*It worked.*

She had doubted Cam's lessons and methods, but they produced results. Her first instinct was to run to him and tell him about her success, but then the reminder of their kiss yesterday came flooding back. Once again, the memory made her hot with embarrassment.

'Miss DeVries, I saw you had an empty hand.' Viscount Palmer offered her a glass of sherry.

'Thank you, my lord.' She accepted it and took a sip, the liquid calming her frayed nerves.

'Now that Lord Annesely has departed,' he began, 'I was hoping to catch your attention.'

'Why would you need my attention, my lord?'

'I thought it would be obvious by now. I wish to know more about you.'

'For what—oh.'

'I regret not going to the Baybrook ball and writing my name on your dance card,' he continued. 'Then, it would have been acceptable for me to pay you a call this week.'

'Well, my lord, you are here now. You could get to know more about me.' Did she just…flirt back with him? *Yes, I did.*

'How right you are, Miss DeVries.'

Confidence surged through Maddie as the handsome Viscount smiled at her. Perhaps those lessons from Cam were worth it. She only had to put those thoughts of that awful kiss out of her mind.

Well, the kiss wasn't awful. No—in fact, it had been wonderful.

At least, up until the end.

Unable to help herself, she looked back across the room at Cam, who was standing by the mantel with Lord and Lady Houghton, the firelight caught in his golden locks. Had they always had a red glint to them? How come she'd never noticed?

*Oh, heavens.*

She had to get that kiss—and Cam—out of her mind. The carriage ride with Annesely would be a good distraction, plus Palmer was right here beside her. Still, why did she wish that it was Cam she'd be out and about with? And Cam right beside her now instead of Viscount Palmer?

'Miss DeVries?' the Viscount asked. 'Would you like another sherry?'

'Er…yes, my lord.' She had to put those thoughts away for now. Of the kiss and of Cam. There was no use thinking of him, as their courtship was all a game. A play they were putting on. She should remember that and instead look forward to her own future—one that didn't include him.

## Chapter Twelve

Cam eased his grip on his brandy glass and unclenched his jaw, fearing both might break if he did not relax.

But how could he relax when he had been forced to watch Maddie flirt with that dandy throughout the entire dinner?

And now, she was deep in conversation with Viscount Palmer.

He wanted to throw the brandy. At Palmer's face. Preferably after filling the glass with hot nails.

Cam was quite relieved that they didn't have to go to another ball this evening. Miss Merton had explained the purpose of this dinner party, which was to invite the gentlemen who were likely to match with the DeVries sisters. He'd even told himself that he was pleased, because this meant Maddie would find a husband soon enough and be out of his reach.

That's why he'd agreed to this fake courtship plan, after all.

Of course, when he'd seen Palmer arrive, he'd been incensed. 'What is he doing here?' he had asked Miss Merton.

'Oh, it's a tragedy, my lord. Sir Alfred was thrown off

his horse,' the companion had cried, then explained that Palmer was not Maddie's potential suitor and only filling an empty seat for the injured Sir Alfred Kensington. While he would never wish anyone harm, Cam couldn't help but feel relieved the man was not here.

*One less suitor for Maddie.*

Downing the rest of the golden liquid, he handed the glass to a footman. 'If you excuse me, Your Grace, Lord Houghton, Lady Houghton, I must refresh myself.' After a nod from the Dowager, he made his way out of the parlour.

Had he not been a guest at Mabury Hall, Cam would have left the dinner party. However, he was the Dowager's escort tonight, so politeness and good manners dictated he stay by her side until the last guest had left. A few minutes of reprieve from having to watch Maddie and the Viscount should help him get through the rest of the evening. Not that leaving the room would be of help, as she didn't even need to breathe the same air for him to think of her. This last day, his thoughts had been consumed by nothing but her and that kiss they'd shared.

Half of him was glad that Persephone had interrupted him. And the other half? Well, that part continued to torture him with the memory of her sweet lips and eager body, as well as images of what could have been. He could have continued to let her slide on his thigh until she shuddered with pleasure. Then he could have pressed her against the wall, lifted up her skirt, and touched her in all the soft and sweet places on her body. Or pulled down the bodice of her gown so he could find out what her breasts looked like.

'My lord, where are you going?'

Cam halted and turned. 'I'm just—Miss DeVries?'

Sure enough, Caroline DeVries stood at the other end

of the hallway, her expression akin to a cat who had trapped a mouse in a corner. 'Are you off to have a secret tryst with someone? With my sister, perhaps?'

'I beg your pardon?'

'Of course, she's occupied at the moment. With Viscount Palmer.'

His fingernails dug hard into his palms. 'If you'll excuse me, Miss DeVries, I should get back to my duties as our hostess's escort.' He attempted to walk past her, but she blocked his way. 'I suggest you move aside, Miss DeVries. Besides, we should not be alone together.'

'*Pfft.* It's just a hallway.' She sauntered closer to him. 'And you've done far worse with other women, I imagine.'

His patience was beginning to wear thin. 'Miss DeVries, this is a completely inappropriate conversation.'

'Do you have these conversations with Maddie?'

'I don't know what you're talking about.'

'What do you have planned for my sister?' Her eyes narrowed into slits. 'You dance with her at every ball, sometimes twice. You've paid a call to her with my father present. And then there was that tryst.'

'Tryst?' He swallowed hard.

'In the garden.'

'Garden?' Relief poured through him as he realised she wasn't speaking of the smoking room. 'My sister was but a few feet away and your mother and Miss Merton could have looked outside the window and seen us.'

Her eyes flashed. 'Do you plan to court Maddie or not? Will you be proposing soon?'

'That is none of your business. Besides, why are you playing the concerned sister now? You do nothing but put Maddie down and belittle her every chance you get.'

'I have not,' she sputtered. 'I am only concerned for

her. Maddie will not be suited to the life of a countess. She's too shy and awkward. She'll only embarrass herself. And you.'

So, that was what this was about. Who did this lass think she was? 'Really now? Tell me, then. Who should be my countess?'

A seductive smile curled up her lips. 'Someone sophisticated. Beautiful. Delicate.' She drew closer. 'You're an earl, my lord. Surely there is someone else you're attracted to? Someone more to your taste?'

'You don't know me at all.' Cam laughed aloud. 'Lass, the last thing I want is to marry someone I'm attracted to.' Never again. Not since Jenny. 'Now—' He towered over her. 'Run along, and do not ever approach me alone again, you *ken*?'

Sidestepping her, he marched away, feeling her hating stare burn a hole into his back.

*She could go jump in the Thames, for all I care.*

How dare she even suggest that she would be a better match for him than Maddie.

As he walked away, he cursed silently as he realised that his only escape from this narrow hallway was blocked by that witch behind him. Now he had no choice but to go back to the parlour and continue to watch Maddie and Palmer converse so closely all night. He couldn't help but wish he was the one in deep conversation with her; he could listen to her ideas and thoughts about anything and everything under the sun all night long. All these boring and tedious parties would be so much more tolerable if could spend them by her side. He could already imagine the little smiles and looks she would flash him, or perhaps she'd have some witty remark she would whisper to him. Lord, she was so pretty when she acted all awkward and shy.

He supposed there was one bright side to this, and that was that after tonight, maybe he would never have to look at that odious viscount ever again.

After running some morning errands, Cam returned to Mabury Hall in the afternoon and asked Eames where his sister was.

'In the library, my lord,' the butler informed him. 'But please do take the entrance through the dining room, as the sitting room is currently occupied by Miss Madeline and Viscount Palmer.'

'Viscount—' Cam couldn't even finish as he marched off in the direction of the sitting room. He flung the door open. Sure enough, there he was—Viscount Odious, seated across from Maddie. Her blue eyes went wide as saucers, while the Viscount's mouth turned down into a disapproving frown.

'My lord!' Miss Merton exclaimed. 'Did Eames not inform you that this room is occupied?'

'I'm afraid I didn't see him,' he lied. 'What's this, now?'

'The Viscount is paying my daughter a call,' Mrs DeVries informed him in an irritated tone.

'Really, now? How much time d'you have left?'

'Five minutes,' the Viscount replied in an irritated tone.

'I see. Excuse me, then.' He shut the door, then spun around, planting his feet firmly on the ground, then took his watch out of his pocket. He watched the second hand like a hawk, tracking its movement until it completed exactly five journeys around the face. Once it was done, he flung the door once again.

'Your call is done,' he announced, much to the shock of Miss Merton and Mrs DeVries.

Viscount—Odi… Palmer got to his feet. 'I had a lovely time, Miss DeVries. Thank you.'

'Thank you, my lord.' She sneaked a glance at him, her expression confused.

Cam glared at the Viscount as he passed by, and to his irritation, the damned man didn't react at all. In fact, he behaved as if Cam weren't even there.

'This is highly unusual, my lord,' Miss Merton began. 'What was the purpose of your interruption?'

Three pairs of eyes stared at him, waiting for an explanation. 'I required…some…' He glanced around and picked up the first thing he could grab—an embroidered cushion. 'This. I needed this.' He waved it around.

'A cushion?' Miss Merton raised a brow.

'Yes. I needed to show my valet the excellent needlework on it.' He tutted. 'The man's been slipping, you know. His stitches have not been up to standard. Now, if you'll excuse me, I must see my sister.'

He stifled the desire to run and somehow managed a dignified stride into the library. Letting out a breath, he called, 'Persephone?'

No answer, but from the way the door that led to the dining room was left ajar, he guessed she had already left.

'My lord?'

His entire body reacted to the sound of Maddie's voice. Slowly, he turned around. 'Miss DeVries?'

She stood by the entrance, looking so lovely in a light blue gown that emphasised the colour of her eyes, the sun shining behind her, lighting her up like an angel. 'Miss Merton and Mama have gone upstairs.'

'And?'

'And I stayed behind because I said I needed to speak with Persephone.'

'She's not here.'

She looked visibly relieved. 'Thank goodness. I was hoping to have a moment of your time.' Stepping inside, she closed the door behind her.

'How may I be of assistance?'

'It's not you. I mean, I—' Her teeth sank into her lip. 'I'm afraid it's my turn to apologise.'

The words had him agog, and for a moment his mind ceased all function. 'Apologise? What for?'

'F-for taking advantage of your kindness.'

He stared at her, still unable to process the words coming out of her mouth.

She sighed and then leaned closer. 'The other day. In the smoking room. Our lessons.'

'You…were taking advantage of me?'

'Our—my kissing you,' she whispered, her entire face turning scarlet.

*Oh.* 'The kiss.'

'Yes. It was just… It was just a lesson after all, correct? And I may have taken it too far and c-coerced that kiss from you. I would just like to say I apologise and I promise it will never happen again.' She wrung her hands together. 'And I would understand if you feel uncomfortable around me and wish to end our fake courtship agreement.'

Cam couldn't quite believe what he was hearing. She thought she had been the one who had wronged him by 'coercing' him?

Somehow, his life had turned into some kind of comedic play.

But he wasn't quite ready to close the curtains.

'I don't think it would be wise.'

'You don't?'

'No. Not at this stage, anyway. I've already paid a call on you, then danced with you several times, sometimes twice. Maddie, if we give up now, then you'll be humiliated. Your other suitors might drop you, wondering why I, an eligible young peer, would suddenly lose interest in you.'

'Oh.'

'Don't you see? It's much too late to quit now. We must see this to the end.' Yes, that was it. They'd done all this hard work, and to bow out now would guarantee defeat. 'So, we must continue on, but you must also allow me to help you. To…sooner achieve your goals.'

'My goals?'

'To marry. I can't be running around pretending to court you forever, after all. Hopefully you'll find a suitable match before my hair turns grey.'

She laughed. 'I hope it does not come to that.'

'I hope so, too. But don't just marry the first man who comes in that door,' he warned. 'You must avoid scoundrels who may take advantage of you.'

'Oh. Like Mr Davenport.'

'Exactly.' He despised hearing that name from her, but in this instance he was the only example Cam could think of. 'As I mentioned, what he attempted with you is not your fault, but you must be vigilant. I'm not worried about what you might do, but rather, I am concerned about other men.' He was one himself, after all, and knew how their minds worked.

'Oh, you should definitely help me, then.' Her voice lowered once more. 'Please, Cam?'

'Help you? With what?'

'Help me avoid these scoundrels. You seem to have a good instinct.'

'Well—'

'You already do it for Persephone, correct? You meet

other gentlemen, examine their prospects, and select which ones would be suitable to introduce to her?'

'It's not quite the same—'

'Then you could do it for me.' She clapped her hands together. 'I mean, you could warn me which gentlemen are scoundrels. You could be like my elder brother, too.'

The mere thought of it made Cam want to retch up his breakfast.

'Yes, that's it. I've always wanted an older brother.'

*If she says brother one more time, I'm going to hang myself.*

'Very well, Maddie.' He cleared his throat. 'Once the time comes and you have a list of gentlemen coming to call, I can help you assess their suitability.'

'Thank you so much, Cam. That truly is very kind of you. If you'll excuse me, I must head upstairs before Mama comes down to find me.'

Cam watched her walk away, his mind still reeling from what had just occurred. He wasn't just deep into this scheme, but rather, he had jumped right into it, head first.

Glancing down and seeing that he held the cushion with a death grip, he tossed the damned thing to the floor.

## Chapter Thirteen

Maddie wasn't certain exactly what had happened this week, but she was flooded with cards, and more gentlemen came to call on her, even those with whom she'd danced but who hadn't shown further interest previously. They hadn't even attended any balls, but she had been introduced to more gentlemen at various events, including at the opera, at one charity art show, and during a stroll in Hyde Park. She had also gone on that carriage ride with Lord Annesely, and despite the first disastrous visit, Viscount Palmer had called once more this week, and they had also spent some time conversing at the art exhibit. He planned to join them at the ballet tomorrow night.

'See, I was right all along,' Persephone had told her. 'It's all about competition. I think news of Cam, Lord Annesely, and Viscount Palmer's interest in you has spread through London, and now all these men are calling around, wondering what the delightful Miss Maddie DeVries has to offer.'

Maddie still wasn't sure how to feel about that. On one hand, she was getting what she wanted, but on the other, all those gentlemen showed interest only because other men wanted her. And not because of her.

'How wonderful,' Mama exclaimed as she went through the various cards that arrived that morning. The DeVrieses, Miss Merton, and Persephone were having breakfast by themselves that morning as the Dowager had an early appointment. 'Both my girls are a success this season.'

'Maybe there won't be a need for a second one,' Papa added, taking a sip of his tea. 'And we can go home.'

Caroline, on the other hand, pouted. 'Ugh. All these gentlemen have nothing to offer. Mama, I cannot go home without a titled husband. I'll be a laughing stock.'

'Caroline, dear, don't you think it's time you made a decision?' Miss Merton said diplomatically. 'At the very least, you should let some of these gentlemen down instead of continuing to receive them week after week. Some might say you are much too picky.'

Caroline's nostrils flared as she shot to her feet. 'Then perhaps you need to find me better prospects!'

'Caroline!'

Maddie jolted in surprise. Papa never raised his voice to them.

'You will apologise to Miss Merton.' His voice lowered in volume but did not soften. 'She is not your servant, but rather, she is doing this family a great favour.'

Caroline's eyes filled with tears. 'I—I apologise, Miss Merton.' She sniffed.

'It's quite all right, dear,' Miss Merton assured her. 'We all lose our tempers.'

'May I be excused?' Caroline jutted her chin defiantly. As soon as Papa nodded, she fled the room. Papa tsked and Mama placed a hand over his in a comforting gesture.

The rest of the breakfast continued in muted conversation, and finally, Papa and Mama excused themselves as well as Miss Merton, so Persephone and Maddie found themselves alone.

'That sister of yours sure has a temper.'

'Caroline's not that terrible,' Maddie found herself saying. 'She was a sweet child.'

'Sweet?' Persephone stuck out her tongue. 'I can't imagine her being sweet, even as a wee child. She's spoiled rotten.'

Maddie had never truly thought about how or when Caroline had become who she was. 'We weren't always rich, you know. But then the furnace became successful and Papa and I worked together all the time, so he made up for it with Mama and Caroline by giving them everything they wanted.' She remembered what Caroline was like as a child and how they used to play together. Seeing her in tears now made her heart clench.

'What time are your callers arriving this afternoon?' Persephone asked. 'Are you having any more of your lessons with Cam?'

'I… I'm not sure, really.' She chewed on her lip. Cam had all but disappeared this week. *And right when I needed him, too.* He'd promised her he would help her weed out the scoundrels from her callers, but now he was nowhere in sight.

'Why don't we go to the library?' Persephone suggested. 'Unless you're much too busy for me now.'

Maddie chuckled. 'For you—never.'

The two women left the breakfast room, and as they passed through the hall, Maddie saw Eames opening the front door, and a familiar dark-haired female figure strolled in. 'Kate?'

'Good morning, Eames— Maddie!' she cried, then rushed over to her. 'You don't know how happy I am to see you.' Kate drew her in for a fierce hug. 'I've missed you so.'

'So have I!' Happiness filled her as she drew back and looked at her friend. 'You're looking so well. But what are you doing here? I mean, I know you can come and go as you please.' This was Kate's home, after all, as she was the current Duchess of Mabury. 'But why didn't you send word of your arrival?'

'I had a meeting with the architects that ended early and wanted to surprise Mama and everyone.' She looked over at Eames. 'Is the Dowager in her sitting room?'

'I'm afraid not, Your Grace,' the butler replied. 'She left early and is not expected back until luncheon.'

'Oh, no.' She tsked. 'But this means I'll be able to spend time with you, Maddie.'

'Wonderful. Will you be staying until tomorrow?'

'I'll have to leave after luncheon, I'm afraid. I promised Sebastian I'd be home in Highfield Park tonight.' From the glow on her face, it was obvious that Kate was very much in love with her husband. 'But—oh, are you Lady Persephone? Mama has told me all about you in her letters.'

'Oh, how rude of me,' Maddie exclaimed. 'Allow me to introduce you. Your Grace, this is Lady Persephone MacGregor. Lady Persephone, this is Her Grace Kathryn, the Duchess of Mabury.'

Persephone curtsied. 'I'm honoured to meet you, Your Grace.'

A mysterious smile touched Kate's lips. 'The honour is mine, Lady Persephone. I've been eager to meet you.'

She blinked. 'Y-you have?'

'Yes. But why don't we sit down for tea in the library.' She nodded to Eames, who immediately set off. 'Come.'

They headed off in the direction of the library and

settled in the wing-back chairs and sofa by the window. 'I hope you can visit us in Highfield Park at some point,' Kate began. 'When I heard Mama had another guest arriving, I thought she might bring you, Lady Persephone, to visit us there to ease you into the season.'

Persephone looked confused, so Maddie began to explain, 'When the Dowager agreed to become our sponsor, we stayed in Highfield Park at first. We weren't quite ready yet for a London season, and she asked us to stay there at first, if only to stop us from floundering.' Maddie sent Kate a smile. 'That's also where Kate met and fell in love with the Duke of Mabury, the Dowager's son.'

'That's the short version of events, anyway,' Kate laughed. 'But let's not talk about me—it's boring. Tell me all about what's been happening with you. You haven't had much time to write letters.' She feigned a pout. 'But I forgive you, because from what I've heard, you've been busy with all your suitors who are lining up outside the door?'

Maddie couldn't help but smile. 'Not quite. A few callers, and two prospects who are serious.'

'Three,' Persephone said. 'Don't forget my brother, now.'

How could she forget?

'Your brother?'

'Yes, Your Grace. Cameron, Earl of Balfour. He's quite mad about Maddie here,' Persephone offered cheerfully.

'Really, now?' Kate's dark eyebrows lifted in question

Maddie wanted to tell her friend about their plan and how Cam was assisting her rather than trying to marry her, but the less people knew, the better. Besides, if she told Kate, she would have to tell the Duke, because they shared everything, and she didn't want Kate to have to lie to her husband.

'And he's taller than her,' Persephone added.

'Then he must be tall indeed.' Kate grinned at her.

'You'll see for yourself soon enough. But, Your Grace,' Persephone began. 'I have heard so much about you from Maddie. Is it true you are a railway engineer?'

Kate's expression changed. 'Yes, I'm designing my own locomotive now, but I helped my grandfather design the Andersen steam engine. It's one of the fastest and most efficient locomotives today.'

Persephone's eyes grew wide. 'But you are working on an engine of your own design now?'

'Persephone's very much interested in mechanics,' Maddie explained. 'Her family runs a whisky distillery.'

'Truly?' Kate leaned forward. 'You must tell me all about it.'

Maddie was glad that Kate was distracted by talk of engineering, and truth be told, she had missed her friend and missed this type of conversation. Though she was not as passionate about the furnace as Kate was about her engines, her work had made her feel useful and productive. There was progress being made in the world, and she couldn't help but feel that someday her own small contributions would somehow make a big difference.

Eames eventually came with some tea, and they continued talking until luncheon. The Dowager arrived just before lunch, and she was thrilled to see Kate. Luncheon was a lively affair, with everyone welcoming the new Duchess back, though Caroline remained muted throughout the meal.

'I hate to leave so soon,' Kate said as she and the Dowager walked to her waiting carriage. 'I promise you, Mama, Sebastian and I will come to stay. Then we can all go to Highfield Park together.'

'I look forward to it, dear.' She kissed Kate on the

cheek. 'I shall head inside so you may have a few minutes of privacy.'

Kate turned to Maddie. 'So, is there anything you need to tell me? About your suitors, maybe?'

'They are all quite agreeable,' she said.

'I'm sure they are, but is there anyone you truly fancy?' Kate leaned forward, her gaze narrowing. 'There is, isn't there? Is it the Earl?'

'What? Uh…' What was she supposed to say? 'I wish we had more time. Then I could tell you everything.' Perhaps by then she would have enough suitors and she could tell Kate the truth. For now, she would delay telling her friend, which would not exactly be lying.

Kate embraced her. 'All right. I'll let you keep your own counsel for now. Just promise me you'll follow your heart, all right? Do not let your mother pressure you into making a decision you might regret later.'

'I won't.' Her throat burned, and she could see Kate's eyes water as well. 'Come now. I'm still going to see you, Your Grace,' she teased.

'Of course.' Kate chuckled as the footman assisted her into the carriage. 'See you soon, Maddie.'

'You too.'

Maddie waved as the carriage pulled away, her friend's words lingering in her mind. She never resented Kate for what she had, but as was the case for anyone with privilege, she sometimes failed to see that not everyone's circumstances were the same. Not all women had the luck of falling in love with the first man they met, and it was even harder for people like Maddie who did not fit society's standards of what a woman should look like.

At the same time, however, she pondered Miss Merton's words about not being too picky. With two potential suitors, Maddie was luckier than most, and she did not even want a title, just a husband who could give her a family she could love and care for.

Cam's face appeared in her mind, but she quickly shook it away. But, just as luck would have it, a familiar carriage was quickly pulling up in front of the house. She froze, unsure what to do. If she were to flee now, he would see her running away from him. But if she were to stay, she would have to acknowledge his presence. Seeing as there was no alternative, she chose the latter.

*Why am I hiding from him, anyway? He promised her he would help her once the time came that she had potential suitors.*

And that time was now.

'My lord, good day,' she greeted him.

Cam had just stepped down the step when their eyes met. His expression faltered for a moment, as he obviously did not expect to see her there. 'Miss DeVries. What a lovely surprise. What are you doing out here by yourself?'

'I was seeing a friend off.'

His lips pulled back. 'I see. You have been popular lately.'

'About that.' She lowered her voice. 'May I walk inside with you?'

'Of course.'

'Now,' she continued as they meandered back into the house. 'I was wondering if you are able to assist me now. In our—' she glanced around surreptitiously '—project.'

'Project?'

'You know. The project.' She leaned closer and whispered, 'To sift out the scoundrels from my list of suitors.'

'I see.' He paused thoughtfully. 'And did you have this list?'

'List?'

'Yes. A list. One that we can go over.'

'I didn't realise I needed an actual paper list.'

'That's what I said, right?' he reminded her. 'Once you have a list, I shall help you. I will need time to learn about these fellows, of course. I do not know every gentleman in London, after all.'

'Oh.'

'I shall see you later, then, Miss DeVries.' He tipped his hat to her, then handed it to Eames along with his coat before striding off in the direction of the smoking room.

'Huh.'

*All right, then. If it's a list Cam wants, then it's a list he will have.*

Marching up to her room, she opened her notebook and wrote down names of all the gentlemen who had shown some interest in courting her. No one had asked her papa's permission yet, but a few had made overtures.

When she finished her list, she hurried down to the smoking room and knocked. When she heard Cam call out, 'Come in,' she opened the door and peeked inside.

'Murray, just put it on the— Maddie?'

'Cam,' she greeted from the doorway. 'I have it.'

'Have what?'

She waved a piece of paper in her hand. 'My list.'

'List—oh. You have it already?'

'Of course.' As she crossed the threshold, he held up a hand. 'What is it?'

'You shouldn't have come here by yourself. Anyone could come in,' he pointed out. 'And find us alone.'

'How was I supposed to give you my list? I couldn't very well ask Eames to deliver it to you.' Before he could protest, she handed him the list. 'Here you go.'

He plucked the list from her fingers, eyes scanning through the list. 'All of these men want to court you?'

'They've implied their interest,' she said.

'How so?'

'Well, everyone on that list has at least paid a call on me at least once,' she said. 'But we've all had a second point of contact. I didn't know how many names you would have time to look into, so I've narrowed it down to a list of five based on a set of criteria.'

'Criteria?'

'Yes. Either they've paid me a second call or we've done an activity, like go for a ride or stroll in the park. Or some I've made plans with.'

'How organised of you,' he commented. 'All right. I will ask around and find out what I can.'

'Thank you, Cam. I'll see myself out.'

Cam knew this time would come.

He just didn't think it would be this soon.

He thought he would at least have two weeks, maybe a month, before Maddie made any progress, especially since they had yet to attend more balls. But apparently it had taken only a matter of days for news of her popularity to spread.

Cam sank deeper into the leather chair, wishing it would swallow him up. He had delayed as much as he could by avoiding Maddie, but he could say no to only so many engagements, as he still had to escort his sister around.

And so, for the next two weeks, he went to the opera with Persephone and attended teas and other socials. All the while, he watched Maddie with other men. Palmer—who was on her list—even joined them in the Dowager's private box at the ballet.

He did, however, make good use of his social activities by enquiring about the men on Maddie's list. Actually, it didn't take much to find useful information—London's gentlemen were as terrible as the ladies when it came to gossip, especially when there were no women around. There were still two more names on the list he could not dig up dirt on, but perhaps he could hire a private investigator.

Cam decided he would ask George Atwell when he arrived for their meeting. And speaking of which, he was due to arrive soon, so he made his way to the smoking room. He barely had time to settle into his usual chair when he heard a knock on the door.

That was probably Atwell now. 'Come in,' he called. When he saw Maddie enter, he groaned inwardly. 'You're not Atwell.'

Her lips were pressed tight together as she strode in. 'I don't mean to be impatient or ungrateful, Cam. But it has been two weeks. I don't suppose you have any information for me?'

'Information about…?' he asked, feigning innocence.

'The list,' she said. 'About the gentlemen.'

'Ah, yes. Actually, I have.' He gestured to the seat opposite him and retrieved the wrinkled sheet of paper from his pocket. 'Baron James Clifton,' he read aloud, then clucked his tongue.

'What's wrong with him?'

'Notorious gambler. He will obliterate your dowry within a year.'

She frowned. 'You do not know how big my dowry is.'

'And you do not know how terrible Clifton is at cards.'

'My father hates gamblers, anyway.' She blew out a breath. 'Who else?'

He looked at the next name on the list. 'Lord Andrew Annesley.' He shook his head.

'What about him? He was at the dinner party the Dowager hosted. You didn't seem to object to his presence.'

'Yes, well, he's a nice fellow. But rumour is, his mother's got him under her thumb,' Cam explained. 'A bit of a harridan, that one. She controls everything he does, from what he eats for breakfast to what articles he reads in the paper. You wouldn't want to live with a mother-in-law who controlled every aspect of your life, would you?'

'I suppose not.' Her shoulders slumped over. 'Who else?'

'Lord Thomas Harver.' He touched his fingers together and placed his forefingers on his chin while drawing his eyebrows together for dramatic effect. 'I do not know how to explain this one, Maddie.'

'Why?' She scooted to the edge of her seat. 'What have you heard?'

'Harver's a widow three times over.' Actually, Cam had heard different versions—some said only twice, and other said four times, so he'd picked the number between them. 'And all his wives died in mysterious circumstances. The last one was found by the butler at the bottom of the staircase.'

She shuddered. 'I always thought there was something strange about him. Who else?'

Cam paused. He didn't need to read the last two names on the list, because he already knew what information he had on them: absolutely nothing. 'Sir Alfred Kensington—he's a little old for you, isn't he? His hair is completely white.'

'Old? It's not like he's decrepit,' she pointed out. 'He's probably only a few years younger than my father.'

'I heard that fall from his horse wasn't that terrible, and he only suffered a sprained ankle.' He tsked. 'But you know, when you get to his age, every little trip and fall brings you closer to your deathbed.'

'Cam!' she admonished. 'You cannot say such things. Besides, I saw him yesterday at Hyde Park. He seemed fit as a fiddle.'

'Did you now?' Damn.

'Well, you know…uh…he…' *Think of something!* He wouldn't lie to Maddie, but he had to say something about Kensington. 'He…he…smells like soup.'

'Smells like—are you jesting with me, Cam?'

'No, I'm not. I swear to you.' He held a hand to his chest. 'Go ahead and take a whiff next time he's around. He's definitely got that aroma of lobster bisque.'

Maddie's face turned green as she covered her hand with her mouth. 'All right. How about Viscount Palmer?'

Double damn.

It had been even harder to find any dirt on Palmer. 'Yes, well… I noticed you have never danced with him. Are you sure he knows how to?'

'No, we have yet to dance, but we have had the most pleasant conversation at the ballet, and he has requested to dance with me first at the Hayfield ball next week.'

*Over my dead body would he dance with Maddie first.* 'But he's quite a bit shorter than you, isn't he?'

'Cam, all the men on the list are shorter than me.' She sighed.

*Except me.*

Cam's stomach flipped at the thought, and the one that came after that.

*Me, Maddie. Put me on your list. Pick* me.

Triple damn.

He curled his hands into fists. No, he had to stop his thoughts from wandering in that direction. This little exercise was meant to help Maddie find a suitable husband

and not expose his own growing need. He only had to think of Jenny to know where this would lead.

'I wish I were shorter.' Her head drooped low, her gaze falling to the floor. 'If I could make myself smaller, I would.'

'No,' he protested. Sliding forward, he got to his knees in front of her and reached over to her so he could tip her chin up. 'Never make yourself small, Maddie. Not for anyone.'

Luminous blue eyes stared up at him, and her plump pink lips parted. 'Cam...'

Slowly, he leaned closer, and she, too, moved her head forward. Time slowed down, and their lips were mere inches away when a knock on the door had him reeling back. He slammed back into the chair but managed to quickly scramble to his feet. 'One moment, Atwell!' he called out. 'Maddie—'

'I... Sorry... I shouldn't,' Maddie stammered as she shot up from the chair. 'Thank you for the information. It was definitely helpful.' She dashed towards the door and flung it open, then ran past a very confused-look-ing Murray.

Cam stared at the door, unsure what to do.

'My lord?' Murray asked. 'Your coffee?'

'No.'

'No?'

'I don't want any coffee,' he bit out.

'What do you want then, my lord?'

*Her.*

*I want her.* 'I want to go out. To the fencing club. Please have my clothing ready. And when Mr. Atwell arrives, tell him I had an emergency.'

'Right away, my lord.'

# Chapter Fourteen

Cam had been a member of the Beaumont Fencing Club for the last few years, ever since he'd started taking regular trips to London. Like many men his age, Cam enjoyed sport, and when most people first laid eyes on him, they immediately thought he preferred boxing. While he could always go a round or two in the ring, Cam actually liked fencing, which required a different kind of grace, skill, and strength from pugilism. He was glad that his mother had insisted he learn the gentlemanly sport, as Cam found he excelled at it. Most of his opponents thought he would be slow and lumbering due to his size, but he quickly proved to be the opposite—fast as lightning, with a deadly reach and accurate aim.

Usually, an afternoon of physical activity was enough to calm him on a stressful day, but it seemed nothing could put him at ease. He'd already obliterated two opponents, and no, his agitation had not abated. Not even imagining Kensington's and Palmer's faces over their helmets could soothe him; in fact, he probably would have seriously injured his sparring partners if it were not for the protective gear they wore.

'Thank you, gentlemen, but I must be on my way,' he

murmured to the other members. He could practically hear all of them sighing with relief as he walked away.

Cam entered the changing rooms, then headed to the first set of benches. He sat down, removed his helmet, and buried his face in his hands.

They'd almost kissed. Again. He was supposed to be helping her find a husband, not lusting after her. Not wanting to kiss those luscious lips or feel her body against his. The only other time he'd been this out of control was with Jenny.

*I cannot do this again.*

'…so, you're really banned from The Underworld for life? Why did Ransom have you tossed out on the street?'

The voices he was overhearing were difficult to ignore as they reverberated round the small room. Rising to his feet, Cam began to undress so he could leave before it got too crowded.

'I was having a bit of fun with one of the whores in the back room. Bitch went running to him, said I roughed her up.'

Cam had the canvas jacket halfway off when he went rigid. He recognised that voice. Viscount Odious.

'When he confronted me, I said, "That's what they're here for, right?"' He spat. 'Then he personally escorted me out and told me never to come back. Stupid whore. And damn that Ransom.'

'He's a ruthless bastard, that one,' someone said.

'Bastard is right,' Palmer scoffed. 'In any case, soon I'll have so much money, all the clubs in London will be begging me to be a member.'

'Your father's nearly at death's door, right?'

'Unfortunately, no. The twisted old git's hanging on for dear life, if only to spite me. No, I've a much better plan.'

'Is it that chit you were with at the ballet? The giantess?'

*Maddie.* They were definitely talking about Maddie.

'She's American, correct?' Another voice piped in. 'Heard her father's richer than sin. But why not go for the sister? She's much more pleasant to look at.'

'I thought I would take a gander at her, seeing as she'd look better on my arm and I wouldn't have to hurt my neck each time I tried to kiss her.' Palmer laughed. 'But word around town is that she's a little tease. Keeps men hanging on with her favours here and there, but ultimately won't let go—of her dowry, at least. No, no. With my father beating off Death at every turn, I cannot wait that long.'

'You almost have her, then?'

'Nearly there. I'll ask her father's permission to court her, and we'll be engaged soon enough.'

'What if she wants a long engagement? Or what if her father says no?'

'Well, there are other ways to speed along a wedding, are there not?'

'Pleasurable ways,' someone quipped.

Laughter rang throughout the room, the sound only making Cam's fury rise.

Palmer continued. 'See, chaps, that's the advantage of homely misses and undesirable wallflowers. They're so grateful for the attention, you'll have them following you around like a bitch in heat in no time. I'll marry her, have a bit of fun, get her with child, and pack her off to the country. Then I can spend her dowry in peace and live to a standard I'd like to get accustomed to.'

'You are a genius, Palmer.'

'Aren't I?'

It took every ounce of strength Cam could muster not to march over there and beat the Viscount senseless. *Or skewer him*, he thought, glancing at his sabre. Unfortunately, he'd dealt with enough Englishmen to know they would never take anyone else's side against their own, especially not a Scotsman. He knew he'd have to rein in his fury—a scandal could ruin Persephone's chances at a successful London season.

Bottling his rage, Cam didn't bother to change out of his fencing clothes and raced out of the club. 'Mabury Hall,' he told his driver as he got in the carriage. 'As fast as you can.'

The drive did nothing to soothe his fury. All he could think of was that bastard Palmer and all the ways he could make him hurt. But first, he had to ensure Maddie never saw him again.

His first instinct was to speak with Mr DeVries and tell him what he'd learned. Unfortunately, Eames had told him that Mr DeVries was not at home.

He had no choice, then. He would have to go directly to Maddie and make her see reason. He had only one guess as to where she could be, so he stormed into the library.

'Maddie?' he called out, shutting the door behind him. 'Maddie?'

'I— Cam?' She rounded the corner from behind one of the shelves. 'Cam, what's the—what are you wearing?'

'It doesn't matter.' He crossed the distance between them. 'You cannot marry Palmer. In fact, you are never to see him again.' He could only guess what kind of 'fun' Palmer had in mind, and he would kill the Viscount first before he touched Maddie.

'What?' She replaced the book in her hand onto the nearest shelf. 'Cam, what happened? You look as if you've run a mile.'

'Are you listening to me, Maddie?' He wanted to shake

her until she agreed but settled to speaking slowly. 'You. Cannot. See. Him. Ever.'

'I don't understand. Where is this coming from? Just a few hours ago, you couldn't find any objectively good reason I shouldn't consider Viscount Palmer. And now I'm to stay away from him?'

'He's a bas—he wants you for your money.'

'They all want me for my money,' she said matter-of-factly. 'That is why women have dowries.'

How could she be so glib? 'You can't marry him, Maddie. He's a foul miscreant. He means to get you with child and forget about you while he spends your dowry. He called you a...'

'A what?'

*Homely. Undesirable. Bitch in heat.*

No, he would not repeat Palmer's awful words to her. Not when she'd worked so hard to build her confidence. And while he didn't want Maddie to marry that bastard, he did not want to destroy her, either.

'Tell me,' she said gently. 'What is this really about?'

He swallowed the lump in his throat as she took a step closer to him.

'What has made you so worked up?'

*You*, he wanted to rail at her. *You have me riled up and twisted me about so I cannot think straight.* But as the air thickened and tension stretched taut between them, neither of them spoke.

Her lips parted, and she let out a breathy, 'Cam?'

His teeth ground together in frustration. 'Tell me, Maddie, do you even like him? Could you even see yourself spending the next twenty or forty years next to him?' Her plump lips parted, and he couldn't help but stare at them. 'Would you even want to kiss him?'

'Not as much as I want to kiss you.'

The last string that held his control together broke. Maddie closed the distance between them and reached up to him, but Cam was faster and caught her face in his hands as he slanted his mouth over hers. Maddie grabbed onto his shoulders and clung to him, opening her lips to his kiss.

He swept his tongue into her mouth and he swore he could taste sweetness. He deepened the kiss, nearly devouring her as she moaned aloud and moved up against him, breasts crushing into his chest. He'd been dreaming about them, wondering what they looked like, how they tasted, and what her colour her nipples were.

As if she'd read his mind, she grabbed his hand and pressed it against her breasts. Needing no further invitation, he delved into the neckline and popped one delectable globe out, then trailed his lips down to her neck so he could look down at her exposed breast.

*Holy hell.* Her nipples were the loveliest shade of brown, dark and taut, while the large areola was a pretty pink. Dragging his mouth away from her neck, he licked at the stiff peak.

'Cam!' Fingers dug into his hair and the scraping of her nails on his scalp made his cock instantly harden.

He suckled and laved her breast, giving it the attention it deserved. Maddie sighed and moaned, and he wondered if she was even aware of how her hips thrust at him invitingly. Sliding a hand down her back, he cupped her bottom and pulled her to him, allowing her to rub herself against him.

Cam teased and tortured her nipple some more, and while he could do this for hours, he wanted to give Maddie the relief she needed. She let out a protesting cry when he released her breast.

'Lord, Maddie... You're too much... You're driving

me wild.' He looked at her, those sky blue eyes fixed on him. 'I could give you so much more…' But he couldn't go on further. In fact, they'd gone on far enough. He loosened his hold on her and took a step back but found himself unable to move as Maddie's arm slipped around his waist, holding him in place.

'Then give it to me, Cam,' she said without hesitation. 'Please. I want it and everything else you can give me.' A hand boldly slipped down to his buttocks and pulled him forward.

Dear God in heaven, she was truly an Amazon goddess. She didn't ask. She *took* what was rightfully hers.

He caught her mouth in a kiss before she could speak further, then walked her backwards against the bookshelf behind her. His hand slipped further down, then bent her leg to plant her foot on the lowest shelf. He grabbed her skirt and lifted the frothy fabric over her knee so he could reach underneath. The first touch of his hand on her warm thigh made her jolt.

His fingers trailed a path up her soft skin, up to the downy triangle left exposed by the slit in her drawers. When she didn't protest, he gently stroked the lips, which were now damp with her desire. His cock swelled, straining against his tight fencing breeches. He parted her and pressed a finger into her, until the first knuckle.

*Dear God, she was tight.*

'More,' she pleaded against his mouth. 'Oh, please, Cam.'

And so he pushed further, until his finger was fully in her, wrapped in her heat and slick. If this is what she felt like with his finger, he would surely die once he was inside her.

Slowly, he moved his hand, sliding his finger gently along her slick passage. Apparently, this was not enough for Maddie, and her hips undulated at a much faster pace than his hand.

*Patience*, he urged silently. Withdrawing his finger, he twisted his hand so he could find that button just above her entrance that he knew would drive her wild. When he brushed his thumb over it, Maddie fell against him, head leaning on his shoulder and fingers digging into his arms.

She panted, her breath hot on his neck, as he continued to stroke her. She grew slicker by the second, so he managed to slip a finger inside her, and then another. 'Cam!' Her hips moved in time with his fingers as he thrust them into her. When her grip on his arms tightened and her spine stiffened, he knew her peak was close.

'That's it, lass,' he encouraged. 'Let go. Let it happen.'

She whimpered loudly as her body shuddered. His cock twitched painfully as she brushed against his hips. He bit the inside of his cheek to stop himself from spending like an untried lad. When it was over, she slumped back against the bookshelves, eyes closed as she breathed hard.

'We must stop now, darling.' Could she even hear his whispered groan? 'We can't be found like this. I'll not have you compromised like this.' She deserved much better than a rut against a shelf.

A loud gasp rang in his ear, and while he was lost in passion, he was still mindful enough to recognise that was not a gasp of pleasure, nor had it come from Maddie. He froze in place.

*What in the world—?*

'You Goddamned bastard, get off her!' A hand grabbed at the straps of his fencing coat and hauled him off Maddie. He barely had time to recover before a powerful fist connected with his jaw, sending pain across his face.

Cam staggered back and miraculously he didn't lose his balance. There were shouts and cries around him, but he was too stunned to make sense of what was happening. When the stars disappeared from his vision, a man appeared before him—dark-haired, dark-eyed, and very, very displeased.

'You bastard,' he raged. 'How dare you do this to Miss DeVries?'

'Do this—who the hell are you, anyway?'

'Sebastian, Duke of Mabury.' Dark eyes flashed with fury. 'Your host and owner of this house.'

'Oh.' *Hell.* 'Your Grace,' he said with a bow.

Mabury lunged forward, and this time, Cam was prepared and ducked away from him.

'Don't, Your Grace!' Maddie shouted as her mother rushed in, sobbed, and wrapped her arms around her.

'Oh, Maddie.' Mrs DeVries was frantically trying to put her hair to rights. 'My poor, poor Maddie.'

Mabury gnashed his teeth. 'What were you doing to her?'

'I was trying to stop her from making a big mistake,' Cam explained.

'By ruining her?' Mabury roared.

'Sebastian!' A petite brunette Cam had never seen before put herself between them. This must be Mabury's wife. 'Calm yourself.'

'Calm myself?' Mabury said in an incredulous tone. 'Did we all not see the same thing? This…this beast rutting on Madeline?' His face was scarlet with wrath, hulking shoulders heaving. 'If I could, I would ensure him a long, slow death, then bring him back to life so I could do it all over again.'

'So would I, darling, but I need to see to Maddie first.' The Duchess sent Cam a seething glare before heading over to Maddie's side. 'Are you all right, Maddie? Are you hurt?'

Maddie shook her head. 'Please, Kate. I don't want any more violence. This is a simple misunderstanding.'

Mrs DeVries pointed an accusing finger at Cam. 'That…fiend has stolen your virtue!'

'Mama, compose yourself. Nothing happened.'

Cam bit the urge to say, *It was not nothing*, except it was obvious whatever he said or excuses he made would not help in this scenario. Indeed, by all accounts, he was the villain here. Maddie was an innocent virgin, and he shouldn't have let passion overtake him. 'I'm so sorry,' he said to no one in particular.

'You should be sorry,' Mabury growled. 'And so you must marry her.'

'Of course, I will marry Maddie.' They had been found *in flagrante delicto* by her mother and the Duke and Duchess, and the Dowager was there in the doorway, too. The only way this could be worse was if Mr DeVries had witnessed this. 'We will get it done as soon as I can procure a special licence.'

Mrs DeVries moaned. 'The scandal. Think of the scandal.'

'Everyone, please.' Maddie disentangled herself from her mother. 'There's no need to overreact.' She sent him a sideways glance. 'If no one says anything, then there's no need to fuss. We do not have to marry.'

'What are you saying, Madeline?' Mrs DeVries planted her hands on her waist. 'I cannot lie to your father.'

'Maddie, think about this—'

'Don't give him a way out—'

Despite the din around him, Cam could not make out what everyone was saying because the only thing he could think of was that Maddie had said she didn't want to marry him.

The truth hit him straight in the chest like an axe.

Of course she didn't want him.

But what she wanted didn't matter. After what they'd done and with all the witnesses here, they would have no choice. Her father would expect that.

'Stop!' Maddie shouted. 'You're not listening to me.'

'Maddie, you must—'

'This bastard—'

A delicate clearing of a throat made the noise cease. The Dowager glided into the room, calm as a millpond. 'Emotions are running rather high at the moment, so I suggest we all take a breath and think about what we need to do. Kate, please escort Mrs DeVries to Miss Merton. I normally wouldn't have the heart to wake her during her afternoon nap, but I'm sure she won't mind, given the circumstances. Explain to her what happened, then come back down here.'

'Yes, Mama.' The Duchess placed an arm around Mrs DeVries. 'Come now, Eliza.'

'B-but what about Maddie? Shouldn't she come with me?' Eliza asked.

'I'm going to arrange a cup of tea for Maddie. Before you go up to Miss Merton, send word to your husband and ask him to return to Mabury Hall at once.'

'Of course, Your Grace.' Mollified, she allowed the Duchess to take her away.

The Dowager went over to Maddie. 'I'll take care of everything, dear.' Looking over her shoulder, she said to her son, 'Sebastian, take the Earl away, please, but do not let him out of your sight. I will send for him after I've spoken to Miss DeVries.'

'Gladly,' Mabury said, glaring at Cam.

Cam evaded the Duke's grasp when he attempted to grab his arm. 'I'll come, Your Grace. No need to shackle me. I'll not run away.' He sent one last glance at Maddie, but she would not look him in the eye. How he wished he could speak to her.

He'd offered marriage, and she'd turned him down. They'd been stopped just in time, and Maddie remained a virgin. *I should never have touched her.* His lust and desire had been overwhelming, and the thought that she wanted him—and that she wanted to kiss him—had been too much of a temptation. *And I didn't want to marry, anyway.*

But then, why did her rejection bring that twisting, painful sensation in his chest instead of gratitude and relief?

He followed Mabury out of the library, down the hall into what he assumed was the Duke's private office. Mabury said not a word, so Cam studied the man.

The Duke was tall, but still a good half a foot shorter than him. He was wide, though, his shoulders straining against his tailored coat, and his skin was sun-kissed, as if he spent a lot of time outdoors. As he strode over to the mantel to pour some brandy from a decanter into a glass, Cam couldn't help but notice that his hands were not pale and soft but, rather, rough and calloused. It reminded him a lot of his own father's hands.

When Mabury turned back to face him, he began with, 'Your Grace, please allow me to apologise for—' Another blow struck him on the cheek, though not as hard as before, as it only sent his head knocking back. 'I suppose I deserve that.' He was definitely going to have a black eye in the morning.

'I needed to do that. For Maddie,' the Duke explained,

his tone curiously polite. Then he handed the glass of amber liquid to Cam.

'And what's this for?'

The Duke shook his head. 'For having your proposal rejected.'

Cam would have smiled, except it hurt to do so. 'Thank you.' The Duke had sounded sympathetic, as if he knew what that particular experience was like.

Mabury folded his arms over his chest. 'Why?'

Such a simple question.

One word.

Three letters.

Yet, Cam couldn't explain it himself.

He downed the contents of the glass in one gulp, the alcohol sliding smoothly down his throat and warming his belly. 'As I said, it began because I was trying to stop her from making a mistake.' With a deep breath, he told Mabury about Viscount Palmer and what he'd overheard at the club.

'Bloody bastard. I always hated that snivelling fool.' The Duke's dark brows slashed together. 'Still, that doesn't excuse why you mauled her against my complete set of Shakespeare's works.'

'You're right.' He pulled at the collar of his fencing coat. 'I wasn't… I didn't think…'

'You'd get caught,' the Duke finished.

Cam placed the glass back on the mantel. 'I was caught up in the passion,' he explained. 'I wanted her.'

'She's an innocent.'

'She is, and that's why I'm not making any excuses.' Maddie could have stopped him at any time, but he was the more experienced between the two of them. 'I should have known better. But I plan to make things right.'

'Oh, you will marry,' he declared.

'Why do you care, anyway?'

'She's my wife's dearest friend and like a sister to me: I'll kill anyone who upsets my wife.' He sounded deadly serious. 'Was she willing?'

'Aye. I would never force myself on a woman.'

The Duke's stare softened. 'Why didn't you say so?'

'And humiliate her in front of her mother, your wife, and the Dowager by implying she's a wanton woman who asked for it? Nay, I'll not do that to her.' Besides, what they had shared was beautiful. He didn't want to cheapen that.

Mabury turned pensive. 'Cornelius won't force her to marry you. You'll have to find a way to convince her.'

Cam was tempted to reach for the entire decanter and pour the entire contents down his gullet. Maddie's rejection had stung more than he'd thought. 'Why did she turn me down?' When the Duke did not answer, he came up with the explanation himself: because she didn't want to marry him.

Plain and simple.

This was like Jenny all over again, but worse. It wasn't that she was in love with Palmer or she would have said so.

She just didn't want *him*.

He wasn't enough for her, either. And why would he be? She was so intelligent and lovely and kind, and he was unworthy of her. He was not smart, certainly not like his mother had been or how Persephone or Liam were. He had the MacGregor charm, yes, but that was it. All charm, but no substance.

'Here, have another.' The Duke offered him another glass. 'You look like you need it.'

'Aye, I do.' He took a sip.

'Even if there are no consequences, you still need to marry her,' the Duke said. 'Her mother—'

'I know. She will force my hand somehow.' He knew Eliza DeVries well enough. She would do anything so her daughters could marry well, even if it meant a scandal. Eliza would go public with Cam's deeds, and if they didn't marry, Maddie would have to either live as an outcast or leave England. He could not let that happen to her.

'It just occurred to me, Balfour, that you simply told her that you were marrying. And if there's something I've learned the past few months as a married man is that women definitely do not like being told what to do. At least, the ones worth having.'

'So, I will ask her again to marry me properly.' *Even if she doesn't want me. Even if I'm not worthy.*

'She still has to accept your proposal.'

'Aye, that she does.' He could only hope he could somehow make her say yes.

## Chapter Fifteen

Everything had happened so fast, it was as if Maddie's mind remained two steps behind her body. One moment, Cam was on her, pinning her against the bookshelf, and the next…chaos.

Oh, heavens. What was to happen now?

'Have some tea, dear,' the Dowager said. 'It will calm you down.'

Maddie blinked, surprised to find herself sitting in the wing-back chair by the window, a shawl wrapped around her and a cup of hot tea in her hand. She did as the Dowager bade and took a sip. The hot liquid was, indeed, soothing. 'Thank you, Your Grace.' She put the teacup down.

'Do not thank me yet, dear.' She sent Maddie a comforting smile. 'But I promise you, we will get everything sorted out.'

'I have taken care of Mrs DeVries, Mama,' Kate said as she entered the library. 'Oh, Maddie.' She dashed to her side and wrapped an arm around her shoulders. 'I'm so sorry. Will you tell us what happened? Did he…force himself on you?'

'No, he did not.' Maddie would have laughed, but the entire situation was already absurd. Cam, force himself on her? Why, she had been a willing participant, from beginning to end.

The pleasure was unlike anything she'd felt before. She wanted it. If anything, she wanted more, and even now, she still throbbed and ached, the dampness between her thighs evidence that the encounter had really happened. His fingers…his mouth…

'*Ahem.*' The Dowager's lips were pressed together, but the amusement in her eyes was clear. 'It's all right Maddie. You know you can trust us. You are safe here.'

'I know.' She smiled warmly at Kate. That's why the Dowager had sent Mama away. She knew the only way Maddie would tell the truth was if her mother were not around. 'I—we—kissed, willingly. It just went a bit too far. But we didn't mean to.' They'd been swept away by the passion, and now that they had been caught, they were trapped.

'But why don't you want to marry him?' the Dowager asked. 'I thought he was interested in courting you. You danced with him at every ball, sometimes twice. He paid you a call. I heard he even interrupted your time with Viscount Palmer. Your mother was practically preening at his jealous rage. I thought for sure you would welcome a proposal from him.'

'Is there someone else?' Kate enquired. 'Perhaps you've recently met another gentleman you prefer more than the Earl?'

Maddie swallowed hard. *Now I know how a trapped fox feels.* Their lies and deception had finally caught up with them.

'It's not what you think.' Having no other choice, she confessed to Kate and the Dowager about the fake courtship plot. The entire time, neither woman said anything, but they looked at each other every so often. '…so, you see, the Earl doesn't really want to marry me.'

'Yet, he ravished you in the library,' Kate said drolly. 'Men always say one thing and mean another. Change their mind at a whim. And they say we are the unpredictable sex.'

The Dowager tilted her head to the side. 'So, the Earl did all of that for you? Pretend to court you so that you may find a husband?'

'Persephone practically had to beg him on my behalf.' She sighed. 'Besides, our plan was working. There were several gentlemen who were ready to ask my father's permission to court me. Why did Cam have to go muck that all up by storming into the library, demanding I not marry Viscount Palmer?'

'You didn't say anything about that,' Kate said.

'Did I not?' She bit her lip. 'I was in the library, and then he came all in a rage. We'd just had a nice conversation about my list earlier in the day.'

'What list?' Kate's eyebrow rose high.

'My list of—' Oh, dear, she kept going backwards. 'Let me start again.' So she explained this time, about her list of eligible men that Cam was helping her with. 'Later, he came into the library, demanding that I not marry the Viscount. He wouldn't tell me why, only that I should never see him again. I asked him what was going on, and then… Then, things just got out of hand.'

Kate and Dowager once again exchanged knowing glances.

'I know what we did was not proper,' she continued. 'But I swear to you, I'm still a virgin, and there's no chance I could be…in the family way, so there's no need for us to marry. Besides, I do not want a pity proposal.'

'Maddie,' the Dowager began. 'I agree that you do

not deserve a pity proposal, but I'm not sure you have a choice.'

Maddie wrung her hands together, feeling the walls closing in on her.

'Your father will not force you, but your mother will be apoplectic,' the Dowager began. 'If you do not marry the Earl, she may well find another way to force his hand.'

Unfortunately, she could not put it past her mother to do something drastic, if it meant Maddie would be a countess. 'So I must marry him now to prevent a scandal or my mother will cause a scandal so he is forced to marry me?'

'You could go back to America,' Kate pointed out. 'Or you could come live with me at Highfield Park. You could focus on the London furnace as you've always wanted. You could run it and we can work together. You won't even have a husband to answer to. You'd be free.'

'Thank you, Kate. You are a dear friend.' But she wouldn't be able to have the family she wanted. No husband, no children. She would be a ruined woman no man would touch.

The Dowager's dark gaze bore into her. 'Tell me, Maddie. Why don't you want to marry him now? You could do worse than a rich Earl.'

Maddie avoided her gaze. 'I told you, I don't want a pity proposal.'

'But if he had got down on one knee, would you have accepted?'

'He does not want to marry me. He has made that clear from the beginning.' That's why they had all those rules. He didn't want her. This was all fake. 'If he's forced to marry me, he'll be miserable.'

The room grew quiet for a moment, then the Duchess said, 'I think it's time you and the Earl have a private chat.'

'Oh, please, no.' How could she possibly face him after all that had happened?

'But you must dear. Explain to Balfour why you do not want to marry him.'

'But Mama and Papa...' Oh, heavens, her father would be home any minute. She could not face him, either, not when she knew how disappointed he'd be with her.

'I'll take care of them. Kate, dear, would you please send for the Earl?'

Kate squeezed her shoulder, then headed out the door.

'What do I say to him?'

'Be honest. Tell him what you told me, and I'm sure he will do the right thing.'

'You think he'll withdraw his proposal?'

The Duchess didn't answer. 'I'll be right outside and ensure no one but Balfour enters.'

Once she was alone, Maddie shot to her feet and began to pace. She practised what she would say to him in her head.

*Obviously, we cannot be forced to marry. My mother can spread all the rumours she wants, but Kate, the Duke, and the Dowager won't corroborate their story. We'll be free and never have to see each other again after today.*

The very thought of never seeing Cam made her heart clench tight. But it would be better that way. Cam would agree, and he'd take it upon himself to go back to Scotland.

The loud creaking sound made her jump, and as she watched the door open, her heart pounded like a drum.

Cam walked through, still dressed in his fencing gear, his hair mussed. Slowly, he approached her. 'For what it's worth, I am sorry,' he said, head bowed low.

'I'm sorry, as well.' She took a deep breath. 'For trapping you in an impossible situation. But don't worry. My father will not force me, and none of those who witnessed what happened will breathe a word to anyone. W-we can still avoid a scandal.'

'You misunderstand me.' His chin lifted and emerald eyes caught her gaze. 'I meant to say that I'm sorry for the terrible proposal and that now you have an even more terrible prospect for a husband in me.'

'You're not terrible, Cam,' she quickly said. Indignation rose in her, hearing him say those words. 'Don't say that, please.'

'I understand why you would say no.' He clasped his hands behind him. 'I'm not intelligent like you. I wouldn't be able to talk about philosophy or geology. I can be impulsive and brash. While I'm indeed an earl, I'm only one generation away from being a tradesman.'

'So am I,' she reminded him. 'But that's not why we shouldn't marry.'

A furrow appeared between his eyebrows. 'What is it then, Maddie?'

'B-because...because y-you don't want to marry me.' She hated it that she stammered and her throat burned with tears as she said it. Even more, she hated that she had to admit it.

'What is that all? Maddie, no.' He was in front of her in an instant. 'Do not think that. Of course, I want you. How could you not believe it, after what happened between us?' A gentle hand cupped her chin, forcing her to look up into his bright green gaze.

'It—it was fake. All pretend.'

'The courting, yes, but not everything else. I want you, Maddie.'

She forgot to breathe for a moment. 'You do?'

'Aye.' A smile curled up the corner of his lips. 'And you want me, too.'

A hot flush spread all over her, reminding her of his kisses and his touch. 'Yes,' she admitted.

'Did you enjoy it?'

She shut her eyes tight but nodded.

'Did you want more?'

Slowly, she opened her eyes. 'Yes.'

A fire burned in his gaze. 'Then you shall have it.'

She tipped her head back as he kissed her, softly at first. Just a brush of his lips. So she angled her head and opened up to him, and to her surprise he groaned into her mouth. Her body ignited once more, the memory of the pleasure he'd given her coming alive and making her want it again. Her arms encircled his neck, drawing him deeper. She wasn't sure how long they were kissing, but eventually, he broke it off.

'I want you, and that's the truth, Maddie. And I hope that's enough of a reason for you to say yes.'

Maddie saw something in his expression that made her pause. It was fleeting, but she was sure it had been there. *Doubt.* Like a chink in his self-assured, brash armour. As if he wanted to tell her more, but exactly what, she didn't know. But she was desperate to find out.

'Yes.' The word came to her without thought.

'Yes?' He seemed surprised, as if he were anticipating the opposite.

'Yes. I will marry you, Cam.'

Before she could gauge his expression, he captured her mouth. She had so many more questions for him, more things she wanted to know, but they all promptly flew out of her mind. All she could think of was Cam's warm, soft lips on hers. Her hands reached up to tug at the hair on his nape as he seemed to enjoy that quite a bit, especially when she scratched at his skull.

'Maddie,' he moaned. 'I—'

The sound of hinges squeaking made them pull apart. 'Is everything all right?' the Dowager asked as she entered. 'I thought I heard…silence,' she said with a wry smile.

Maddie smoothed her hand down her skirt. 'Yes, Your Grace.'

Cam took her hand into his. 'You'll be happy to know, Your Grace, that Maddie has accepted my proposal.'

'Splendid news!' The Dowager hurried over, then kissed Maddie on both cheeks. 'Congratulations, my dear.'

'Thank you, Your Grace.'

'We must tell everyone,' she continued. 'And tonight we will celebrate.'

'You're too kind, Your Grace.'

As Cam's grip tightened around hers, Maddie sneaked a glance at him.

*He's going to be my husband.*

The thought sent a giddy feeling through her. However, there was a nagging feeling in the back of her mind, and her earlier questions came flooding back.

*He wants to marry you*, that logical voice in her mind said. *He said so. He showed you.*

Yes, but was that enough?

*Oh, bother.*

What more did she want? Cam would be a fine husband, despite his own objections. He would give her the family she wanted. She couldn't possibly hope for more than that.

## Chapter Sixteen

'Oh, think of it. My daughter, a countess!' Eliza DeVries's attitude had completely reversed once the Dowager had announced to everyone that Cam and Maddie would be married. 'I knew she would make a good match. We are so happy we will have you as our son-in-law, my lord.'

*Less than an hour ago, you called me a fiend.*

But Cam bit his tongue and said, 'Thank you, Mrs DeVries.'

Cornelius DeVries on the other hand, was strangely calm for a man who'd received news that his daughter had been ruined.

'You have my blessing, of course,' he said. 'But all that matters is that Maddie has fully accepted your proposal.'

'Yes, Papa.' Maddie looked up at Cam. 'I fully accepted.'

'Oh, Cam,' Persephone exclaimed as she embraced him. 'I'm ecstatic for you both, but—' She lowered her voice. 'I thought this was all pretend? What happened?'

Cam wasn't exactly sure how to explain it to his sister.

*Well, Seph, I ruined your friend in front of her family and our hosts. So now we must marry or her mother will ensure there will be a scandal.*

'I'll explain later,' Maddie whispered. 'I promise.'

'Congratulations, my lord, Maddie.' Miss Merton was next to offer her felicitations. 'Oh, my, another wedding to plan. How lovely.'

'I can help,' Kate said. 'I'm a veteran of speedy wedding preparations.' She looked up wryly at her husband.

'I'm telling you, Balfour, there's no need to wait,' Mabury said. 'You'll thank me for it.' For a man who had been ready to kill him, the Duke was now awfully chummy.

'We have only been engaged for a few minutes,' Cam pointed out. However, marrying sooner than later definitely appealed to him. Then he could have Maddie in his bed for the rest of his life.

How Maddie could think he didn't want her, he didn't know. Lord, he wanted her so much, he would expire from it. He could not wait to give her endless pleasure, night after night, until it made both of them mindless.

He'd thought he wouldn't be enough for Maddie, but then she'd admitted that she wanted him only on a physical level.

*Yes,* she said when he asked her if she wanted more.

Now, that, he could live with.

*Things couldn't have turned out better,* he thought smugly. The physical side of their relationship would keep their marriage strong, much better than any other kind of entanglement. Their marriage would have a sturdy foundation on mutual desire, and nothing more.

He'd broken every rule he'd set from the beginning of their fake courtship plot, but not the very last one he'd added for himself.

He would not fall in love. Not with anyone, and certainly not with Maddie.

'Surely you would want to be wed in Scotland, Balfour,' the Duchess said. 'So you could be surrounded by your family?'

'I only have my brothers and Seph, I'm afraid, as my father did not have any siblings,' he said. 'On my mother's side, we have an uncle and some cousins, but they're all here in England. I would be just as happy to wed here.' *As long as the wedding takes place.* 'Besides, Maddie will be living in Scotland soon enough.'

'And travelling back to England with you regularly, I hope?' Cornelius asked. 'I could use her talents and advice once the furnace is up and running.'

'You know, you could build a furnace in Scotland, too,' the Duke said.

'Industry isn't only booming in England and America,' Cam added.

'Really?' Her face was all aglow. 'Is that possible, Cam?'

'Aye.' If it weren't, he would make it so. Cam knew Maddie would be happy if she had her work to occupy her. And Maddie happy would make him happy.

'Let us have a toast to Maddie and Balfour,' the Dowager said as Eames and a footman arrived with a chilled bottle of champagne and a tray of flutes.

Everyone was surprisingly cheerful, considering what had happened earlier. Almost everyone, anyway, as Caroline was conspicuously missing. Cam couldn't help but remember their encounter a few weeks ago. Lord, she was going to be his sister-in-law. He had a feeling this marriage would stoke her ire and she would lash out at Maddie even more. *I will have to keep an eye on that one.*

'To Maddie and Balfour.' The Dowager raised her glass and everyone followed suit.

'To Maddie and Balfour,' everyone cheered as they clinked glasses.

As Cam sipped his champagne, he couldn't help but think of the time he had announced to his parents that Jenny had accepted his proposal. Their reaction had been quite different from everyone's tonight and there certainly had been no champagne.

*No, don't think of that,* he chided himself. He would not have memories of Jenny sully tonight. He already had the perfect arrangement in place with Maddie. A mutually beneficial physical arrangement in private, and on the outside, they would be a respectable couple. And that's all there ever would be between them.

'I am utterly exhausted,' Maddie said as she, Persephone, and Kate settled into the carriage and a footman closed the door. 'How did you manage to survive your engagement?'

'I'm exhausted, too,' Persephone chimed. 'And I'm not even the one getting married.'

Kate laughed. 'You must learn to pace yourself and keep your strength up.'

Once news of the engagement had spread, the invitations to various events flooded in. Of course, while Cam and Maddie were not a sought-after couple, their connection to the Mabury title still held weight. The last few days had been occupied with balls, trips to the opera and plays, tea parties, and other such events. Just now, they had just left Lady Farrington's tea party, a long and boring soirée that was attended by many matrons and mamas, all of whom wanted to hear all about Maddie's engagement.

'I don't know how long I can do this,' Maddie said.

'You haven't even started with preparing for the wedding,' Kate reminded her. 'There's the trousseau to think about, the guest list, the engagement ball, the church, the breakfast. I'm just so glad Sebastian insisted on a short engagement and we married within a month.'

'Why so soon?' Persephone asked. 'Did you not want to wait and become better acquainted with your fiancé?'

'My Sebastian is an impatient man,' she replied with a smile. 'And he could not be swayed.'

Persephone sank back into the plush seating of the coach and crossed her arms over her chest. 'I should like a long engagement. Six months, at least. Maddie, how long do you plan to be engaged to my brother?'

'I…' Maddie frowned. 'Actually, we haven't discussed details yet.' In fact, they hadn't discussed anything at all, as they had not had a moment to themselves. They had attended several parties and balls, but they had never been alone. They hadn't even set a wedding date or decided exactly where they were getting married.

'As long as you come live with us back in Scotland, I'll be happy.' Persephone hooked her arm into Maddie's. 'I've always wanted a sister.'

She leaned against Persephone. 'I'm so glad you approve.'

'Aye, of course. I just wish you two had told me that in the midst of that fake courtship plan, you two were already falling in love.'

Maddie's mouth pulled back into a tight smile. She didn't want to disillusion Persephone, so she didn't deny it. *But love?* Could it even be possible?

Kate was in love with her Duke, and he was obviously besotted with her. But again, a love match was not very common among the British aristocracy. In fact, she'd seen how they almost frowned upon it. To them, marriage was about preserving wealth and titles. Perhaps in time, she and Cam would grow to love one another, in a respectable way.

Of course, there was nothing respectable about how their courtship had begun. Not with the way he'd kissed and touched her. How she'd missed being alone with him, but he'd been the perfect gentlemen the entire time. He didn't even dare touch any part of her body except her gloved hand.

'*Ahem.*' Kate sent her a knowing glance, then turned to Persephone. 'Lady Persephone, how are you enjoying your season so far?'

Persephone slumped in her seat further. 'I'm afraid, Your Grace, I am not enjoying it at all.'

*Oh, dear.* Maddie had been so caught up in her fake courtship with Cam, she had been ignoring her friend. 'I'm sure it will get better.'

'I'm not sure. And… I don't even know if I want a husband.' She sighed.

'Then why come to London?'

She worried at her lip. 'Because of a promise.' And so, she told them about her mother's dying wish for her to have a London season. 'She'd been planning it even before I was born. While she had no regrets marrying my Scottish father, she did worry that it would decrease my chances of making a good match. A season in London was to make me a more desirable wife. And Cam wanted to carry out this wish for her.'

Maddie clutched a hand to her chest. *Poor Cam.* The loss of his mother must have been devastating. 'It sounds like he loved your mother so much,' she managed to say through the tightness building in her throat. But how could she even doubt that? From the beginning, she had seen how devoted he was to Persephone.

'I'm just glad all this wedding planning is distracting Cam and he's not been bothering with making me dance at balls.'

Kate chuckled. 'Well—' The coach slowed to a stop, indicating they had arrived back at Mabury Hall. 'Oh, we're home. Thank goodness. I need a nap before tonight's dinner.' The Dowager had invited a few close friends over tonight to welcome Kate and Sebastian back into town.

'I could sleep right through until morning,' Persephone declared.

'A nap sounds heavenly,' Maddie agreed.

Once they were inside Mabury Hall, they all went to their separate rooms. Maddie was about to ring for Betsy when she heard a knock on the door. *Who could that be?* When she opened the door, she was surprised by the sight of her sister.

'Caro. How, uh, lovely to see you.'

Caroline had all but disappeared the last few days. On the day Maddie got engaged, Mama had said she was taken to bed with a cold. Maddie suspected that had been a lie. Knowing her sister, news of her engagement to Cam had probably stung, so Maddie had not verbalised her suspicions. However, Caroline hadn't emerged from her room until now.

'Hello, Maddie. May I come in?' She didn't bother to wait for an answer as she barged right inside.

'How is your cold?' she asked politely. 'You look healthy and lovely.' As always, her sister was impeccably dressed in a striped blue-and-white gown, a matching jacket, and a feathered hat atop her artfully arranged locks.

'Much better, thank you.' Caroline made it to the middle of the room before spinning around to face her. 'It seems congratulations are in order.'

'Thank you.'

'Hmm.' Her eyes turned to slits. 'I don't see it.'

'See what?'

'What Cameron sees in you.'

Caroline could be incredibly cruel with her barbs, but never quite so direct. 'I beg your pardon?' *And why did you call him by his first name?*

'You know, we were speaking the other day.' She glanced down casually at her nails before lifting her chin up to meet her gaze. 'He told me the most curious thing.'

A knot formed in her chest. 'Caroline, I think you should leave—'

'He told me he would only marry someone he *didn't find attractive*,' she drawled.

Now that was a lie.

*Wasn't it?*

That split second of doubt was all Caroline needed and she took the opening for her next jab. 'His exact words were said, "Lass, the last thing I want is to marry someone I'm attracted to."'

Maddie wanted to kick herself. 'I don't believe you. Cam said he wants me. He even proved it,' Maddie added for good measure, though admitting it to her sister made her wince.

'So I've heard.' Caroline covered her mouth with her hand in feigned surprise. 'I didn't think you'd have the guts to actually throw yourself at the man. I thought it was all made up, but Mama was inconsolable, so I knew it had to be true.'

'Which disproves your point.'

'Ha!' Caroline crossed her arms over her chest. 'That's different. When it comes to screwing, a man's not picky. Any body will do.'

Her sister's language sent an uncomfortable shock through her. Where did she learn such words? 'That doesn't change the fact that we are engaged.'

'Really? Tell me, when is the wedding? Are you having it here or Scotland? Will his family be coming?'

'W-we haven't decided yet,' she said. 'We've been much too busy.'

'Or is he simply stalling? Think about it.' Caroline's smug smile made that knot in Maddie's chest grow tighter. 'Can't you see, Maddie? He doesn't want to cause a scandal, and you know Mama will do anything to force him to marry you. He's stringing you along to keep Mama quiet.'

'Why would he do that?'

'To prevent a scandal from besmirching his sister.'

The breath left Maddie's body. *Persephone.* 'Y-you know about that? About his promise to his mother?'

'Of course I do,' she said confidently.

*Cam must have told her.* How else would Caroline know? And what else could they possibly have talked about? Or done. The image of Cam and Caroline together made her want to retch.

'He's probably on his best behaviour, too.'

Now, that made her flinch. Cam had been the perfect gentleman since their engagement. He hadn't even tried to kiss her.

'He won't risk Mama's wrath or give cause to hasten your wedding,' Caroline continued. 'Once he's married his sister safely off, he won't need you any longer.'

Maddie bit the inside of her cheek. 'I think you should leave, Caroline.'

'I'm only looking out for you—'

'Leave,' she repeated. 'Now.'

Caroline sent her a withering look before she turned to leave.

Once Maddie was alone, she staggered backwards to her bed, her thighs hitting the mattress before she sat down.

It couldn't be. Caroline was lying.

*I want you, Maddie.*

Had he been lying about that? But then again, she knew Caroline was right; men were often not very picky with their bed partners. He could want her in that way—just not in any other way.

He didn't find her attractive at all. Why would she even think he did? He'd called her an Amazon the first time they'd met.

*He finds me repulsive.*

A tear ran down her cheek. Good enough to…to screw, but not to marry. Then his hand had been forced, and he didn't want to hurt Persephone's chances of making a good match.

She fell on her back on top of the mattress, then curled up into a ball. Cam had made her feel wanted and beautiful. But reality sank in. At the end of the day, she was still plain, shy, and awkward Maddie. Nothing could change that.

## Chapter Seventeen

Cam didn't want to attend another boring dinner party, but he had his obligations to his host and hostesses. Now that the Duke and Duchess were in residence, it seemed their social activities had only doubled, and he was getting damned tired of it.

The only bright spot of his evenings was Maddie. Now that they were engaged, they could be seen together in public, and so he escorted her to all the social events. He could be by her side, in front of all the ton, and no one would question it. He could look at her all he wanted and soak in her beauty without having to worry about who was watching. Just being with her, around her, made his evenings enjoyable.

How he wished he could be alone with her. Even for just for one minute. He would make every second count. But he swore he would be on his best behaviour as he would not take any chances with her reputation.

And once they were wed—which he would ensure would happen as soon as possible—she would be all his.

'Where is your lovely fiancée?' Lady Bestwick, whom he had been introduced to earlier that evening, asked.

Everyone was gathered in the foyer for aperitifs before dinner.

Cam frowned. 'Perhaps she is still getting ready.'

'I was so looking forward to meeting her.'

'Dinner is served,' Eames announced to the guests.

As Cam took his place, he glanced around. Where was Maddie?

The doors to the dining room opened, and the Duke and Duchess strode in first, yet Maddie was nowhere to be found.

'Apologies, my lord.'

The murmur made him start, then he let out a relieved sigh when Maddie appeared by his side. 'There you are.' She looked incredibly lovely in a pale green silk gown. As he took her hand into his arm, he leaned down and whispered, 'That is not chartreuse, is it?'

Maddie stiffened and did not smile or laugh.

A feeling stirred in his gut at her reaction. *Perhaps she's just tired*, he told himself. Even he was being worn thin by their nightly events.

All the guests took their seats and dinner began. As usual, the guests *oohed* and *ahhed* over Monsieur Faucher's delectable creations. Seasonal roasted vegetables, braised meats falling off the bone, succulent fresh fish, lobsters with butter—a magnificent feast by all accounts. However, Maddie hardly touched anything and instead only pushed her food around. Not to mention, she responded with only single syllables whenever someone asked her a question, which was also the only time she participated in conversation.

'Are you enjoying your dessert, Maddie?' he asked.

'Yes, my lord.' But she only stabbed at the *pain à la duchesse* and did not take a morsel into her mouth.

When dinner was over and the men and women went

their separate ways for cigars and brandy with the Duke and tea and sherry with the Duchess, Maddie did not even acknowledge him. Then, there was the fact that Caroline, whom he had not seen in days, was strutting around like she'd been crowned Queen of England.

*Something was very wrong.*

And Cam intended to find out what.

For the rest of the evening, he went through the motions and pleasantries with the other guests and their host. However, he was already forming a plan in the back of his mind.

When the evening was over and the guests had dispersed, Cam rushed up to his room. He dismissed Murray even before he'd had a chance to finish undressing him, so he was left in only his shirt, trousers, and bare feet. Checking his valise, he found the flask of Glenbaire whisky he kept there and then took a swig. He hauled a chair to the door and sat there, listening for all the sounds outside. When it grew silent and no more light seeped through the tiny gap between the floor and door, he grabbed his candle and headed outside.

According to Persephone, Maddie had the room directly across from hers. So, he made his way to the other wing and found Persephone's door, then turned to the one opposite. Hopefully, he'd heard Persephone correctly and he wasn't about to barge into an empty room, or worse, any of his future in-laws'. He extinguished his candle before putting it in his pocket.

'Betsy?' came Maddie's voice.

Relieved that he was in the correct chamber, Cam ventured further in. The room was dimly lit, with only a single candle in the corner by the plush reading chair where Maddie sat, book propped on her crossed legs. The candlelight set her creamy skin and golden hair aglow, and with her chin resting on her palm and one shoulder bared, she looked like a Botticelli painting. He nearly forgot himself—that is, until her head lifted and her eyes went wide as dinner plates.

'Cam—'

He crossed the room in seconds, kneeling in front of her to cover her mouth with his hand. 'Shh... Or we'll be caught.' When her eyes blinked in understanding, he put his hand down.

'What are you doing here?' she hissed low. 'Did anyone see you?'

'Of course not,' he said.

She pushed at him, then uncrossed her legs. 'You shouldn't be here.' Planting her feet on the ground, she made a motion to get up but quickly toppled over. 'Oh!'

Cam quickly caught her, then hauled her up to him. 'What's wrong?'

'Foot...pins and needles...' She huffed against his chest. 'My lord, please leave before anyone discovers you here.'

'No.'

'No?'

Cam slid his hands down to her waist and pulled her even closer. While he was taking advantage of her temporary lameness, he didn't give a whit. He didn't risk coming here only to leave without answers. 'What's wrong with you tonight, Maddie?'

'W-wrong?' She turned her head away from him. 'I don't know what you're talking about.'

He sighed. 'You were quiet and morose all evening. You didn't say a word. Didn't even laugh at my fashion joke.'

She huffed but said nothing.

'I know something's the matter, darling.' He moved a hand down to her buttocks, cupping her through the thin fabric of her night-rail. That elicited a gasp, and Cam counted that as a small success. 'Tell me what's wrong. Tell me how I can make it better.'

'I...'

'Yes?'

'My lord... Cam.'

He played with a ringlet of her golden hair. It was like gold silk. 'Hmm?'

'I think we should reconsider the engagement.'

'I beg your pardon?'

The shock of her words was enough to make him loosen his grip, and she wiggled away from him. 'I said we should reconsider the—'

'I bloody well heard what you said,' he shouted. 'I want to know why you're saying it.'

'Shush!' She put a finger to her lips. 'Or someone will hear you.'

'I don't care if the Queen herself hears me.' Confusion, indignation, and hurt swirled inside his chest. 'Now, tell me what the hell this is about. Did Palmer get to you? Did he convince you to say these things?'

'No, my lord. I—I just feel perhaps we've rushed into this and we should think—'

'Who, then? If it wasn't Palmer, who?' He curled his hands into tight fists to stop himself from grabbing her shoulders and shaking some sense into her. 'Tell me why, Maddie. You owe me at least that.'

'You don't really want to marry me.'

'This again?' He let out an exasperated sigh. 'Woman, how can I get it into your head that I want you?' *And you want me.*

'You're only doing this for Persephone.'

'What?' He scratched at his chain. 'Now I am truly confused. Start again, please.'

She sank back down into the reading chair. 'If you do not marry me, my mama will cause a scandal. And that would ruin Persephone's chances this season.' She swallowed. 'And you couldn't fulfil your promise to your mother.'

Cam's spine went rigid and his voice turned hoarse. 'How did you…'

'Persephone told me just today. And Caroline, too.'

Caroline? *Of course.* Just as he suspected, it was that damned sister of hers. 'Whatever it was she told you, it's a lie.'

'That's what I thought, but how did she know about your promise to your mother?'

'I don't know.' He threw his hands up. 'She could have been bluffing. Did she say the exact words to you, about my mother's promise? Or did you?' Maddie didn't speak, but he saw the doubt cross her face, so he continued. 'Your mother probably told her or she overheard of her plan of starting a scandal about us, hoping it would force my hand to marry you. Then you mentioned my promise to my ma, and she ran with it.'

Lord, he was so glad he would be away from Eliza and Caroline once he and Maddie married and moved to Scotland. If there was truly a merciful God, the rest of the DeVries family would leave and go back to America. Still, he wasn't sure if an entire ocean was far away enough. 'I swear to you, Maddie, I spoke to her one time and that's it. A few sentences in the hallway.'

'A-and what else did you say to her?'

'I don't know.' He shrugged. 'But she was insisting that you could never be happy as my countess. That I should instead find someone else who I was attracted to who would be more suitable.' What a joke. 'And then—'

He halted, his jaw snapping shut as he saw the tears pooling in Maddie's eyes.

'And then you told her you would never marry someone you found attractive.'

*Double damn.*

'And so you decided to marry me.'

Without explanation, the words did sound dreadful. He had to explain. To give context. But to do that, he would have to tell her about Jenny. To open those wounds that had been sealed for so long.

'Maddie.' The ache in his chest made it difficult to breathe, but he would get through this. 'Maddie, please...' He bent down and folded his legs underneath him, sitting by her feet so he could look up at her. 'Let me explain.'

She did not say yes, but neither did she turn away. So with a deep breath, he began to speak. 'Nearing ten years ago, I had been engaged to a lass in our village. Jenny. The moment I laid eyes on her, I was smitten. The attraction was overwhelming. She was like a siren who enchanted me.' The corner of her mouth twitched. 'I pursued her. Wooed her. Showered her with gifts. Followed her like a lovesick fool. Miraculously, she agreed to marry me. Ma and Da did not approve, but I continued with my pursuit, and eventually she said yes when I proposed. Looking back, I should have heeded my parents.'

Bitterness and regret rushed back through him, as it did each time he remembered. 'But I was too lovesick, unable to see her unhappiness. She'd had her doubts from the beginning, but her parents wanted her to be a countess, so she accepted my proposal anyway. Then she'd been caught up in the wedding planning and felt like she couldn't back out. But then... Well, she fell in love. With my best friend. They told me the day before the wedding, on their way to Gretna Green.'

A small gasp escaped from Maddie's lips.

Cam did not want to see the pity in her eyes, so he bowed his head. 'They loved each other. True love. Their relationship was much deeper than mine and hers. Of course she would prefer Kirk. He was everything I was not. I was just a charming rogue, with nothing to offer but my good looks and a title I didn't even earn. Fool's gold—all glitter but no value. And since then, well, I told myself I would never marry someone I was that attracted to. I would never be blinded that way again nor allow myself to forge on with only obsession keeping me going.'

'I'm so sorry, Cam,' she said. 'They betrayed you and scarred you so deep. And I want you to know... It's all right if you don't find me attractive.'

'Maddie, I was so attracted to you that day you walked into the Duchess' private sitting room that I got tongue-tied.'

'So you are attracted to me?'

'Yes.'

'Yet you still want to marry me?'

'Of course. I want you, and you want me. That should be enough, right? What we shared in the library is more than what most married couples have. You don't know how glad I am that you felt that way too. We are physically compatible in every way.'

She seemed to ponder his words. 'Cam... I don't want to break our engagement.'

Relief washed over him, loosening all the knots and tension in his body. 'Thank God.' He got to his knees and scooted forward, wrapping his arms around her. 'I want you. You are one of the most attractive women I've ever laid eyes on. Let me show you. I promise you will never doubt me again. And you won't regret wanting to marry me.'

'I… Yes.'

His heart leapt into his throat. 'Are you sure? You understand what I'm trying to say?'

Her pupils blew out. 'Yes, Cam. Please, make love to me.'

Cam needed no further invitation. Nudging her knees apart, he knelt between and lifted the hem of her shift slowly up her legs and soft thighs, torturing himself by revealing her skin slowly, then finally, the soft curls that hid her sex.

'Beautiful,' he declared. Maddie's face was all flush, her eyes shut tight, her breathing heavy. He wished she would look at him, but seeing as this was her first time, he had to be more patient and understanding.

'You must relax for me, Maddie. You'll want to close your legs, but fight the urge as much as you can. All right?'

She nodded wordlessly.

Placing a hand on her knee, he skimmed his fingers upwards over her inner thighs until he reached the downy triangle between them. When he touched the curls, her body twitched, but her knees remained spread.

'This will feel good. You remember, right?' He interpreted her quick intake of a breath as a yes, so he probed her soft nether lips, stroking them up and down until she was slick, her hips squirming invitingly. He pushed one finger in.

'Oh!' Her hands gripped the sides of the chair. 'Oh, Cam.'

'I love hearing my name on your lips.' He pushed the finger deeper still, moving it around. She was sopping wet but still so tight. He would have to make sure she was prepared for him.

'Maddie, darlin', I'm going to kiss you…'

Her eyes flew open.

'Down here,' he continued, then leaned forward before she could protest. He touched his lips to her sex, moving over them in a soft caress. Her entire body went rigid, and she let out a soft cry. But he did not stop and instead licked at her, tasting her sweetness and lapping up her juices while inhaling her womanly scent. His cock twitched inside his pants, and so to relieve the pressure, he reached down to unbutton his falls and stroked himself while he continued to devour her.

'Cam!'

Fingers dug into his hair, scraping at his scalp. Cam slowed down his strokes, lest he spill without warning. He swirled his tongue around her entrance, then probed her with it. Releasing his cock, he moved his hand up to search for the little bud hidden above her folds. When he found it, he stroked it gently with his thumb at first, teasing the bud back and forth until she was moving her hips against him, seeking more friction. She moaned in disappointment when he released it, but then he quickly switched around so his mouth latched onto the bud and his finger entered her again, thrusting in and out, stretching her to capacity.

Her pants came at a faster pace and her hips rose to meet his tongue and fingers. He increased his pace incrementally, tuning his rhythm with hers, and when her body shuddered, he pressed on, letting her ride her wave of pleasure before she went all limp.

With a deep sigh, he laid his cheek on her thighs, enjoying the sight of her damp sex and the scent of her permeating the air. Feeling her hips shift, he rocked back on his knees so he could look at her, looking so satisfied and soft and sleepy as she lay back on the chair, head thrown back and eyes closed, one shoulder still bared.

'You were magnificent, Maddie.' Rising to his feet, he caught her hand and pulled her up. He undid the ribbon at the neckline of the night-rail, then tugged it down to her waist, revealing her breasts and those delectable brown nipples. He cupped one breast in his hand, testing its weight, and gave it a gentle squeeze.

Her mouth parted slightly. Unable to resist, he slanted his mouth over hers. She opened up to him, leaning back and allowing his tongue to enter her mouth. When his thumb brushed over her nipple, she let out a little gasp.

Cam didn't want to let go of her lips or breast, but he knew that he could not take long as he had to leave while the house was asleep. Reluctantly, he pulled back. 'Maddie, are you ready?'

Sky blue eyes stared up at him, luminous in the candlelight. 'Yes.'

*Yes.*

How she could ever say no to this man, Maddie didn't know. But with her body coiled with anticipation, she knew she wanted him.

He kissed her again, softly, then led her away from her reading chair and towards the bed. He guided her on top of the mattress and broke their kiss. Wordlessly, he began to strip away his clothing, starting with his shirt, then trousers. She couldn't help but gasp at the sight of his body—long and muscled all over, with hair on his chest and lower arms. Her gaze continued lower to his trim waist, to the erection jutting out of his body. Her heart pounded in her chest as he approached her, raising a knee up on the mattress to join her on the bed. They lay down on their sides, facing each other.

'Do you want to touch me?' he asked, voice low and husky.

There was only one answer she could give him, but it was stuck in her throat at the sight of him, so she nodded instead. Taking her hand in his, he guided it to his taut, muscled belly and pushed it lower. Her fingers moved past the wiry dark mat of hair before reaching the rigid length of his erection. He moved her hands up and down slowly. His skin was silky, yet the flesh underneath was hard as iron. Even as he removed his hand, she continued to stroke him, fascinated by the length and feel of him, starting when she felt the bead of wetness at the tip.

'Maddie, I'm not sure I'm going to last if you keep that up.'

She withdrew her hand.

'Are you ready?'

'Yes, Cam.' Oh, yes.

He wrapped an arm around her, then rolled himself over her, murmuring sweet words in that soft burr of his

Maddie found herself spreading her thighs so he could settle between them.

'This will hurt a bit. I'm sorry.' Lifting his head, he stared down at her. Though she couldn't see his emerald eyes, she imagined them, blazing hot with desire.

A pressure pushed at her entrance and the tip of him probed her slowly, dipping in and easing forward. He filled her, and Maddie found it wasn't painful—at least, until it was. She winced as the pressure turned into a stinging ache.

'Maddie,' he groaned. His hand reached down between them to where they were joined, then spread her nether lips. He rocked back and forth, getting halfway into her. His fingers once again found the bud at the crest of her sex and teased it slowly, sending little shocks of pleasure through her body.

'Yes,' he moaned. 'That's it.' He pushed further in.

The fullness was a strange sensation, yet her body seemed to crave it. Her hips pushed up at him, drawing him deeper. When she once again reached that peak, he drove into her, drowning her mixed cry of pain and pleasure with his mouth.

Her body fully accepted him, his driving thrusts pushing her to new heights. The length of him stroked places she'd never been touched before as his fingers continued to play with her with the skill of a virtuoso, plucking and tugging and pressing like she was an instrument bound to his whims. Maddie didn't care—all she wanted was that feeling to never end.

Cam's breathing came in uneven spurts as her body gripped him. He pushed at her, riding her hard until that wave arrived, moving from the tips of her toes and washing over the rest of her, smothering her in pleasure. When it was over, Cam let out a strangled growl and rocked his hips hard. She felt the strangest pulse inside her as he gave one last push before going completely still.

With a deep sigh, he withdrew from her, then rolled to his side before gathering her close. Seconds passed. Or it could have been longer—Maddie couldn't really tell, as her senses had ceased to function.

'You must marry me now, darling.' He kissed her soft skin, then slid a hand over her belly. 'You might be carrying my bairn at this moment. We will be married as soon as possible.'

She hummed in contentment. That didn't sound too bad at all.

Sleep came and went, but the awareness of him in her bed never left her. A cycle of sleep had settled over her when once again she awoke, this time from the sleep-roughened voice in her ear.

'Maddie.' Arms held her tight and the hard male body

behind her pressed closer. Lips caressed her ear before Cam released her. 'Your maid will be by any moment.'

Unfortunately, he was right. 'You must leave.'

'For now.'

The mattress shifted as he left her bed. The rustling of fabric told her he was getting dressed, and she turned to face him.

'You were amazing, Maddie,' he said as he buttoned his shirt and leaned down to kiss her temple. 'As I knew you would be.' A hand cupped her cheek and she nuzzled at his palm, the calluses tickling her skin. 'We are making the right decision, you know.'

She paused. 'We are?'

'Mmm-hmm. I knew we would be physically compatible in every way, and our marriage will be a success. I thought with Je— I thought I wanted more in a marriage when I was first engaged. Like what my parents had. But this, between us, is much better.' He rose up. 'I will see you later.'

Maddie could only watch his shadow move in the darkness. When he was gone, she lay on her back, looking up at the blackness above her.

Hearing about his former fiancé had sparked jealousy in her. The emotion was ridiculous; he was a man, and of course he had a past. But to know that there had been a woman before her that Cam wanted to marry made her chest ache. Then he'd told her his story and the pain had deepened—for him.

*Oh, Cam.*

All the parts were coming together, like assembling a piece of machinery. He hid behind that brash and charming façade so no one would see the hurt. He'd made that vow to never marry anyone he was attracted to because he was afraid it would turn into obsession. And she didn't blame him, because he had been burned so badly.

Still, Maddie couldn't help but feel there was still more. Cam might think he's a man with no substance; yet, she'd been peeling back layers only to find more.

But would she ever get to the core of him?

## Chapter Eighteen

After the night they'd made love, plans for the wedding quickly took shape. Cam wanted a firm wedding date and he wanted it as soon as possible. He was ready to obtain a special licence—hell, he would have eloped with her to Gretna Green, but Cornelius would not allow it. And since he was the only other DeVries Cam respected, he did not insist on it.

And so he settled for six weeks, which would be enough time to have the banns read and for his brothers to settle business at the distillery before they travelled to England. He agreed to have the wedding in London, as it would be inconvenient to have everyone travel back to Scotland, which would only delay the wedding. Besides, after what Maddie had endured in London, he wanted the ton to see that she was a desirable bride and make every man and woman who laughed or jeered at her regret their words.

'Must we attend another ball?' Cam asked as he and Maddie waited for everyone in the foyer.

'I'm afraid we must.'

'Why?'

'So I can show off my new gown.' She twirled around,

sending violet tulle fluttering around her like a cloud. 'And my fiancé.'

'You are beautiful in that gown. But—' he leaned down '—it would look much better on the floor.'

'My lord,' she admonished, a pretty blush creeping up her bare shoulders and neck. 'We are not alone.'

'Later, we will be.'

Cam had been visiting her room every night since the first time. The first few nights, he still believed he could resist her siren call, but after wearing the carpet in his rooms down with his pacing, he would eventually give in, anyway. He came to her after everyone was asleep and left before dawn. Their time together was much too short, but they made the most of it. Maddie was eager to please him, and in return, he brought her to peak after peak of pleasure. He was surprised either of them managed to stay awake the rest of the day.

'Oh, here we are,' Eliza announced as she, Cornelius, and Caroline descended the stairs. 'My lord, don't you look handsome tonight.'

'Thank you, Mrs DeVries.'

'You know, if it's just us, you may call me Mama.'

Maddie groaned loudly.

'What?' Eliza snapped her fan open. 'In six weeks, he will be my son-in-law.' Her eyes gleamed. 'And you will be Madeline, Countess of Balfour.' She waved her fan. 'Your Ladyship.'

Maddie looked to her father pleadingly. 'Come now, dear,' Papa began. 'No need to be so dramatic. Right, Caro?' Caroline merely sniffed and didn't say a word.

*Good*, Cam thought. Had Caroline been a man, he would have called her out for pistols at dawn for trying to get between him and Maddie. Hopefully, this was the last of her antics, as even he had limits on his control.

Once the Duke, Duchess, Dowager, Miss Merton, and Persephone came downstairs, they all left for the Devonshire ball. As his betrothed, Maddie was permitted to ride in his carriage and he to escort her to events. So he, Maddie, and Persephone all rode together to the Duke of Devonshire's grand home on Park Lane.

'Cameron, Lord Balfour! Lady Persephone Mac-Gregor! Miss Madeline DeVries!'

They descended the steps, all eyes were on them, and in particular, on Maddie. Cam himself couldn't take his eyes off her, and from the way she blushed, she enjoyed the attention. *Who's the awkward giantess now?* he wanted to shout at these silly Englishmen and women.

'Come,' he said. 'Let us greet our host and hostess.'

One more advantage of having Maddie on his arm at these events was that Persephone no longer disappeared. As long as Maddie was there, she stayed by his side and allowed him to introduce her to eligible gentlemen. Cam was pleased that his sister and fiancée got along, as they were the two most important women in his life.

As he did at every ball, he danced the first dance with Maddie. He held her close, much closer than permitted, which raised a few eyebrows from some eagle-eyed matrons, but Cam didn't care. How he enjoyed feeling her body next to his—whether they were making love or dancing—and he would not let anyone shame him into stopping. Besides, only Maddie's opinion mattered to him. She had only to turn those sky blue eyes at him and the feelings of doubt disappeared.

Once they were finished dancing, they joined Persephone, who stood by the sidelines with Miss Merton.

'Maddie,' Persephone began. 'Would you mind coming with me so I may freshen up?'

'I shall join you, as well,' Miss Merton said.

'Cam?'

He nodded. 'I'll come find you later.' When the three women left, Cam glanced around the room, hoping to find Mabury or the Dowager, but before he could locate them, he felt a tap on his arm.

'Oh, here's my daughter's fiancé.'

Cam winced at the sound of Eliza's voice. 'Mrs DeVries,' he greeted.

'My lord, I have brought over some friends who would like to make your acquaintance.' She nodded to the couple next to her. 'I told them, you simply must meet my future son-in-law, the Earl of Balfour. My lord, this is Viscount and Viscountess Shelby. My lord, my lady, this is Cameron, Earl of Balfour.'

Irritation pricked at him, but he politely said, 'How do you do?'

He chatted with the Viscount and Viscountess for a few minutes before excusing himself. 'I see an acquaintance whom I promised to introduce to my sister. I must find her.' Scanning the room, he saw the Duchess, Maddie, and Persephone speaking to a gentleman he'd never seen before. However, before he could reach them, the gentleman took Maddie's hand and led her to the ballroom floor.

'Who was that?' he asked the two women when he did arrive at their side.

'She's just dancing, Balfour,' the Duchess informed him. 'Not eloping with him.'

But he kept his eyes on her the entire time—and his hands.

*One wrong move*, he swore, *and I will rip those hands away from his wrists.*

After what seemed like an excruciatingly long dance,

Maddie and her partner returned. 'Thank you, Mr Thomson. I enjoyed the dance.'

'As did I, Miss DeVries.'

'I— Cam, you're here.' Her face lit up. 'I was just dancing with Mr Thomson. Kate—Her Grace—introduced us.'

'How nice,' he said through gritted teeth.

She quickly introduced them. 'The Earl is my fiancé,' she added. 'And Lady Persephone is his sister.'

'Pleased to make your acquaintance,' he said.

Cam merely nodded.

'Mr Thomson.' The Duchess began to lead him away. 'I believe I see Sir and Lady Walker talking to my husband and his mother. I'd like to introduce you.'

'Who was that?' Cam asked once the Duchess and Mr Thomson were out of earshot.

'A friend of Kate's.' Maddie slipped her hand into his arm. 'I'm parched. Shall we go get some lemonade?'

'I'd like some, too,' Persephone said.

Cam put Thomson out of his mind for now. This was a ball, after all, and Maddie loved to dance. She was allowed to dance with anyone she wanted. Several more times throughout the evening, gentlemen came and asked Maddie to dance, and etiquette dictated she accept their invitations, since she had already danced with Cam and Mr Thomson. Still, he did not have to like it and showed his displeasure by scowling the entire time Maddie was with another.

'You could ask any lady to dance,' Persephone pointed out.

'Why would I?' he bit out.

'Oh, how romantic,' his sister sighed.

He stared at his sister. 'Romantic?'

'Yes. Your jealousy. You really are in love.'

In love? Was she mad? No, he definitely was not in love with Maddie. He was going to marry her. He wanted her. Hell, he admitted he was attracted to her. There was no way, however, that he would fall in love with her.

But he would not stand another minute of watching her dance with other men. 'Persephone, will you please find Miss Merton or the Dowager? There is something I must attend to.'

Cam made his way out of the ballroom and away from the crush of guests, not really caring where he was going, just following one random hallway after another.

'Cam! Wait!'

He halted in his tracks and spun on his heel. 'Maddie?'

Sure enough, there was Maddie, running towards him. 'Lord, you're fast,' she said, huffing and puffing as she stopped and braced herself against his chest. 'Where were you going?'

'Nowhere,' he said. 'The ballroom was getting much too stuffy.'

'There was hardly any room for dancing.' She wrinkled her nose.

'You seemed to be enjoying yourself with all your partners.' That came out harsher than he wanted it to. Jealousy was a big, green-eyed monster that demanded retribution. Stepping forward, he caught her arm. 'Come with me.'

'Where?'

'Anywhere.' Tugging at her arm, she followed him as he led her down the darkened hallway to the first room they reached. Darkness concealed what type of room it was, exactly, but all he needed to know was that it was empty.

'Cam,' she gasped when he backed her up against a wall. 'What are you doing?'

'I want you.' He nipped at her lips. 'Now.'

'But we're not in my bed,' she protested. 'How can we—'

'I'll show you.' It was too dark to see her face, but that was part of the thrill. 'If you let me.'

'Show me.'

His mouth was upon her, devouring her. She let out a squeak as he lifted her skirts up over her waist and pressed two fingers into the slit in her drawers. There was no time to make her come first, unfortunately, so he stroked her until she was more than sufficiently wet and grinding into his palm.

'That's it,' he growled against her mouth.

One arm hooked under her knee, while the other unfastened the falls of his trousers, releasing his cock. After a few tugs with his hand he was completely erect and he slid into her in one smooth motion.

He smothered her cry with his lips, his tongue pushing in to her mouth with the same motion of his hips. Jealousy rode him hard, urging him to mark her. Make her his. Only his. When she clasped around him and her body vibrated, he let go, spilling inside her. His pleasure came in a quick fury, sweeping over him until he was drained.

'That was…' Maddie slumped against him.

'…phenomenal,' he finished. Withdrawing from her, he helped her with her gown, smoothing down as much of the wrinkles as he could. When he looked up at her face, all he could see was pure satisfaction.

'You enjoyed that,' he said.

A lazy smiled curled up her lips. 'Of course. I didn't think it would be possible…anywhere except on a bed. Where else can we do it?'

Ideas flooded into his mind. 'I'll show you. Don't worry.' He brushed away an errant curl stuck to her cheek. 'Now, if you head back into the ball first, I'll follow in a few moments.'

She nodded, then dashed off.

Cam righted himself, then leaned an arm against the wall, taking a deep breath. Nothing like a hard tupping to prove that all that was between them was physical. He would not allow any more than that. Not after Jenny.

Had he forgotten her and how she had left him a broken man when she and Kirk had eloped? He'd barely survived that first time; he wasn't sure he could do it again. Not with Maddie.

With the wedding now fast approaching, Maddie's days were a flurry of fittings, shopping, and appointments. As if that weren't enough, there were also other social obligations expected of the bride, such as going to teas and paying calls to the ton's most important members.

'Why must we attend all these events?' Maddie asked Miss Merton as they were on their way to the Viscountess of Lattimer's home for afternoon tea. 'I am already so busy with planning for the wedding.'

'I completely understand, dear. All this must be taking its toll on you.' Miss Merton patted her hand. 'But, as a future countess, you must make the right impression and connections. You shall be the Earl's most important social asset. He will be judged by how you act and conduct yourself, as will his family.'

'His family, too?'

The companion nodded. 'Most definitely. You will essentially be the matriarch, after all.'

Maddie had never thought of it that way. She had to do better.

No—she had to be perfect.

Just like with her dancing lessons, Maddie would not buckle under the pressure. She would work hard. She owed it to Cam and Persephone. If she were a success as Countess of Balfour, then Persephone's chances for a good match would increase.

*And Cam would fulfil his promise to their mother.*

That was the only thing she wanted.

*Well, not the only thing.*

Maddie could not help but notice the nagging feeling that something in Cam had shifted. Or maybe there had always been something different with him. His confession that night they'd first made love clarified some things for her, but there were still pieces missing.

Hate was a strong word, but she could categorically say she hated his former fiancé. With her actions, that woman had left deep scars in Cam, which may have healed but nevertheless had left their mark. That was what she had seen on his face the day he'd proposed; it was no chink in his armour, but rather, Cam had wrapped himself in this protective gear to stop anyone from getting too close and hurting him.

Maddie had hoped that a physical relationship would be enough. It should have been, but now she was wanting more. There was potential there—she just knew it. But Cam's emotional scars were preventing that from happening.

'We are here,' Miss Merton announced as the carriage slowed to stop. 'Come.'

Despite the fact that she was exhausted, Maddie put a smile on her face and did her best to charm all the important ladies of the ton. She drank her watered-down tea, pretended to be interested in conversations about shopping and fashion, plus feigned interest in the juicy gossip about whichever lord and lady were having an affair this week.

She hated every moment of it, but endured, for Persephone and Cam. Once they were on their way home, she breathed a big sigh of relief.

'You should have a nap, dear,' Miss Merton suggested when they arrived at Mabury Hall. 'Tonight's dinner is very important. The Dowager Duchess of Durham is a powerful figure in society, and the fact that she's hosting a dinner in honour of your engagement is monumental. Everyone's eyes will be on you tonight.'

'I understand.' Maddie was nervous just thinking about it. 'I will be the perfect future countess.' However, that nap would have to wait. She had one more important task.

'Hello, dear,' Papa greeted as she entered the library. 'Glad to see you're not too busy for your father.'

'Never.' Bouncing over to him, she kissed him on the cheek.

'I'm glad. Though I'm afraid I don't have anything as fun as wedding dresses and cakes to show you today.'

'Oh, please. After this wedding, I never wish to see anything white ever again.' Maddie could not say yes fast enough when her father had asked her to meet at the library when she returned from Viscountess Lattimer's tea party to look at the furnace design plans. 'Now, where are those drawings?'

For the next few hours, Maddie forgot all about wedding planning as she poured over the sketches with her father. They still weren't quite right, and while she was frustrated the designers did not listen to her suggestions, she was still glad for the distraction.

'This is good practice for you, Maddie,' Papa said. 'I've been thinking about building a furnace in Scotland.'

Maddie held her breath. 'And?'

'It might be an excellent idea, a few years down the line. We need to get the furnace here up and running, but once that's proven to be a success, we can start planning for this next venture. Perhaps by then you'll have a child or two, and they'll be old enough that you can put more time into the business.'

'Really, Papa?' Excitement made it difficult to breathe.

'Yes. Your future husband has such a way with words that it makes it difficult to say no,' he said with a chuckle.

'Cam convinced you to start a forge in Scotland?'

'He has convinced me something I already know—that with you at the helm, it will be a success.'

Maddie had no words to say after that. Cam had that much faith in her? He had never even seen her near a furnace.

'But first,' Papa continued, 'let's get this one off the ground, shall we?' He shook his head as he rolled up the plans and put them aside. 'I don't know how I'm going to do this without you, Maddie. But parents cannot hold onto their children. We must eventually let go, especially if that means our child's happiness.'

Tears stung the back of her throat. 'Thank you, Papa.'

'Are you, Maddie?'

'What, Papa?'

'Happy.' He qualified that with, 'Truly happy?'

Puzzled, she asked, 'What do you mean?'

'I know you, dear.' He walked over to her, guided her to a settee, then sat down. 'And I see you. You always put aside your own wants to make others happy.'

'That's not true.'

'Oh? Did you really want to come here and find a husband in the first place? Or did you do it because Caroline and your mother wanted to?'

'I—'

'And what about when you wear the dresses your mama chooses? And go to these events she plans? Do you do them for yourself or to please her?'

'She's my mother. Of course I want to please her.'

'But what about yourself? What about what you want?'

Maddie didn't know how to answer that.

'You've always been so selfless, Maddie. Even with Caroline. When you were younger, you would give her everything she wanted, even your prized clothes and toys.' He tsked. 'Anyway, I hope you think about what I said, Maddie.' He kissed her cheek. 'Because you deserve all the happiness in the world.'

'Thank you, Papa.' She embraced him, then got to her feet. 'I'm afraid I must be going. Mrs Ellesmore is coming over and I'll be poked and prodded with needles and pins all afternoon.'

He laughed. 'Good luck, dear.'

Maddie made her way out, but as she opened the door and crossed the threshold into the silence of the hallway, her father's words came back to her. Was she happy? And did she think she deserved happiness? But what would make her happy in the first place?

In the beginning, she'd thought all she wanted was a husband and a family. Now that she was to marry Cam, she would get her wish, and even more than that—fulfilling work to fill her days once her children were old enough.

But why did it feel like there should be more?

## Chapter Nineteen

'Which dinner are we attending again tonight, Balfour?' Mabury asked as he handed Cam the glass of whisky.

'Damned if I know. They're all the same, aren't they?' He nodded his thanks and accepted the glass. The Duke had been kind enough to invite Cam to his private study for cigars before they left for tonight's activities, and so he'd brought a bottle of Glenbaire single malt to share.

'Do not let my mother and Miss Merton hear you. Cheers.' The Duke clinked his glass to Cam's and took a sip. 'Now, that's damned fine whisky.'

'Thank you, Your Grace.' The familiar taste of the buttery, malty liquid was a comfort; it made him think of home. A sudden pang of homesickness hit him. *I can't wait for all this to be over.* All he wanted to do right now was to take Maddie back to Scotland and be away from London. To have her to himself, day and night, instead of sneaking in a few hours with her from midnight to dawn. To make love to her every evening and then sit next to her at breakfast the next day.

'From the look on your face, I can guess you cannot wait for all this wedding madness to be over,' the Duke said.

'You guessed right.' He downed the rest of the whisky. 'If I had my way, we'd be on our way to Gretna Green now.'

'There's still time.' The corner of Mabury's mouth quirked up. 'But, once things settle down, you'll look back on all of this with fondness.'

'Liar,' Cam said with a chuckle.

'I was trying to cheer you up, old chap.'

'I appreciate it.'

Despite having been punched by him twice and his threatening to kill Cam, he quite liked the Duke. He could definitely see them becoming good friends over the years, which was a real possibility since the Duchess and Maddie were as close as sisters.

'I promise you, Balfour, it will all be worth it.' Mabury put his glass back down on the mantel, then looked at the clock. 'We should get going or we'll be late.' They left the study and made their way to the hall where everyone was waiting for them.

As ever, the others faded in the background as Cam's gaze sought out Maddie. Tonight, she wore a delicate, light pink silk gown that only enhanced her natural beauty, while her golden hair shone like a halo around her. She smiled shyly at him as he came to her. Why was it that she only had to glance his way and everything seemed right in the world? All those fears and doubts— thoughts he hadn't realised had been plaguing his mind— would all but disappear when she was around.

'Good evening, my lord,' she greeted.

'Good evening, Miss DeVries.' Taking her gloved hand, he kissed it. 'You look beautiful tonight.'

'Thank you,' she said, her skin turning nearly the same shade of pink as her gown.

'I hope you never stop blushing for me,' he said in a low voice, ensuring only she could hear it.

'Everyone.' Miss Merton clapped her hands to get their attention. 'We must make haste.'

As usual, Maddie and Persephone rode with Cam, though when they sat down, he made Persephone switch places with him so he could sit beside Maddie. He reached over and took her hand in his.

She cocked her head to the side. 'Is everything all right, Cam?'

'Yes.' No, it wasn't. He didn't want to be here. All he wanted was to go back to her rooms and be alone. 'I just want to hold your hand, that's all.'

'Of course, but—oh!' She scooted a few inches away from him. 'Please mind my dress. Silk easily wrinkles.'

He chuckled. 'Forgive me. I'm afraid I'm not well versed in the properties of fabrics, except maybe for their tensile strength.' Or lack thereof, as demonstrated last night when, in his impatience, he'd rent her night-rail down the middle. Maddie apparently had picked up his meaning, and once again a pretty blush coloured her cheeks.

'Why would you know that, Cam?' Persephone asked, blinking owlishly behind her spectacles.

'Never you mind, Seph.' But Maddie's blush deepened. 'By the way, where are we going again?'

'You don't know?' Maddie asked in an exasperated tone.

He shrugged. 'All these dinners, parties, balls... They're all melding together and I can't keep my head straight.'

She sighed. 'The Dowager Duchess of Durham is throwing a dinner in honour of our engagement.'

'Wait, we're the guests of honour?' First he'd heard of it.

'Yes.' Reaching over, Maddie brushed a stray lock of hair from his temple. 'It's very important. *She* is very important, and we must make a good impression on her.'

Cam frowned. Important? Since when did Maddie care about all these so-called doyens of the ton?

'Cam, how old is this tail-coat?' She clucked her tongue as she plucked a stray thread from the lapel. 'You must get some new ones made. Would you like me to speak with Murray?'

'I'll speak with him,' he muttered, then snatched the thread from her fingers.

'Everything must be perfect.' Maddie wrung her hands together. 'We cannot make a mistake.'

Irritation rose in Cam. 'What's the matter with you, Maddie? You're acting very strange.'

'Strange?' Her head snapped towards him, her eyebrows slashing downwards. 'I'm fine. Just tired from all the wedding planning.' The carriage halted and her body went rigid. 'We're here. Come or we'll be late.'

Cam had sensed the vexation in her tone, which was unusual for her. But perhaps all this madness was affecting her more than he thought, and now she was on the verge of breaking. *I shouldn't have insisted on having the wedding so soon.*

He wanted to apologise to her, but as soon as they entered the Dowager Duchess of Durham's home, they were swept up in a flurry of introductions, good wishes, and congratulations from people he hardly knew and, to be honest, likely never wanted to know. Cam was relieved when they finally sat down to dinner, as at least he had to endure conversations from only the Dowager Duchess and a few of her close companions. That, and Maddie was by his side.

'Lord Balfour, is it true you've decided to hold your nuptials in England?' came a question from the well-dressed man on the Dowager's right.

Cam searched his memory for his name. *Forsythe.* They'd been introduced as soon as they arrived and he claimed to be the Dowager's dearest friend. 'Aye, Mr Forsythe, it's true.'

'How lovely. And why not back in Scotland?'

'It seemed simpler,' he replied. 'If we held it back home, we'd have to prepare at least three households for travel. My sister is already here and so it would only be my three brothers making the journey, which makes a wedding in London much simpler.'

'Ah, yes. Preparing a trousseau and then having to travel for a few days would indeed be taxing,' Forsythe said. 'Not to mention, a grand wedding in London is nothing less than what your lovely fiancée deserves.'

'Aye, for sure.'

Maddie had never expressed her desire for a grand wedding, but he supposed that it would have to be a large gathering since it would be in town. 'And really, once my brothers have settled business at the distillery, they can make the journey anytime.'

'D-distillery?' The Dowager's hawk-like stare narrowed at him. 'What do you mean, distillery?'

'My family business, Your Grace,' he said proudly. 'Glenbaire Whisky Distillery.'

'Whisky? Business?' she echoed.

'It's been in my family for generations,' Persephone piped up. 'Even before it was legal—'

'Mr Forsythe,' Maddie interrupted. 'Her Grace tells

me you have the most divine collection of rare French paintings. How did you come to have an interest in art?'

'I'm glad you asked, Miss DeVries. You see, I was but a young lad when....'

Cam tuned out Forsythe and instead, for the second time that evening, was searching for an explanation for Maddie's odd behaviour. Persephone could sometimes launch into inappropriate discussions, but Maddie acted as if she would send the ladies in the room for their smelling salts if she spoke about the distillery.

At first he thought it might have been a fluke, except that as the dessert plates were being cleared, the Dowager's sycophants had launched into a discussion about the latest scandal in the gossip columns.

'So, who do you think is this Mr R caught by Lord M in bed with his lady wife?' Forsythe asked.

'Who else?' the woman on his right—Lady Christine or Cassandra—said. 'The writer describes this Mr R as a "dark god."'

'God of The Underworld, then?' Forsythe waggled his eyebrows knowingly. 'Have you read the column, Miss DeVries?'

Cam almost laughed, imagining Maddie poring over those sordid anonymous gossip columns.

Maddie put her napkin down on her lap. 'I'm afraid not. But I heard the most interesting tidbit at the Viscountess Lattimer's tea today.'

'Well? Tell us,' the Dowager pressed her.

'Apparently, a certain Viscount G and Lady Q have started their affair again.'

Forsythe gasped. 'No.' The rest of the flunkies let out gasps of disbelief.

Maddie smiled. 'Oh, yes, according to some reliable sources.'

Cam could only stare at Maddie. But before he could say anything, the Dowager spoke. 'Dear guests, thank you for coming tonight, especially our honoured guests.' She nodded at Cam and Maddie. 'Now, the evening is not over yet. As a surprise for the happy couple, I have invited Signora Carmina Giuselli, the London opera's prima donna, to sing a few songs for us in the music room.' The guests *oohed* and *aahed* in delight. 'But while we wait for her, there will be coffee, tea, and digestifs in the parlour. Please do join me.'

Everyone stood up and followed the Dowager out of the room. Cam fell behind as their hostess and her friends surrounded Maddie, ushering her along. He trailed after them to the parlour, which was now filled with the other guests. With Maddie occupied, he decided to seek out some friendlier company, scanning the room for Mabury until he found the Duke with his wife and Persephone speaking to a few other guests. *Thank God.*

As he crossed the room towards them, he halted when he heard his name.

'Why, yes, my future son-in-law is the Earl of Balfour.' *Oh, hell.*

Eliza DeVries continued, 'I'm so lucky, aren't I? And this is Maddie's first season, too. I just knew she would succeed. Just think, in a few weeks, we'll all be calling her *my lady*.'

Irritation grew in him. This night was turning into some sort of farce, and he just wanted to leave. Turning on his heel, Cam changed direction and marched towards his fiancée holding court at the other end of the room.

'Maddie.'

'So he told—Cam?' A smile lit up her face. 'Where were you? I thought you were just behind us?'

He was surprised she'd noticed he was gone. 'Might I have a word? In private?'

'Now?'

'Yes, now.'

She hesitated, glancing at her new friends. 'Of course, my lord. Would you excuse us?' Her flock parted to let her through, and she took the hand he offered. 'Cam, what is it?'

Cam ground his teeth together as he pulled her along, away from the guests and out into the hall.

'Cam? Where are we going?' She tugged her hand from his. 'Cam, what's the matter?'

He spun around to face her, unable to tell her the words that were really on his mind. 'Come away with me, Maddie,' he said, his voice hoarse.

'Away? What do you mean? And where?'

'Back to your room. Or to Scotland. We can go to Gretna Green and be married in days.' On impulse he wrapped his arms around her and crushed her to him. 'I don't care, as long as it's not here.'

'Cam!' she admonished, wiggling away from him. 'What are you doing?' she hissed, anger flashing in her eyes. 'We cannot do this here. Someone might see us.'

'Who cares what these silly fops and matrons think?' His chest tightened.

'You should care,' she said. When he made a motion to take her in his arms again, she raised her hands. 'And I told you, this gown wrinkles easily.'

'I don't give a damn about your infernal gown.'

'Cam, language.' She placed her hands on her hips. 'Can't you see? We have to be on our best behaviour. We must be *perfect* tonight.'

'Perfect? For these fops and fools?'

'Cam, shush. They might hear you.' She glanced

around. 'Please. Can't you just be on your best behaviour tonight? I've worked so hard. I don't want to give up now. I just need a little help from you…just need a bit more.'

She needed more.

That's all he had to hear.

Something inside Cam shrank and contracted and a cold wave washed over him. 'Of course, Maddie. What was I thinking? Forgive me.'

Maddie's shoulders sank. 'You don't have to apologise, Cam. Truly.'

'You should go back inside. Before they miss you.'

She bit her lower lip. 'I—Yes, you're right. I shall see you later, then, my lord.'

Cam watched her go, his chest tightening. When he tried to go after her, he found that his feet would not move. He hated that room and didn't want to go back, so he walked off in the opposite direction. Seeking solace, he found the glass doors that led to the garden. He inhaled, but the cool night air did nothing to soothe him.

Maddie needed more.

'All alone, my lord?'

Caroline DeVries.

He had no patience for her tonight. 'Miss DeVries, we are soon to be family, so I will get straight to the point. Your malicious attempts to drive Maddie and I apart will never work. So please, stop.'

She laughed mockingly. 'Yet here you are, all by yourself.'

He curled his fingers into his palm. 'Goodnight, Miss DeVries.'

'I can see why Mama likes you,' she began. 'You're like a shiny bauble she can show off. Perhaps that's why Maddie accepted your proposal. She's always wanted Mama's approval because I'm her favourite.'

'I do not see the point of this conversation, so I shall bid you goodnight.' Without another word, he walked past her and back into the house.

Caroline's maliciousness had nearly cost him Maddie, and Cam knew better than to listen to her. However, her words buried themselves in his mind, and considering Maddie's behaviour tonight, they somehow made sense. And it wasn't as if Caroline was lying; she was merely giving her observations.

Observations that were somehow in tune with his and explained why Maddie was suddenly acting strangely.

*A shiny bauble*, he thought bitterly. That was all he was.

## Chapter Twenty

Maddie's jaw ached from smiling for hours, but she endured it, as well as the mindless conversation and the spiteful and venomous people around her.

*It will be worth it*, she convinced herself.

When she was small, Papa had worked long hours at the furnace, and sometimes they wouldn't see him for days. But his persistence and tenacity had paid off, and now the DeVries Furnace and Iron Company was one of the most successful furnaces in America and they would soon be making their mark in England, as well.

Her small sacrifice now would pay off later.

*For Cam and Persephone and their dear mama.*

Once she and Cam were married, she would take Persephone under her wing, and between Kate, the Dowager, and herself, no one would dare laugh at or mock her friend. Maybe she might even stop hiding behind foliage and statues and find someone who could cherish her and love her for who she was, quirks and all. Someone who would give her the same sense of self-worth Cam gave Maddie.

Maddie's heart slammed in her chest and urgency and dread rose in her, like she had just realised something important, but she couldn't name it. Maybe it was Cam's strange behaviour when they spoke earlier outside.

*Come away with me, Maddie.*

In the moment he had said it, it had sounded preposterous. Mad, even. Leave the party—their party—and run home to make love? Or elope to Scotland? Was he crazy? The ton would have eaten up that gossip, and then her work would have been for naught. All she needed was for him to put in the least bit of effort. Just a little more, she'd asked.

But now, part of her wished she had said yes to his proposal to run away. Not just yes, but *oh, yes!*

'Miss DeVries, did you hear what I said?'

Mr Forsythe's question yanked her back from her thoughts. 'What? I—I'm sorry. I must go.'

Maddie ignored their protests as she walked away. She needed to find Cam. Right now. But where was he? A pit in her stomach formed, and so she headed off in search of him. A quick scan of the room told her he wasn't in the parlour, but she did spot Kate and the Duke.

'There you are,' Kate said as Maddie approached them. 'Are you enjoying yourself?'

She wrung her hands together. 'Have you seen Cam?'

'I haven't. Sebastian?'

The Duke shook his head. 'I thought he was by your side?'

'He…left,' she replied, her voice trembling. 'Excuse me.'

'Maddie, wait—'

Whirling around, she sped off, heading out of the parlour to where she had last seen Cam. 'Cam!' she called, but the hall was empty.

'Maddie!'

Kate? She hadn't even noticed her friend was right behind her, face filled with concern. 'What's the matter?'

Maddie sniffed. 'Oh, Kate, I can't help but think… I think I've done something wrong. Everything is spinning out of control.' Defeat weighed down on her. 'I can't do this anymore.'

Kate's arms came around her in an embrace. 'Maddie,' she soothed. 'It's all right. Tell me what's wrong.'

Gathering her thoughts, Maddie told her what had happened with Cam. 'I just have this feeling, you know… I was a bit short with him, because I've been exhausted and I just wanted everything to be perfect tonight.'

'Perfect? Why would it matter if tonight were not perfect?'

'Because they're counting on me.'

'Who?'

'Cam and Persephone. And their mother. Don't you remember what Persephone said in the carriage? About Cam's promise to their mother? If I make the right impression, then Persephone will surely have a successful season. In the ton's eyes, I must be *perfect*.' Like gold. Precious and with no impurities.

'That's preposterous,' Kate huffed.

'But it's true. Cam and Persephone will be judged according to my actions.'

'First of all,' Kate began, 'who cares about what these biddies think? And second, that all shouldn't be on your shoulders. Yes, Cam promised his dying mother, but why on earth is that your responsibility? Did he ask you to do all this?'

'No.' In fact, Cam hadn't even asked her to help Persephone. 'I just wanted to do it for him.'

Kate smiled sadly. 'You've always been so sweet and unselfish, so of course you would do this for Balfour, no matter what the cost to you. But if he's the man that deserves you, then that shouldn't matter to him. All he would want is for you to be happy. Maddie, dear, are you happy?'

*Happy.*

This was the second time today anyone had asked about Maddie's happiness. She thought she was, but then that feeling came back from earlier today. That feeling that she wanted more.

*I love him.*

Oh, Lord, why hadn't she realised it before? She wanted more, wanted Cam—all of him. She wanted to have a true marriage with him. Not just the physical part, but on every level. But that armour he wore kept him from opening up to her. He didn't want to leave his heart open because it had cost him too much the first time.

'I think I know where he is—or where he's going. Thank you, Kate.' She quickly embraced her friend, then raced out the door. Sure enough, Cam was there, about to get into his coach, one foot on the step.

'Cam!' she called, chasing after him. 'Stop, please.'

He froze, but kept his back to her. 'What do you want, Maddie?'

The iciness in his voice did not escape her. 'I'm so sorry I was acting strange this evening.'

His shoulders slumped, then he turned to face her. 'It's all right. I understand now.'

'You do?'

'Yes.' A smile that did not reach his eyes formed on his lips. 'I'm sorry, too. That I cannot give you what you want. That I cannot give you *more*.'

Oh, that damned word. Why had she said it? 'Oh, no, Cam. It's not what you think—'

'Perhaps you should find someone else, someone worthy of you. Someone more your equal and not just a shiny, charming object with nothing else to offer.'

She stepped forward and gripped his arms. 'But I want you. All of you.' For the first time in her life, she wanted to be selfish, to take what she wanted. And she wanted all of him.

'I know you do. I told you we were compatible in that way.' Wrapping his hands around her wrists, he put her hands away from him. 'I shall miss your sweet little body when we part.'

It sounded like he meant to hurt her, as if to push her away. But it did not work on her— not anymore. Not now that she understood him. All the missing parts were complete and she could see him for who he truly was.

'Cam,' she began gently. 'I am not Jenny. I will not leave you at the altar. I hate that she's turned you into this. But I promise you, I will prove to you that I'm nothing like her.' She didn't know how, but she would find a way.

His jaw ticked, but otherwise he remained unmoved. He was still processing what she had said. But she had to have faith in him. And he had to find that faith in himself. The next part would be the hardest, but it had to be done.

'And now I'm walking away from you, Cam. Not running away. Not forever. Just for now. Because you've taught me that I, too, am worthy.' Going on her tiptoes, she kissed his cheek. 'So when you are ready, come and find me.'

Turning away and leaving Cam was the hardest thing she'd ever had to do in her life. Each step was like slogging through mud, but somehow, she was doing it. She'd done her part, and hopefully, he would know to do his. When she entered the house, she saw Kate was still in the hallway, waiting for her.

'How did it go?'

*Trust Kate to know exactly what was going on.*

'I've done what I can, but now I must wait.' How long, she didn't know.

'I hope he's worth it.' Kate took her hand. 'In the meantime, what do you think about coming back to Highfield Park?'

She smiled weakly at her friend. 'I think that would be a splendid idea.'

# Chapter Twenty-One

'Are we headed back to Mabury Hall, my lord?' John, Cam's footman asked.

'Yes,' Cam replied curtly as he climbed back into his carriage. Taking his hat off, he flung it across the empty seat and sank back into the plush upholstery. Removing his left glove, he pressed a naked palm where Maddie had kissed him on his cheek. The freshly shaven skin was cool and smooth, but he felt as if she had branded him there. And she had branded him—not just on the cheek, but all over.

A damned fool, that's what he was, for not learning his lesson. He would never be enough. He hadn't been for Jenny, and he wasn't for Maddie. Not even she could prove otherwise.

He knocked on the roof of the carriage. As it slowed down, he opened the window. 'John, I've changed my mind.'

'Where shall we go, my lord?'

He thought for a moment. Going back to Mabury Hall was not an option, at least not for now. He did not want to be somewhere that reminded him of Maddie. He needed distraction. An evening of diversions. 'St James's.'

'Where in St James's?'

'Just go, John,' he said impatiently.

'Right away, my lord.'

Cam drummed his fingers on the seat as the carriage sped along. He watched the outside, waiting until they reached the notorious street filled with gaming hells and bordellos and high-end gentlemen's clubs that were just covers for expensive—and legal—gaming hells and bordellos. Tonight, however, he was looking for a particular one.

*Why did I not ask my man of business, Atwell, for a damned address?*

They drove by a few establishments, but Cam felt they were not the right place. With his patience growing thin, he knocked on the roof. When the coach stopped, he did not bother to wait for John to get the door and instead flung it open, hopping out by himself.

'My lord?'

'I think I shall go for a walk.' John looked like he wanted to protest, but Cam waved him away. 'It's all right. Just wait for me at the corner.'

'Of course, my lord.'

Cam pulled the collar of his shirt over his neck to protect him from the cool, damp London air. He shoved his hands in his coat pockets and began to walk in no particular direction, just following the streets, ignoring the drunken gentlemen stumbling out of bawdy houses and well-dressed women trying to catch his eye as they sauntered by. He was nearing the end of the street when he stopped as something drew his attention.

*There.*

Up ahead was perhaps the most enormous building Cam had ever seen. It wrapped around the corner and probably took up an entire block, though he could not be certain because the street lamp extended its illumination only so far. That, and the entire structure was black.

If that place was not called The Underworld, Cam would eat his hat.

He hurried over, climbing up the grand black marble steps, then knocked on the heavy, stained oak door. To his surprise, a slot opened up in the middle. A pair of menacing-looking eyes peeped through.

'Password?'

*Password?* 'I don't know any password.'

The slot slammed shut with a sharp snap.

Undeterred, Cam knocked again.

The slot slid back open. 'Password?'

'I told you, I don't know it. How can I get it?'

'Only members 'ave the password for the day.'

'I'm not a member.'

*Slam.*

He took a deep breath and rapped his knuckles on the door.

'Pass—'

'I was invited,' Cam quickly said. 'By your owner. Ask him yourself. I'm Cameron, Earl of Balfour.'

'Where's yer invite, then?'

'In—' *Oh.* He reached into his pocket, his fingers searching around. *Damn.* He couldn't remember where he'd placed it. *Murray must have put it away.* 'I seem to have lost it.'

*Slam.*

He knocked his forehead on the door and took a deep, calming breath.

'Sir, do you mind?' came a well-spoken voice from behind.

Cam straightened up and stepped aside. 'Be my guest,' he said to the gentleman on the step behind him. With a frustrated groan, he raked his fingers through his hair and bit out a curse under his breath.

'Are you all right?'

Cam's head shot up. 'I beg your pardon?'

'I asked if you were all right.'

Cam's eyes narrowed at the man. His blond hair was cut in the latest fashion, clothes impeccably tailored and made with expensive materials, which meant he was rich, likely titled. He also had the face of an angel, with fine features and eyes the colour of sapphires. 'I'm fine.'

'On the contrary, you look like you could use a friend.' Those twin sapphires twinkled with amusement.

'We are not friends.'

'You know, I get told that a lot.' He tsked. 'But that has never stopped me. Strangers are just friends you've never met, you know. Devon St. James, Marquess of Ashbrooke.' He held out his hand.

Cam looked at it suspiciously but took it anyway. 'Cameron MacGregor, Earl of Balfour.'

'Scottish, eh?' Ashbrooke said.

'Aye. Will that be a problem?'

'No, no.' Ashbrooke waved him away. 'Not at all. The fact that you're not English actually makes you even more desirable to me as a friend. I've never had a Scottish friend before, you see, so you'll make a fine addition to my collection.'

'Well, show me my place on your shelf and I'll make sure to take my place, then.'

Ashbrooke grinned. 'See? We're already getting along smashingly.'

'So, friend,' Cam began. 'Any chance you can get me in there?' He jerked his thumb at the door.

Ashbrooke frowned. 'You are not a member?'

'Nay.'

'And you do not have the invitation?'

He shook his head.

'Then I cannot bring you in with me, I'm afraid. Rules of The Underworld are strict.'

'Could you somehow get me past the doorman?'

He shuddered. 'You can't pay me enough to try to sneak you inside. If our dear Charon doesn't want you in, believe me, you are not getting in.'

'I— Wait, his name's really Charon?'

'Yes. Maybe. I don't know. That's what most people call him.'

Cam thought for a moment. 'The owner. I was invited by the owner on business. Perhaps you could speak to him and tell him I've misplaced my invitation.'

'Talk to Ransom?' Ashbrooke stared at him as if Cam asked him to cut off his right foot. 'No, thank you. I shall take my chances with Charon.'

Cam rubbed his jaw. 'Damn. There really is no way I'm getting in?'

'Not without an invite.' Ashbrooke took his elbow and guided him down the steps. 'Look, this street has dozens of other establishments where we can carouse all night and forget whatever's troubling you.'

'I suppose you are right.' Cam gestured to the street. 'You seem to know your way around here, Ashbrooke, so lead on.'

'All right, but do call me Ash.' He flashed Cam a roguish smile. 'I think we may become best friends before the night is through. Come!'

As Cam suspected, Ash did indeed know his way around St James's. In fact, he strutted around like he was its lord mayor, waving to the ladies looking out their windows, tipping his hat at all the bouncers, and even stopping to chat with a few suspicious-looking figures scurrying about.

Ash first took Cam to a brothel, but he immediately vetoed the idea. Despite what had happened with Maddie, he could not bring himself to be with another woman. So, Ash led him to a gambling house. Which one it was, Cam didn't know or care, because he spent most of the evening watching Ash play round after round of faro while drinking whatever liquor he was handed. Whatever it was, it was ghastly, but he didn't care, as long as it dulled his mind and senses.

'Well, the standards here really must have slipped if they're letting the likes of you in here.'

The sound of that voice was enough to get Cam's blood boiling. Rising to his feet, he shoved his chair back and spun around. He staggered as the world wobbled beneath his feet but braced himself against the faro table. 'You.'

Viscount Palmer glared at him. 'You think you're so clever, Balfour? Stealing Miss DeVries from right under my nose?'

Cam ground his teeth. 'It's not my fault she prefers me.'

'I need her more,' the Viscount snarled.

'Her dowry, maybe,' Cam slurred. His tongue felt thick and unwieldy.

'You're already wealthy. Why couldn't you let the rest of us have a chance?'

'Gentlemen,' Ash interrupted, getting up from his game and standing between them. 'Is there a problem here?'

'Step aside, Ashbrooke. This is not of your concern.' Palmer's hateful stare never left Cam's. 'I didn't want her, anyway. Who would want someone like her?'

Cam made a fist with his hand. 'You'd better watch what you say next.'

He huffed. 'Tell me, is it true what they say about plain and homely girls? Are they as eager to please in bed? Because from her looks, I bet she's probably giving you a grand old time.'

Rage fuelled Cam as he shoved Ash aside and lunged for Palmer. His fist connected with the Viscount's nose with a satisfying *crack.*

'You broke my nose!'

'I'll break more than that!' Cam reached for him again but, with his senses dulled, missed completely. Seeing an opening, Palmer grabbed him by the shoulder and pulled, then punched him in the jaw. Cam's head ricocheted back and he fell to the floor, but not before he managed to drag Palmer down with him. The Viscount landed on top, and they scrambled on the floor, trying to get the advantage.

Shouts and screams rang around them, along with breaking glass, smashing chairs, and general havoc. Palmer managed another blow to Cam's cheek, but he could hardly feel the pain anymore. With one last push, he rolled the Viscount under him, then let his fists fly once more.

'How. Dare. You!' he bellowed, punctuating his blows with every word. 'She is an Amazon goddess and you are not fit to speak her name!' He punched him one more time, and Palmer let out a pained moan before his head knocked back on the floor.

'Damn it, Balfour!' Ash cursed as he helped Cam to his feet. 'This was all about a woman?'

'Aye,' he slurred. *Maddie.* 'S-sorry about the fight. And ruining your evening.'

He let out a *pfft.* 'Evenings at St James's are pretty much the same night after night. At least you've provided some novel entertainment, though just to inform you, a fist-fight at a gambling den hadn't been on my list of things to do tonight.'

Ash guided Cam outside, away from the chaos. Cam hissed and lifted a hand to his face as the sun dug into his eyes like claws. 'What the—What time is it?'

'I don't know. Seven? Eight?' Ash hailed a passing hackney cab. 'Are you renting a terrace somewhere? Or staying with family or friends?'

'Mabury Hall. In Mayfair.'

'Mabury—as in the Duke of Mabury?' Ash looked at him disbelievingly. 'You're staying with my best friend?'

'I thought I was your best friend, Ash? *Oi!*' he protested as Ash packed him in the cab and climbed in. 'Where are we going?'

'I'm taking you to Sebastian.'

Cam frowned. 'I don't want to go back.'

'Whyever not?'

*Because she is there.* Cam leaned back into the cab's seat, feeling the rush of energy from the fight drain away from his body. His jaw hurt and blood trickled down from a cut above his eye, but he didn't care. *Punching Viscount Odious was definitely worth it.* Especially after what he'd said about Maddie. If there was anyone who didn't deserve her, it was Palmer, who couldn't see how beautiful and magnificent she was.

The lurching motion of the cab made Cam's head spin, so he closed his eyes. The alcohol still numbed his senses, so the next few minutes blurred together. Before he knew it, he was being ushered past a confused-looking Eames across the Mabury House threshold and into the Duke's private study.

'Where the hell— Ash?' Mabury's face turned comically confused. 'What are you doing here?'

'I met a new friend.' Ash gestured to Cam. 'Who's apparently a friend to you, too.'

Mabury sighed. 'Bring him to the sofa. I'll send for coffee and some hot towels and bandages.' He called out and a footman immediately entered.

As the Duke whispered instructions to his footman, Ash assisted Cam to the dark leather sofa, then headed to the mantel to pour himself a drink. 'I know it's early for a drink, but—' He stopped as he took a sip. 'This is divine. Whisky, eh?'

'The finest,' Cam interjected. 'Single malt scotch.' The room spun as he tried to lift his head, so he lay back down once again.

Mabury walked over and knelt by Cam. 'What the hell happened, Ash?'

'Do you want the short or long version?' The Duke lifted a dark brow. 'Right. Well, after Cam and I met outside The Underworld, we decided to band together for a night of carousing and general mischief. Then he got stinking drunk, started a fist-fight, all the while screaming about some Amazon goddess.'

'He deserved it, that bastard,' Cam spat. '*Ouch!*' Pain throbbed on the left side of his face.

'Started a fist-fight—' Mabury gritted his teeth. 'What the hell were you thinking, Balfour?'

'It was Viscount Odious—*Palmer*.'

'I see.' The Duke's obsidian eyes turned even darker. 'I hope you made him hurt.'

Cam grinned. 'I did.'

Mabury stretched up to his full height and smoothed his hands down his trousers. 'So, this is about Maddie. I should have guessed. What happened between you two?'

'None of your business.'

'It is my business, Balfour, because she's my guest and

therefore under my protection, and more importantly, it has upset my wife.' Dark eyes blazed with a quiet anger. 'Kate was tight-lipped about it, so you'd better tell me now what's going on.'

'We had a fight.'

'So you go off and get drunk and start a different fight,' Mabury said sarcastically. 'How did that work out for you?'

'Bloody well great, thank you very much.' Cam attempted to sit up. 'Now, if you don't mind, I shall—'

Mabury pushed him back down. 'No, you will not ignore Maddie, nor pretend nothing happened. You're going to get cleaned up and dressed and make up with her.'

'Why on God's green earth would I do that?'

'Because for some reason, she's in love with you, you nitwit,' Mabury roared. 'Anyone with eyes could have seen that.'

'Then I advise you get some spectacles, Your Grace, because there is no way she is in love with me.' Bitterness coated his tongue. 'Why would she be?'

'A pitiful fool you are, Balfour. Why don't you think she is?'

Cam's mouth pulled back. Was Mabury really going to make him lay out all his flaws? Did he need to list all the reasons why someone smart and beautiful like Maddie would not want him? 'She needs more than I can give her.' *More than I am.* 'I told her she should find someone else.'

Mabury huffed. 'And why the hell would you do that?'

'Because I am not enough for her!' he snarled. 'That's why she could not possibly love me. She told me herself she needed more than I can give her.'

'Is that so? What made her say that?'

His head pounded and all he wanted was to lie down

in a bed in a dark room and never emerge. 'All this time, I thought she didn't care about my title, but just last night at the dinner party, she was playing the part of the perfect society lady. I thought it was just the stress of the wedding planning, but when I tried to get her to leave with me, she told me that everything had to be perfect. And that I had to step up and give *more*. Then when I told her I couldn't give her more, she walked away from me.'

'Balfour, you idiot!'

All three men paused, then looked towards the source of the voice.

Kate, Duchess of Mabury, who had apparently been standing by the doorway the entire time, came down on them like an avenging angel. She dropped the tray of towels and bandages on the coffee table with a loud bang that made Cam's head pound.

'Your Grace, how lovely you look this morning,' Ash greeted cheerfully. 'Even lovelier than usual. Did you do something with your hair? New gown? Or perhaps it's the seething rage you're channelling to my best friend?'

'I thought I was your best friend,' Mabury said.

'New best friend,' Ash qualified. 'I'm allowed more than one.'

'Your Grace,' Cam said to the Duchess. 'I would stand, but as you can see, I am injured.'

'Good.' Her blue eyes blazed with fury. 'And to think I was worried about you. But now I know you're just a numbskull!'

'Maybe you are right, Your Grace. Otherwise, Maddie would have stayed.'

'You told her that she should find someone else.'

'And then she ran away from me.'

'She did not—' The Duchess threw her hands up in the air. 'Were you not listening to her? Or were you so

caught up in pitying yourself that you did not comprehend what she was trying to tell you?'

'Aye, I was there, remember? And, as I recall, Your
Grace, you were not.'

'She told me everything about what happened.' She
plopped down ungracefully on the armchair across from
him. 'Maddie was doing all that for *you*. The big society wedding. The tea parties. The gossip. Kissing up to
that puckered old Dowager. Maddie hated every minute
of it, but she did it so the ton would look favourably on
her and, in turn, you and your family.'

Disbelief struck him like another blow to the head.
'Why would she do that?'

'So that Persephone may have a successful season and
then you can fulfil your mother's dying wish.'

'You are— Wait, you know of that?'

'Yes, your sister told us. And when dear, sweet Maddie found out, her first thought was how she would help
you fulfil that promise.'

A sense of dread pooled in his chest. Of course that's
what Maddie would do. She'd done it all for him. 'That's
preposterous. She didn't need to take on that burden.'

'That's what I said.'

'And I never asked her to—' He shot to his feet, ignoring the pain on the left side of his face. 'I thought... I
thought she was doing it because she wanted her mother's
approval. Lord, I've been an idiot.'

'I'm glad we agree,' Mabury added.

Maddie thought he was pushing her away because she
was like Jenny. In what way, exactly? In no way. Jenny
could not compare to her.

*But I promise you, I will prove to you that I'm noth-
ing like her.*

He let out a laugh. Prove to him? What a joke. She had nothing to prove to him.

Cam turned to the Duchess. 'I must speak with her.'

'She's not here.'

'Not here?'

'She's gone.'

*No.* His throat burned as if he'd swallowed a bad batch of whisky. 'Where is she? Did she go back to America? I must find her!'

'She did not leave England,' the Duchess said. 'Only to Highfield Park. She and Mama left at around dawn. I was supposed to join them, but I had to delay because of a problem at the factory.'

Relief swept over him. 'Thank God. I'll call my carriage and leave at once.'

'Not like that, you won't.' Mabury wrinkled his nose. 'You look like death and smell like a public house. And Eames told me this morning your carriage had not returned.'

'Damn.' He had forgotten about the instructions he'd given his footman. 'My carriage should be somewhere in St James's.'

'I'll have Eames send someone to find them,' the Duke offered.

'And I'll call Murray so he can draw you a bath and prepare some fresh clothes,' the Duchess added.

'And I'll stay here and drink more of this fine whisky,' Ash quipped.

Cam looked at Mabury. 'Is he always like this?'

'Worse,' was the Duke's only answer.

Cam excused himself and headed up to his room. Maddie had probably arrived in Surrey by now. He wished she hadn't left, wished he'd come to his senses sooner, and wished he hadn't let her walk away last night. But after everything, he now understood why she'd had to do that. It was not to teach him a lesson or make him chase after her. No—by walking away, she was telling him that she deserved more. That she now had confidence in herself and she would no longer accept anything less from him.

But at the same time, she also told him to come seek her out when he was ready because she trusted he, too, would have confidence in himself. That he was more than just a charmer with no substance.

Maddie had walked away because she believed in him. He just hoped he could prove her right.

Maddie was in the orangery at Highfield Park, enjoying the warm, citrus-scented air wafting up through the iron grates on the floor. How she loved this place, with its lovely brickwork walls, high glass ceiling, tiled paths, and abundance of exotic plants.

She and the Dowager had arrived at Highfield Park early that morning from London. After napping for a few hours, she'd had a cold lunch in her room then decided to go to the orangery. This place reminded her of another world, which was one of the reasons she went there. Here, she could imagine she was someplace else.

Still, she could not quite enjoy the peace and tranquillity—not with the turmoil inside her.

*Please*, she said in silent prayer. *Please, make him understand what I was trying to say.* How long that would take—if he realised it all—she didn't know, but hopefully it wouldn't be too long. She hated leaving him, but she'd done this for him and for herself.

The sound of footsteps from behind made her pause. Who could be here? *Perhaps it was the gardener.* She hurried deeper into the orangery, hoping to avoid whoever it was so as not to disturb their work, but the footsteps followed her. Frowning, she halted and turned around. 'Who's— Cam?'

Her heart stopped beating as she soaked in the sight of him standing a few feet away, golden hair glinting in the sunlight, emerald eyes bright. Then she noticed the cuts and bruises on his face. 'Oh, heavens! What happened to you?'

'It doesn't matter, darling,' he said in that soft burr that smoothed over her like velvet. 'I'm here.'

'You're here,' she breathed.

He took slow, unsure steps towards her. 'You said I should come find you when I'm ready.'

She barely managed a whisper. 'Are you?'

'I'm not sure I'm that man you think I am,' he said. 'Not yet, anyway. But walking away from me was the right thing to do. However, know this. I will always come after you. You could walk halfway across the world and I would be right behind you.'

A breath hitched in her throat, and she clutched a hand to her chest.

'You're not Jenny,' he continued. 'Never were, never could be. But her actions wounded me so deeply, I couldn't see what was happening before my very eyes.'

'And what was that?'

'That slowly, carefully, you were getting past my defences and making me fall in love with you.'

*Did he really say…?*

'Cam…'

'I was scared, plain and simple. That you, too, would run away from me. But you have nothing to prove to me. In fact, I should be the one proving myself worthy of you.'

She lifted a hand towards him. 'I shouldn't have said—'

'I was wrong.' He caught her hand and pressed it to

his bristly cheek. 'I have done you wrong, Maddie. Accusing you of awful things when all you wanted to do was help me fulfil my promise to my ma.'

'I just want Persephone to have the London season your mother envisioned.'

'I didn't know that's what you were doing. Maddie, you don't have to do anything you don't want, especially if it makes you miserable.'

'I wanted to do it for you.'

'And I just want you to be happy.'

Tears gathered in the corners of her eyes at his words. 'I am happy.' She knew now that was the truth. 'Because of you.'

'Ma would have loved you, you know.' He kissed her palm, then turned his beautiful emerald eyes to her. 'And I do. Love you.'

*This wonderful, beautiful, broken man.* Cam challenged her and made her look at herself through his eyes and built her confidence. How could he not see himself in the same way? She searched for the right words, to tell him what he needed to hear.

When she finally did speak, she said, 'Iron pyrite.'

'I beg your pardon?'

'Iron. Pyrite. That's what fool's gold is called.' Her teeth sank into her lower lip. 'Cam, you're not iron pyrite. And you're no fool.' She cupped his face with both her hands. 'You're smart, in your own way. After all, you've managed your business and estate by yourself, I presume? Your fortunes haven't disappeared, nor has the distillery gone bankrupt?'

He shook his head.

'There are different kinds of intelligence, according to my father. Some people can calculate figures in their head, others can repair machinery. Then there are those who inspire others, true leaders who make others want to follow in their lead. Trust me, Cam. Those kinds of skills are worth their weight in gold. So no, you are not without substance.'

'How can you—'

'I'm a metallurgist —trust me.'

The corner of his mouth quirked up.

She continued, 'The day you proposed, you asked me if wanting you was reason enough to marry you. I realise now what you were really asking me.' Maddie felt as if she were standing at the edge of a cliff, not knowing what was below, though in this case, she didn't know if her hunch was correct. 'What you were really asking me is if *you* were enough.' Her throat tightened and her heart pounded so loudly she was nearly deaf, but she forged on. 'And the answer is yes, you are enough, Cam. Enough for me, for a lifetime. For two lifetimes, even. I've fallen in love with you, you see.'

'Maddie, I love you, too,' he said in a hoarse voice. 'And I will tell you and show you every day, until the last breath leaves my body.'

Arms came around her, pulling her close to his chest before his mouth came down on hers. His firm mouth moved over hers, caressing her softly before it turned deeper. Maddie tipped her head back to give him full access, opening up to him and basking in the love he showered on her as his kisses overwhelmed her. This kiss was not their first, and certainly not their last, but to Maddie it felt like something special.

It felt like true happiness.

# *Epilogue*

The incredible beauty of the Scottish Highlands, with their rolling hills, verdant valleys, and wild landscapes, was a sight to behold.

At least, that's what Maddie heard, because she had yet to leave the master bedroom of Kinlaly Castle, her new home since taking the title of Countess of Balfour.

'Cam?'

'Hmm?'

'Cam!' She playfully grabbed a handful of his hair to get his attention.

Cam looked up at her from between her legs, annoyed. '*Oi*. I was busy with something.'

She giggled. 'Not that I don't appreciate your efforts, but don't you think it's time we left the room?'

'Nay,' was his answer, and he proceeded with the work she had interrupted. Maddie mewled and moaned until pleasure wracked her body and she lay back on the pillows, wrung out and boneless.

Cam crawled up her body, trailing kisses upwards over her belly, stopping not so briefly at her breasts, nibbling at her neck before finally capturing her mouth with a deep kiss.

'Satisfied, wife?' he asked with a cheeky grin.

'Very.'

Maddie could hardly believe they were finally married. After he'd come to her in Highfield Park, he'd offered to delay the wedding, if only to relieve the pressure on her. However, Maddie would not hear of it. So instead, they'd compromised with a smaller wedding held in Highfield Park. Frankly, it had been even more beautiful and meaningful to Maddie than some society wedding, especially since all the people they cared about had been there, including all three of Cam and Persephone's brothers.

A week after the wedding, she, Cam, and her—now hers, too, she supposed—brothers made the trip back to Scotland. Persephone opted to stay behind to finish out the season under the sponsorship of the Dowager. Maddie was thrilled for her, though puzzled—Cam had asked Persephone if she wanted to come back home with them and try again next season, but for some reason she wanted to remain in London.

Maddie was sad to be away from her friend, but then they wouldn't be parted for too long, because they had more reason to return to London, not just with Glenbaire business. The construction of the DeVries London Furnace and Ironworks would be finished in a few months and they would begin operations soon. Her father had asked her to return to help, and of course, she'd said yes.

So it seemed the DeVrieses would be in England for a while longer, much to the delight of Mama and Caroline. Despite her antics, Maddie had no ill will towards her sister, as she'd decided to focus on her own happiness with Cam rather than spend time and energy on her sister's bile. However, during the wedding breakfast, Caroline had attempted to steal the limelight from Maddie by orchestrating a fist-fight between Viscount Gilbey and Lord Finlay over her.

Thankfully, Cam and the Duke of Mabury were able to stop them in time. However, when Caroline's involvement had been discovered, Papa had finally put his foot down and given her an ultimatum: there would be no more stringing along an endless parade of gentlemen. She would have to either settle down or decline all her current suitors and wait for the next season. Papa had warned her, however, that the next one would be her last, and if she didn't find a husband, he would send her back to America. By the time they'd left, Caroline had not decided, but knowing her sister, she would not pass up a chance to have another year of balls and new gowns and suitors. But Maddie still had hope that perhaps her sister would somehow mature before then and, somehow, find happiness, if not satisfaction and peace.

'You seem far away,' Cam said as he positioned himself beside her so they lay face to face. 'What's on your mind, darling? And how can I make you forget it so that you're only thinking of me?'

How she loved the way his burr had become more pronounced as soon as they'd got here. 'I am always thinking of you.'

A hand traced up her hip, all the way to her breasts, to the brass object that lay between them—the assayer's blowpipe that Cam had given her. While she was out shopping with Kate one day, she had found a thin gold chain at a jewellery shop and threaded it through the pipe so she could wear it close to her heart.

'You know I could buy you jewellery worth thousands more than this, right?'

'I know,' she said. 'But this is a special piece. It's the first gift you ever gave me.'

'An apology gift,' he reminded her jokingly. 'A reminder of our fake courtship.'

'Which became a real marriage.'

'True. *Hmm.* I think it's time we put it to the test.'

'Test?'

'Aye, I was told it was useful in finding precious metals.' Scooting closer, he took the pipe and placed one end over the left side of her chest, then the other end by his ear.

'That's not how that works, Cam,' she pointed out.

'Shh… I'm doing serious work here.' His brows drew together as if he were in serious thought. 'Yes… Mmm-hmm… Just as I thought.'

'Really? What does it say?'

Bright emerald-green eyes looked back at her, filled with love and happiness. 'That you, darling, are priceless.'

\* \* \* \* \*

*If you enjoyed this story, be sure
to read Paulia Belgado's debut*
May the Best Duke Win

COMING NEXT MONTH FROM

*All available in print and ebook via Reader Service and online*

## THE NIGHT SHE MET THE DUKE (Regency)
by Sarah Mallory

After hearing herself described as "dull," Prudence escapes London to Bath, where her new life is anything but dull when one night she finds an uninvited, devastatingly handsome duke in her kitchen!

## THE HOUSEKEEPER'S FORBIDDEN EARL (Regency)
by Laura Martin

Kate's finally found peace working in a grand house, until her new employer, Lord Henderson, returns. Soon, it's not just the allure of the home that Kate's falling for...but its owner, too!

## FALLING FOR HIS PRETEND COUNTESS (Victorian)
*Southern Belles in London* • by Lauri Robinson

Henry, Earl of Beaufort and London's most eligible bachelor, is being framed for murder! When his neighbor Suzanne offers to help prove his innocence, a fake engagement provides the perfect cover...

## THE VISCOUNT'S DARING MISS (1830s)
by Lotte R. James

When groom Roberta "Bobby" Kinsley comes face-to-face with her horse racing opponent—infuriatingly charismatic Viscount Hayes—it's clear that it won't just be the competition that has her heart racing!

## A KNIGHT FOR THE DEFIANT LADY (Medieval)
*Convent Brides* • by Carol Townend

Attraction sparks when Sir Leon retrieves brave, beautiful Lady Allis from a convent and they journey back to her castle. Only for Allis's father to demand she marry a nobleman!

## ALLIANCE WITH HIS STOLEN HEIRESS (1900s)
by Lydia San Andres

Rebellious Julián doesn't mind masquerading as a bandit to help Amalia claim her inheritance—he's enjoying spending time with the bold heiress. But how can he reveal the truth of his identity?

---

# Get 4 FREE REWARDS!

## We'll send you 2 FREE Books plus 2 FREE Mystery Gifts.

FREE Value Over $20

Both the **Harlequin® Historical** and **Harlequin® Romance** series feature compelling novels filled with emotion and simmering romance.

# Get 4 FREE REWARDS!

**We'll send you 2 FREE Books plus 2 FREE Mystery Gifts.**

FREE Value Over $20

Both the **Harlequin® Desire** and **Harlequin Presents®** series feature compelling novels filled with passion, sensuality and intriguing scandals.

---

**YES!** Please send me 2 FREE novels from the Harlequin Desire or Harlequin Presents series and my 2 FREE gifts (gifts are worth about $10 retail). After receiving them, if I don't wish to receive any more books, I can return the shipping statement marked "cancel." If I don't cancel, I will receive 6 brand-new Harlequin Presents Larger-Print books every month and be billed just $6.30 each in the U.S. or $6.49 each in Canada, a savings of at least 10% off the cover price, or 6 Harlequin Desire books every month and be billed just $5.05 each in the U.S. or $5.74 each in Canada, a savings of at least 12% off the cover price. It's quite a bargain! Shipping and handling is just 50¢ per book in the U.S. and $1.25 per book in Canada.* I understand that accepting the 2 free books and gifts places me under no obligation to buy anything. I can always return a shipment and cancel at any time by calling the number below. The free books and gifts are mine to keep no matter what I decide.

Choose one:· ☐ **Harlequin Desire**
(225/326 HDN GRJ7)

☐ **Harlequin Presents Larger-Print**
(176/376 HDN GRJ7)

Name (please print)

Address                                                                                        Apt. #

City                                          State/Province                          Zip/Postal Code

**Email:** Please check this box ☐ if you would like to receive newsletters and promotional emails from Harlequin Enterprises ULC and its affiliates. You can unsubscribe anytime.

> **Mail to the Harlequin Reader Service:**
> **IN U.S.A.:** P.O. Box 1341, Buffalo, NY 14240-8531
> **IN CANADA:** P.O. Box 603, Fort Erie, Ontario L2A 5X3

**Want to try 2 free books from another series!** Call 1-800-873-8635 or visit www.ReaderService.com.

*Terms and prices subject to change without notice. Prices do not include sales taxes, which will be charged (if applicable) based on your state or country of residence. Canadian residents will be charged applicable taxes. Offer not valid in Quebec. This offer is limited to one order per household. Books received may not be as shown. Not valid for current subscribers to the Harlequin Presents or Harlequin Desire series. All orders subject to approval. Credit or debit balances in a customer's account(s) may be offset by any other outstanding balance owed by or to the customer. Please allow 4 to 6 weeks for delivery. Offer available while quantities last.

**Your Privacy**—Your information is being collected by Harlequin Enterprises ULC, operating as Harlequin Reader Service. For a complete summary of the information we collect, how we use this information and to whom it is disclosed, please visit our privacy notice located at corporate.harlequin.com/privacy-notice. From time to time we may also exchange your personal information with reputable third parties. If you wish to opt out of this sharing of your personal information, please visit readerservice.com/consumerchoice or call 1-800-873-8635. **Notice to California Residents**—Under California law, you have specific rights to control and access your data. For more information on these rights and how to exercise them, visit corporate.harlequin.com/california-privacy.

HDHP22R3

# HARLEQUIN
## PLUS

Try the best multimedia
subscription service for romance
readers like you!

---

## **Read, Watch and Play.**

Experience the easiest way to get
the romance content you crave.

Start your **FREE TRIAL** at
<u>www.harlequinplus.com/freetrial</u>.